D0441999

Meant to Be

Meant to Be

JULIE HALPERN

FEIWEL AND FRIENDS
NEW YORK

A Feiwel and Friends Book
An imprint of Macmillan Publishing Group, LLC
175 Fifth Avenue, New York, NY 10010

Library of Congress Cataloging-in-Publication Data is available.

ISBN 978-1-250-09498-8 (hardcover) / ISBN 978-1-250-09499-5 (ebook)

Book design by Carol Ly

Feiwel and Friends logo designed by Filomena Tuosto

First edition, 2017

10 9 8 7 6 5 4 3 2 1

fiercereads.com

For Matt, Romy, and Dean

We were meant to be

CHAPTER 1

My boobs don't look any different. Not that I expected them to melt or explode or turn into origami swans. Are they a smidge bigger? That's just what I need. It took me six months just to find a proper wrangling bra that doesn't give me uniboob and also allows me to run in gym class without getting a black eye.

Gym class. There's some bullshit I will never be forced to endure again. No more lunchroom shenanigans, or hall passes, or "I swear I turned that in!" when I know I didn't. All those insignificant, overdramatized moments end today the second the final bell of high school rings.

How fitting that it's also my eighteenth birthday.

I examine my reflection again. It's not like the Name is going to pop up on my nipple. At least, I don't think so from the other Names I've seen: on my mom, on my best friend, Lish, and on countless celebrities wearing shirts low enough to show off the glamorous script above their impossibly perky décolletage. Supposedly it will materialize over my heart, near the center of my chest, favoring the left side. Countless Instagram stories exhibit the variations of Name locations: smack-dab in the center of collar bones; written in loop-de-loop cursive like a carefully designed tattoo; horizontally, or diagonally, or arcing like a rainbow, or haphazard and scrawly like the signature of a serial killer.

"Where the hell are you?" I ask my chest. It itches back its answer. Something is going on underneath that pasty white skin of mine.

I try to distract myself by digging out my clothes for the day. From the depths of my t-shirt drawer I select a shirt with a once-red Monkees logo, one my mom gave me from her childhood when it was already considered vintage. The fabric is nearly worn to sheer, and my black bra peeks through in certain light. It's a look I've worn before, mostly because I like the t-shirt, but also because I could get away with it. Before I turned eighteen. Before the Name emerges.

Maybe it won't happen.

There *have* been cases. Not many, but they exist. A Name doesn't materialize on a body, and those lucky individuals never have to deal with figuring out who the person is, spending way too much time trying to find someone who may or may not be *that* person. Maybe I'll luck out and be one of those freaks.

Or maybe it's over. Maybe this preternatural phenomenon that blew in out of nowhere a mere six years ago to wreak havoc on the very soul of humanity will stop with me. No one will ever have to read a Name on their eighteenth birthday again.

But, no, I can feel it forming. I have all the typical signs: redness, itching, a warm, tingling sensation over my heart.

Lish claims it's like getting your period: One minute nothing's there, and the next you have a coppery stain in your underwear and your mom is taking you to the grocery store for pads and crying about how you're not her little girl anymore. Only this stain is permanent and isn't just something that makes you feel extra snacky once a month.

This is etched into my skin. This is real. This is forever.

This is a stranger's name.

I scratch at my chest, egging on the words. Maybe if I squeeze the area like a zit, it'll pop out. My skin forms a minuscule mound as I push together the space under my collar bone. "Arise!" I shout dramatically. Definitely one of those moments when I hope no hidden cameras are in my bedroom.

"Aggy! Birthday breakfast!" my mom calls from downstairs. I keep forgetting it's my birthday. I let go of my flesh, now blotchier than ever, still void of the Name. There's too much going on for this to be taking so damn long: the last day of school, turning eighteen, the wheel of fortune that's supposed to magically show up but seems to be taking its sweet time. Who can eat breakfast under such trying circumstances?

I walk into the bathroom. Once a mere closet, my uncle Jim converted it to allow me more privacy. Or so he said. I think it got too awkward once I went through puberty to see me walking around in a towel. Can't complain. I have my own bathroom. My cat, Rugburn, a grunchy old mackerel tabby who can't decide after ten years if he likes me or loathes me, curls up on the wet bath mat.

I check myself in the mirror again. Nothing visible through the shirt. I tie my shoulder-length hair into a messy topknot and slide in some earrings shaped like arrows, my favorite pair. Look at me, getting ready like it's any other day.

But it's not any other fucking day.

I lift my shirt.

"Asshole," I chide the Name, then elicit help from my boobs. "Can't you do something about this? Use your massive girth to bully it out of me?" My boobs don't answer. "Thanks a lot. See if I let Jesse Rothem touch you again anytime soon."

I sit on the toilet and force myself to pee. Only ten minutes have passed since my last go, but I tend to pee more when I'm anxious. I cut my nails. I attempt to apply eyeliner in a sexy cat-eye fashion, only I don't ever actually wear makeup and I end up looking like that Egyptian king from *Night at the Museum*. It takes forever to wash off the mishap, and by the time I'm done the area around my eyes looks like I lost a brawl with my Build-a-Bear.

And then I see it. A shadow through my shirt. It's faint, but it's there.

My heart plummets into my gut, and I fight the urge to kneel in front of the toilet. Hands trembling, I peel up the bottom of my Monkees shirt. I think about a slow reveal, like they always do when someone first sees their Name in the movies, but this is real life and I've had years of anticipation. Or is it dread? I fling my shirt over my hair, and Rugburn complains loudly, zipping out of the bathroom when the shirt lands on top of him. Undeterred, I examine my chest, and there it is: a name written on my body. The font is neat, his handwriting at age eighteen (one fact scholars agree on). I can't imagine what he thinks of the mess that is my signature. The Name is smaller than I expected. An *H* starts below my left clavicle, where my cleavage begins its long descent. The letters continue in a horizontal path over the top of my left breast.

I don't hate how it looks. It's like my first tattoo that I accidentally got while drunk. Idiots do that all the time. What they think reads *love* in Chinese really spells out *moo shu pork*. But I'm not a heavy drinker, and these letters are in English.

I read the backward Name in the mirror.

Hendrix Cutter.

Am I reading that correctly?

I say it aloud.

"Hendrix Cutter."

Interesting? Weird? Kind of cool? Does it even matter? I sigh.

"Nice to meet you, Hendrix Cutter," I speak to my reflection. "I'm Agatha Abrams, and I'm your soul mate."

CHAPTER 2

Soul mate is a stupid term. Six years ago, before Names began invading the human body with no discernible explanation, *soul mate* had implications of sap. People believed or didn't believe, and it more or less felt like a concept made up for rom-coms and Hallmark cards. How could there possibly be only one person on this bloated planet whose destiny it was to be with another person?

Until the idea becomes science. Or an act of God. Or a blip in the evolutionary chain.

The world is full of hypotheses. Scientists tried to prove it has something to do with pheromones and hormones and homophones. Maybe not homophones. It's so blahblahblah, I stop listening. The religious zealots are no better. God, tired of seeing humans destroy a planet with murder and crime and all manner of catastrophic hate, created the meant-to-be (the preferred term over *soul mate*, so as not to be confused with its prior connotations). The True Lovers (the zealots' name for themselves, which I find ironically sexual-sounding for a group of religious devotees) believe that God wanted us to discover our meant-to-bes in a more direct fashion than, say, online dating or Craigslist ads, making it much easier to find contentment, procreate, and bypass all the suffering that comes with heartbreak. And think of how much faster everyone will have babies! The population will explode! Love will flourish! We'll all be so fucking happy and sexually satisfied that there will never be war again!

I call bullshit. There are so many things wrong with this logic (logic? How is any of this ever going to be logical?), so many holes in this fabric of reason. One of my theories, and I have many, is that somehow a sinister corporation determined a way to taint our water supplies, or vitamins, or the air we breathe to disfigure the entire population with random letter configurations. It would explain why the term *soul mate* turned into *meant-to-be*, turned into *MTB*, officially trademarked by the world's largest and most commonly used search engine. Now everyone calls the names on their bodies *Names*, and the people *MTBs*. And instead of mass quantities of research and billions of dollars being thrown at science facilities to figure out why we suddenly *have* MTBs (I like to call them *MTs*, pronounced "Empties." Maybe I should trademark that), Urban Outfitters sells YOUR NAME HERE shirts for thirty-five bucks. The majority of the world accepted its cruel and unusual fate and stopped caring about why the hell it's happening and how we can stop it. Like in the beginning of *The Walking Dead*, where everyone wants to know why people are all of a sudden zombies and if they can find a cure. Eventually they realize it doesn't matter why and instead have to figure out a way to survive in the new world without starving or being eaten.

I'd rather have a zombie apocalypse.

While it may make a modicum of sense for anyone who was under eighteen when the MTBs hit to learn they'd acquired a soul mate, it sure as hell rocked the fuck out of a lot of worlds for people older than that. Millions with marriages and partners and promising second dates had to learn that the person with whom they were cavorting, possibly for decades, wasn't the person with whom they were meant to spend their lives. Sure, some people could pretend they disregarded this brand-new development in their petrified existences, but a good portion of them couldn't ignore the temptation. Let's take, oh, I don't know, my mom and dad. Ellen and Arnold. High school sweethearts who followed each other to college, married soon after, and gave birth to the most adorable, hilarious, slightly-obnoxious-but-in-a-good-way daughter. Me. Their marriage wasn't perfect, but whose parents don't fight from time to time about dinner or where to go on vacation or who forgot to sign who up for soccer?

The second my dad discovered what *Florence Hildebrand* meant after it mysteriously appeared on his chest, he skedaddled to Atlanta and cohabitated with the hag. My mom was left to wonder about her generically named MTB, John Taylor. A quick Internet search listed millions of possibilities, from an economist to a jazz musician to a member of the ancient band Duran Duran. Overwhelmed, she gave up on her search before she even started. Mom wanted nothing to do with "this BS soul mate business" anyway. Her brother, my uncle Jim, younger by six years and battling crippling agoraphobia since his teens, moved in with us to help with the bills and fill the void that Empties created in our home. Uncle Jim was satisfied setting up his bedroom in our finished basement and his office in our attic, ensuring he wouldn't have to leave the house and, god forbid, connect with another human being. He is far more content writing romance novels under the pseudonym Savannah Merlot. They're wildly popular, even though he refuses to write any in the newest, beloved MTB genre. "I write about true romance, not some zit formation that happens to resemble a name." I do so love my uncle Jim.

The fact of the matter is that a Name is here. My Name is presumably somewhere out there. People believe that if the Names match (and they pretty much always do), then that person is your MTB. My best friend, Lish, had been obsessively counting down the days until her Name appeared, and when it did she paid big money to use the Signature Analysis Website. You've seen their commercials on TV. "We scan so you can find your man. Or *wo*man." Clever. But the product sells itself: For a small (read: first-year-of-college-tuition-sized) fee, Lish entrusted a "trained technician" to scan her naked top half with a lubed-up wand in order to enter her name into the International Database of Signatures. Currently, the database only includes signatures of registered voters and military personnel, but governments around the globe are gunning for mandatory signature entry from every person over the age of eighteen.

It's like being drafted into love.

That's why I just can't get myself to buy into all of this. I don't want to be forced to do anything, be it scan my Empty's Name, wear sunblock, or go to college. I like having choices. Or, I like the idea of having choices.

It's been the one point of contention in my long friendship with Lish, which began the second she moved in two houses down and her dog pooped on our mutual next-door neighbor's lawn.

"He always gives out circus peanuts for Halloween," I informed her. "They're not even wrapped. He totally asked for this poo." Instant friendship. When in fourth grade her family moved to a new subdivision with homes twice the square footage of my family's modest 1989 classic, we stayed best friends through cell phones, bike rides, and slumber parties.

The arrival of MTBs screwed up marriages, but it also wedged a chasm in the friendship of two little girls who used to merely want their Equestria Girl dolls to make it back to Ponyville.

Lish was smitten with the concept of *meant-to-be*, while I grew more skeptical. She believed the word *fate* was the antithesis of hate. Destiny was the final destination.

Fuck fate. Screw destiny. I'm team free will.

CHAPTER 3

Lish and I sit at a cafeteria table during first period. We officially have classes we're supposed to be in, but when an ass-backward administrator sets the date for the graduation ceremony three days before the actual last day of school, I think we're golden. The only reason we're here is to pick up our report cards during final period. And for the ritual of it all, I suppose.

"Show it to me now." Lish is tugging on my shirt, not at all taking into account how many other seniors are ditching first period to hang out in the cafeteria.

"Dude. I'm not lifting up my shirt here. I don't need everyone crowding around me pretending to read the name of my Empty but really ogling my tits." My brain flashes to the last person who saw me topless: one Jared Mason who charmingly dumped me on his eighteenth birthday. I wonder how many people have been dumped on someone's eighteenth birthday in the last six years. What do the True Lovers have to say about that? Probably, "It's all for the greater good. When you meet your meant-to-be, there will never be pain again."

Gag me with a spoon.

"Can't I just tell you the name and show you when we're alone?" I wrestle the bottom of my Monkees shirt out of Lish's hand. "You're strong for a midget," I tell her.

"*Little person* is the correct term." She lets go of my shirt but remains ready to pounce. "For which I am not. Nor are you."

"Hey, don't drag me into your old-timey circus act. I am a whole half inch taller than you. It's an entirely different world up here at five feet one inch."

"Wow, I bet you really thought talking about my height for the six trillionth time was going to make me forget about your MTB." Lish dives for my shirt again.

"Okay. Okay," I concede, grabbing her wrists and twisting upward. Lish yelps and crosses her arms into a pout. "I will tell you the name of my *Empty*"—I emphasize the derogatory word—"and then we sneak off to the bathroom and you can fondle me there."

"I'm not going to fondle you in the girls' bathroom!" Lish announces a tish too loudly, drawing the attention of everyone within a thirty-foot radius. I laugh at her indiscretion. "You can lift your own shirt," she whispers, then says, "Besides, I showed you mine." She winks at me. We laugh at our titillating conversation, and Lish prods me to disclose the name.

"Are you ready?" I ask.

"Do you see me salivating?" Lish confirms.

"His name is . . ." Pause.

Long pause.

Excruciatingly long pause.

Lish punches me in the MTB.

"Ow! I think you punched my Empty off."

"Tell me the name, or I am not inviting you to my wedding."

"You do realize that's not really a threat to me."

"Aggy, I'm about to take an X-acto knife out of my art box and cut a bitch, so you best be telling me his name."

"Hendrix Cutter," I cough.

"What?" Lish scrunches up her nose.

"Hendrix Cutter," I enunciate each sharp syllable.

"Really?" She looks disturbed.

"What? What's wrong with his name? Do you know him?" I panic.

"No. No, I don't know him. It's just . . . interesting, you know? Intriguing. Mysterious." Lish changes her face from distressed to aroused. "Sexy. Domineering."

"Lish!" I chide her. "You can't get all of that from a name. I will remind you that his parents gave it to him when he was a tiny baby who was most definitely not sexy or domineering."

"Is his signature cool?" Lish's eyes attempt to burn a hole through my shirt. "I can't make it out enough through that crusty shirt of yours."

"It's not crusty. It's classic," I defend the ancient, frayed assemblage of fabric.

"Just make sure you don't wear that when you meet

Hendrix for the first time. Or the second time. Maybe it's time for the Monkees shirt to go into retirement."

"Considering I'm not going to meet him, I guess the Monkees shirt doesn't need to worry about retirement."

"Aggy!" Lish scolds. "We've talked about this."

Since the MTBs first appeared, Lish and I have debated what we would do when ours materialized. From day one, Lish knew she wanted to find hers. Back then, of course, she assumed it was her latest YouTube obsession. I secretly wished for Rupert Grint in his *Goblet of Fire* years. As we aged into our teens, and real dating prospects materialized, Lish was constantly guessing which schoolboy would ultimately be her MTB. The thought that any one of these gangly douchecarts might be the guy I am supposed to spend the rest of my life with paralyzed me for years. Until I decided I wasn't going to let a wacked-out version of destiny determine who I want to hang out with.

You'd be surprised at how open teenage boys are to helping me rebel against society's constraints on companionship.

Or maybe you wouldn't be.

I will admit that I used my newfound stance on free will somewhat liberally my sophomore year and made the pool of guys who hadn't seen my boobs practically kiddie-size. But that's as far as I let them go. Until junior year. I really thought Jared Mason and I were in love. I sapped out and dreamed of the day his name would manifest across my chest as my MTB. Lish was on best-friend cloud nine, cutting out articles on MTB weddings, decoupaging lamp shades with pictures of us and overlaid wedding dresses. I don't think I was as ready as she was for marriage, but I let Jared go further than anyone before him. So we said I love you. We had sex. We made plans for our future: to move to Australia and pick fruit and roll around with wombats.

I shit you not that his Empty bulged out in the middle of us doing it. Not rolling with wombats; having sex. He was on top of me, and I watched, mystified, as the name "Alanna Silverman" bubbled forth. He had no idea, of course; he was too busy enjoying himself. It took Jared a good three minutes to notice I was crying. I pointed to his chest, not wanting to say the Name, and he bolted off his bed to examine himself in the mirror.

"Alanna Silverman." Jared spoke her name aloud, and by the excited hitch in his voice, I knew we were over. And so was any commitment I had to the idea of One. True. Love.

Guys are fickle. My dad can't even bother to remember my birthday since he left my mom for his Empty. Every year he calls me exactly one day before, which I suppose I could be grateful for. I mean, at least it's early, right? But it's fucking wrong. He abandoned our life because of some stupid biological or celestial anomaly. I refuse to let it rule me.

"No, Lish, I don't want to meet him. I want to find love based on personality and common interests and sexual chemistry—"

"But I'm sure you'll find all of that in your MTB. That's why he's supposed to be your meant-to-be, right?"

"Who can really say for sure, Lish? It's only been six

years! That's not enough time to know if what these people's names represent is about 'forever' love. What if it's actually the name of your future assassin? Or the person you *think* you love but after *x* number of years you hate more than anyone else on the planet? What if the Names go away? Or change? Nobody knows the answers, and I don't trust anyone who claims they do."

The second period bell rings, and Lish gathers her bag, plump with remnants of overused school supplies and an underwashed gym uniform. "Way to keep an open mind," she jokes.

"Yeah, well, I hate people telling me I don't have a choice," I counter.

"I get that. So don't try and find *Hendrix Cutter*." She says his name with a sultry breath. I laugh. People pass us as we exit the cafeteria, people I have seen every day of my life and am completely okay with never seeing again.

As Lish and I depart for our respective classes, she calls down the hall to me, "Just because you don't want to meet Hendrix Cutter doesn't mean he's not going to try and find you!"

Well, shit.

CHAPTER 4

The last few periods of the final day of high school are spent playing Hangman on whiteboards and chatting about summer and beyond.

"Why don't you want to go to college again?" Finley Ellis chastises me while filing her nails. Do people actually do that? File their nails? Isn't biting them more efficient?

"It's not that I don't want to. Eventually. I'd rather do something else right now. Like see all the world's finest amusement parks."

"You're kidding, right?" Finley continues. I consider taking the nail file and buffing off her eyebrows.

"I most certainly am not. You'd be an asshole if your life's goal wasn't to visit Ocean Park in Hong Kong so you can work at a roller coaster called the Hair Raiser. It has a terrifying-slash-happy walk-through entry face." Finley blank-stares me down. I switch gears to her average-person way of thinking. "I'm just not ready to commit to giving up my life's savings or putting my mom in debt because I feel obligated to continue the prison term that is sitting in classrooms." My calc teacher gives me a look that reads, *You're not out the door yet.* "You know what I mean," I backtrack to Mrs. Drew. "I'm sure you feel that way, too, sometimes." I see the look on her face soften a bit with a relinquished nod. It's not like we haven't all seen the Countdown to Summer Vacation clock in the corner of her computer screen.

"Isn't your mom shitting bricks?" Finley asks. Finley, in all her white-blond blunt-bobbed glory, has been asking obnoxious questions since she transferred to our junior high from California. At first, we were mesmerized by her exotic accent and the albino-esque hair until we realized she was the plant at slumber parties who forced us into admitting that we once stole a pack of gum from Circle K and that we did, in fact, shave our pubes once with our dad's face razor.

"No, she isn't shitting bricks," I retort. "Because she doesn't know."

"Such the rebel, Agatha." Finley taps her newly shorn nails on her desk.

I have accumulated an arsenal of insults aimed at Finley for just this type of occasion, but seeing as there are two minutes left to high school and probably the only time I will ever see her again is when she returns home from her college break fifteen pounds heavier with a raging yeast infection, I stop myself.

None of this lame local life matters because for years I've been secretly planning my escape. First stop: Australia.

I really wasn't kidding about visiting the world's amusement parks. I have a soft spot for the carny life, and what better way to learn about foreign lands than by visiting their most heightened and stimulating destinations of pleasure? Junk food in Korea? Yes, please. Ferris wheels in Peru? Fo sho. Luna Park in Melbourne, Australia, has a ride called the Ghost Train, described thusly on their website: "I ain't afraid of no ghost! . . . until I rode the Ghost Train at Luna Park." Obviously, as close to heaven as one can get. I figure I can score a job at Luna Park no problem based on my buff amusement park résumé, work until I'm bored, then pick a fresh amusement park in a completely different country and start anew.

It doesn't hurt that Australia is conveniently on the other side of the world. If someone were to die back home it would literally take me no fewer than twenty-four hours to return for their funeral, that's how far away it is. Remind me not to use that as an argument to convince my mom that moving to Australia before settling down and going to college is the greatest idea since slicing your *own* bread (thicker slices, duh). Very cool films come out of Australia, as do megahot actors, and they have all those wacky animals you can only find down there. Kangaroos! Koalas! Wombats! I imagine myself strolling along a billabong (I don't even know what that is), kangaroos piling on top of me while I giggle uncontrollably from their tickly tails, the intense sounds of a didgeridoo emanating from somewhere unseen.

Shit like that happens every day in Australia. I'm guessing.

The inspiration originally came when I saw the hybrid cartoon/real-life Australian film *Dot and the Kangaroo* as a kid. I read up on the unique species of creatures that live there, including 100 poisonous snakes and 520 poisonous spiders. The dream solidified itself in my subconscious when, upon the first drips of anesthesia during wisdom teeth surgery, I announced, "I wanna go to Australia." The oral surgeon humored me in my drunken state. "Oh yeah, and why's that?"

"They have all different animals there," I slurred. "It's like a whole 'nother world." And then I was out. Just think: If I'd had an adverse reaction to the anesthesia, those could have been my final words.

But they weren't. I'm guessing my last words will more than likely be, "Mom, I'm not ready to go to college, and instead I'm moving to Australia to work at an amusement park. Okay, bye!" She's already got the nasty aftertaste of moving out from my dad, just another way the asshole fucked me over. I have to figure out how to convince her that moving to Australia is me taking control of my life and making it my own, not me destroying any chance I have of living a successful existence.

Assuming I can save my last words until a much later date.

CHAPTER 5

Lish, teary-eyed from a blast of sentimentality, drives us home one last time from high school. "I can't believe he gave me an A," I marvel. "I thought Mr. Mistrata hated me. At least since I wrote that essay comparing high school to the nine circles of hell in Dante's *Inferno*."

"That was a very well-written essay." Lish nods. "I mean, Mistrata does kind of look like a three-headed dog. With one head."

"How'd you do?" I ask her.

"Straight As, son."

"It's weird, isn't it? Why does it even matter? If we've already been accepted into college?"

"Maybe jobs look at your grades when you're older?" Lish guesses.

"That's ridiculous. Why should any job I have as an adult give a flying fuck that I got a C in gym because I refused to participate in the swimming unit while I had my period?"

"Maybe someone will hire you *because* you refused to swim in gym class," Lish notes.

"Maybe. But then I'll have to explain in the job interview that I don't like tampons. I hope that's not a deal breaker."

"Your phobia of toxic shock syndrome is not unfounded."

"Thanks for having my vagina's back." I pat Lish on the shoulder.

A twinge of melancholy hits, and it has nothing to do with the end of high school. In a few days, Lish's meant-to-be, Travis (*that name*), will move in with Lish's family, and our slow crawl from best friends who have a slight difference in opinion will turn into a sprint to two friends who can't agree on major life decisions. Life was so much simpler when we were merely drowning in high school hell.

We enter my house, like so many after-schools before this one, and pretend life is the same, *we* are the same. The opening of the front door activates our ritual: eating microwaved hot dogs and watching reruns of '70s TV.

"What should we dip our wieners in today?" I ask, scanning the fridge for saucelike items, ignoring the weight of the Last Day of High School and Beyond. "Our neighbor brought us back some sick salsa from Door County."

"I finished that off today. Sorry." Uncle Jim saunters into the kitchen in his ubiquitous pair of pocketed gray sweatpants and Mr. Bubble t-shirt. It's not that he wears the same clothes every day; it's that he owns at least seven identical sets of those exact clothes. He collected my empty Mr. Bubble bottles just to order t-shirts off the back label. Admittedly, the most recent bottle was polished off last week. I'm a sucker for the gentle fragrance and abundant froth Mr. Bubble provides.

"How are you so skinny when you seem to only eat entire containers of food?" Lish asks Uncle Jim.

"It's all in moderation. One container at a time. Plus, I walk up and down the stairs at least a hundred and thirty-seven times per day."

Uncle Jim can be odd, although Lish is more than used to him. He's funny, but not always on purpose. He looks much younger than his thirty-five years and at the same time acts like a seventy-five-year-old man. Plus, the whole romance novel thing. When he writes, he keeps a pair of half-moon reading glasses perched on his nose, and when he's not writing they dangle from a beaded chain around his neck. I guess you could call it nursing-home—slash—museum-archivist—slash—five-year-old-in-a-bathtub chic.

"Enjoy your lips and assholes," Uncle Jim salutes our snack of choice and retreats to his writing cave.

Both Lish and I understand the obvious phallic hilarity of eating hot dogs, sans buns, while dipping them into liquidy condiments, but that doesn't stop us from partaking. No one can deny the processed joy of snarfing hooves and anuses with your best friend. Lish and I are slaves to rituals, and this is one of our finest. *Was* one of our finest.

"Ah, here's some horseradish mustard." I grab the jar from the fridge. "Coke?" Part of our process normally involves a tossed-and-caught can of Coke, but today Lish holds up her hand like a stop sign.

"I think I'll have water today," Lish says coyly. When I arch my eyebrows in question, she admits, "Travis said I should stop drinking Coke. It's like pouring battery acid on your teeth." And so it begins.

"Travis said that?" I emphasize his name, *Travis*, probably a little more childishly than I mean. Or at least more than I want Lish to hear.

"Yes. He is studying to become a dentist. He is concerned for my teeth's well-being."

"My teeth are perfectly happy disintegrating if it means they can continue drowning in the sugary goodness of Coke. Hell, when they start to decompose I can get dentures out of Coke cans. Bling!" I tap my front tooth and ring out the shiny sound effect.

"It's not just Travis who thinks actual teeth are important." Lish glares at me. "I would say ninety-nine percent of the population is pretty attached to their teeth. I'd go as far as saying ninety-nine-point-nine-nine-nine-nine-nine-nine"—she repeats the number for eternity—"would prefer their own teeth to Coke-can teeth."

Any mention of Travis makes me completely prickly. Lish seems absolutely mad about him in a very Hatter-like way. After she had her chest scanned into the International Database of Signatures and Travis came up as her MTB, his name manages to slink into nearly every conversation we have.

Travis likes when I wear my hair like this.

Travis always says that.

Travis has been to Australia before. He can tell you all about it.

That last one chafes me the most. I know Australia is an entire country—hell, a continent—and that people besides me visit there, but part of me feels like when I go, I will be a pioneer. I will survive and conquer. Not actual people, but more like live the shit out of life in a way that I could never do trapped by the constraints and expectations of our lame new world.

All Travis did was visit a couple of zoos on a family vacation when he was twelve.

"It's almost three o'clock," I interrupt the Travis static in my brain when I realize we're about to miss the opening credits of *Sanford and Son*, possibly for the last time together. Once Travis arrives, I can't imagine Lish will have time for our rituals.

We bolt into the family room and flip on the television. *Sanford and Son*, the show, is brilliantly hilarious, but the show is nothing without the funky junk of the theme song. Lish grabs a gray tasseled throw my mom knitted back when she had time to knit, and I swoop a green fleece blanket over my shoulders. The *bwakabwaka* starts, and Lish and I strut around the room, tossing the blankets up and back like they're extensions of our dorky appendages. Completely straight-faced because, naturally, this is very serious, we dance like the world is watching. Rugburn, initially drawn to the meaty hotdog scent, dashes out of the room for fear of being trampled.

Half a minute later the performance is over, and we sit down with our hot dogs and mustard to watch the show.

"I still haven't decided if I'm going to let Travis see me do that," Lish muses.

"(a) No, you are not, because no one in the entire universe has ever seen you do that but me and my reclusive uncle, and (b) If you can't show him the dorkiest side of you, then he's obviously not your Empty, is he?" My voice escalates, as it is wont to do whenever I speak of Travis. I should probably get better at hiding my emotions.

"You just completely contradicted yourself, Aggy," Lish fires at me.

"What? No, I didn't."

"Yes, you did. You said I couldn't do the dance in front of anyone but you, and then you said that if I can't do it in front of Travis, he's not my MTB. Which is it?" She eyes me scoldingly.

"It's both. Neither. I just meant that you are only *allowed* to do it in front of me, but if you were, like, forced at gunpoint to do the *Sanford and Son* theme-song dance in front of Travis, he'd be a dick if he didn't see its brilliance," I argue.

"Aggy, how can you hold anything against Travis when you haven't even met him? He's supersweet and nice, and we're so compatible."

"When did 'so compatible' become the criteria of an eighteen-year-old's love life? Aren't we supposed to whore around and make mistakes and think we're in love and realize the guy's a dick sandwich and then fall in love again and really think he's the one and then get cheated on and then swear off men forever until we crash into someone while chasing down Twinkies at a mini-mart at two-thirty in the morning and fall in love at first sight?" I'm a tad out of breath.

Lish laughs (*at* me, I would like to note, not *with* me. Because I'm not laughing). "Aggy, that sounds awful. I'm much happier knowing that I found the right guy. Now. Forever. Period."

"Allegedly," I enunciate each rolling syllable. "We don't know that for sure."

"Does anybody? Ever?"

"Maybe not. But doesn't it feel boring to you? Unromantic? Where's the exploration? The possibility? The tension? The hunt?" I enthuse.

"The closest I ever want to get to hunting is biting the end off this hot dog," Lish proclaims dramatically, tearing the hot dog wildly with her teeth for effect.

"Don't quit your day job," I say.

Lish chuckles, then looks at me with her big brown eyes and requests, "Can you save your judgment for Travis until after you meet him? No, wait. Like after you hang out with him a few times just in case he doesn't make a good first impression?"

"Fine. But only for you. Not because I believe Empties are real."

"You have three days to prepare your most sincere fake smile. I suggest you practice in a mirror."

We watch *Sanford and Son* for a while, and I try my best to live in this moment. Just me, my best friend, some hot dogs, and classic TV. Fred shouts to his dead wife, "This is the big one, Elizabeth!" always a favorite gag on the show, but I lose to my brain, stuck on Travis.

"What kind of name is Travis anyway?" I turn to ask Lish.

"What kind of name is Hendrix?" she blows back.

"I don't know. Nor do I care."

"Mmmhmmm." She side-glances at me. "Just keep telling yourself that, Agatha." Lish uses my full name when she thinks she's being wise. "You know you want to meet your MTB. Even if you don't want to spend your life with him, you've at least got to be intrigued. I bet you search for his name on the Internet tonight. How many Hendrix Cutters can there be in the world?" Lish is such a sensible pain in my stubborn ass. How am I going to resist the lure of an Internet search? Not a full-on Signature Scan, but just a basic Google search of his name? It couldn't possibly bring up very many hits. And what about *my* name? Agatha isn't weird, but I've never met another person named Agatha who isn't over seventy-five.

God. There is a person out there with my horribly illegible signature scribbled onto his body. Is he looking for me? What if he finds me? What if he wants to get married right away and settle down and have babies and, God forbid, wants to be a stockbroker? Or worse: a dentist?

I refuse to look him up. I will use all my willpower and

only touch the interwebs for important things like movie times and Kylo Ren fan fiction.

Good thing I start work tomorrow. That should keep my mind off Empties. Because no one I work with is over eighteen and thinking about their Empty, too.

CHAPTER 6

I wake up the next day with the gross remnants of an early-morning dream about a man named Hendrix Cutter who was bordering on ninety years old. And we still made out. The spray of the shower does little to cleanse my mind, and I keep reliving the feel of his wrinkly, soft lips. How do Hugh Hefner's wives handle this?

Only one case of Empties with a massive age gap has made front-page news—most Empties' ages fall within ten years of each other. What's kind of cool, or could be construed as cool if I cared about this MTB nonsense, is that the Name seems to always correspond with a person's signature at eighteen years old. I'm not quite sure how that fact was discovered. Were scientists digging through boxes of old math tests? Drivers' licenses make some sense, although that's sixteen in Illinois. I think it's different in every state. Every country? Maybe an assumption was made because the Name presents itself upon your eighteenth birthday. In the same vein, if you are eighteen and a person's signature appears on your chest, it may be possible that the person whose signature you see is not yet, in fact, eighteen.

Maybe not even born yet. Much of this is speculation, since the disease (phenomenon, whatever) has only been around for six years. Time will tell, I suppose. Out of curiosity, I grab a piece of scrap paper from the kitchen junk drawer and sign my name as though signing a letter to a relative. I sign again, this time as I would sign the late sheet in my high school office. Still legible, although less so. Finally, I sign my name the way I had on multiple college applications: scattered, angry, willy-nilly. Which one does Hendrix Cutter see? What Hendrix Cutter am I seeing?

I sure as hell hope Hendrix Cutter isn't ninety. Or four.

Not that it matters.

Time to shift gears into work mode. This marks the third summer I've worked at a semilocal (i.e., far enough away that people from my school don't work there, but close enough that I only have a half-hour drive) kiddie amusement park called Haunted Hollow. The park opens in June and closes Labor Day, when all the high school and college kids can dedicate ten hours a day, six days a week to shilling Halloween-themed snacks, like Hag's Hot Dogs and Freaky Fries, and escorting children onto rides with clever titles like Voodoo Vehicles, Spook Spinner, and the Carousel of Decline. Ironically, the park shuts its doors before its holiday inspiration, although I suppose it's no different from the year-round Christmas shop, Jingles, or Fireworks, the Fourth of July–themed restaurant that never made it to its first Fourth of July celebration. Who doesn't want to be scared shitless every fifteen minutes by a mock fireworks display while they're eating their sliders?

Haunted Hollow is run by a man named Sam Hain (always hoping, but pretty sure it's not his real name), a beefy, tattooed man with sideburns that are so close to touching that some may consider them a poorly manscaped beard. He is both terrifying and divine, and, really, who else could own a Halloween-themed amusement park for kids?

And I must emphasize the *for kids* part. No ride would accommodate a person of adult size (although I can squeeze my compact frame into some of the rides, and often do, after hours).

I tug on my glaring orange, ahem, *pumpkin*-orange Haunted Hollow t-shirt, one of about sixteen I've snagged for myself during my two-year tenure. I made it a habit to grab discarded t-shirts from any employee who (a) was fired for insubordination, slacking off on the job, eating all the rainbow-flavored Dippin' Dots, or pilfering funds from concessions, or (b) left for college and wanted no tangible proof that they ever worked at such a subpar amusement establishment.

I, on the other hand, fucking love the place. Halloween is incontestably the best holiday of the year, and it's two trillion times better when you're a kid. Add to that the gluttonous paradise of snacks, the blatantly rigged game stalls, and the questionable safety of the rides, and Haunted Hollow is essentially paradise.

Plus, Luke Jacobs works there.

Luke runs the park's only roller coaster, the Ghoster Coaster with the Moster, usually referred to as the Ghoster by kids and carnies alike. The ride resides directly next to the ride I helm, the Devil's Dinghies. Some people consider the Devil's Dinghies a shitty ride to work on; it's slow-loading, kids are always dropping things into the water, and the tracks are so rusty that half the time the maintenance crew is grumbling their way through knee-high water to save the whimpering kids who are trapped in the tunnel.

I don't mind it. I like to find the tiny toys that have slipped out of kids' hands and sunk to their watery graves in the nuclear-blue water. I enjoy lifting toddlers under their innocent armpits when their parents are too busy on their phones to notice they need help. And I know it drives everyone batshit crazy, but damn if I don't love the Devil's Dinghies song that reverberates through the tunnel from dawn until dusk. The tune is ridiculously peppy, but the lyrics are pretty wicked if you actually listen to them.

Oh, the devil knows where you are.
You're not on a train or a bus or a car.
You're not on a bike or a plane.
Beware of the rattling chain.
The devil's dinghies,
The devil's dinghies,
The evilest boats around.
The devil's dinghies,

The devil's dinghies,
Next stop: be-low ground!

Written and recorded by Mr. Sam Hain himself.

Luke and I spent many a night together over the summers amassing lost toys and belting out the Devil's Dinghies song like a couple of drunk pirates. The fun invariably ended when his girlfriend of four years, Jenny Butor, picked him up from work, and our potentially romantic moment would disappear until the next night.

At the end of each summer, Luke and I hugged goodbye, painfully platonically, promised to keep in touch, and promptly forgot once our respective school years started. At least, he would forget. My itchy texting finger frequently hovered over the desperate send button, but I never pulled the trigger. For all I knew, he turned into a werewolf once he left the park. And there was the whole girlfriend thing.

Like me, Luke turned eighteen this year. Which means Luke has an Empty, too. I wonder what that implies for ol' Jenny Butor. Maybe he won't even work at Haunted Hollow this summer. Which would suck.

Uncle Jim scuffs into the kitchen in decaying moccasins and his Mr. Bubble uniform. The shirt is one of his older editions, shrunken down by too much time in the dryer. A lot of his shirts are too small for his lanky frame, as though he didn't realize he was going to grow to be six feet and stopped clothes shopping when he turned sixteen. I am enamored with the entire concept of my uncle Jim: a tall man with red hair and beard, his bubbly clothing ensembles and his coffee addiction, and his chosen career as a shiller of romantic fantasy reads for women. The man himself is pretty badass, too. He's a rock-star chef, built me a friggin' bathroom, and is damn funny.

But I can't help feeling sorry that he won't leave the house. Like, ever. Sure, he goes into the backyard and sometimes even stargazes from the roof. He'll get the mail after surveying the area to ensure no one is around to attempt small talk. But the only face-to-face human interaction he gets is with me and my mom, plus Lish, due to their shared love of *Degrassi*.

Other than hanging out with us, he writes in his attic studio and keeps to himself. Unless he has some secret online existence I don't know about, Uncle Jim is pretty much crushed by his anxiety. Which is a damn shame. I think he'd love the Devil's Dinghies theme song live and in person.

"My eyes!" Uncle Jim shrieks, shielding his face with his bathrobed forearm. "You can't wear that color at six in the morning," he scolds.

"This is what all the cool kids are wearing. You'd know this if you left the house." Even though I know his agoraphobia is essentially debilitating, I can't help but want more for him. Sunshine streaming through an attic window is hardly a viable source of vitamin D.

Plus, he refuses any sort of help. He won't talk to a therapist or go on medication, no yoga or exercise of any real kind (I don't think climbing up and down the attic ladder to use the bathroom counts). He could be way decent-looking if he shaved his lumberjack beard, fixed his hair, and changed his clothes once in a while, and he is wasting his life living inside our house.

The only piece of his lifestyle that I support is that he is *choosing* to live it his way. He is not abiding by any preset notion of what a man in this freakishly new age should be doing. Empties be damned, my uncle doesn't give a shit that he could be out there finding his supposed true love. He'd rather be holed up, sipping his black coffee from a *Reading Rainbow* mug, and writing cheesy fiction to get off unsatisfied housewives.

This is not to say I don't die of curiosity every time the mention of Jim's MTB comes up and he instantly shuts it down. Uncle Jim would sooner go to the grocery store than walk around without a shirt on.

Maybe that's the real reason he built me my own bathroom.

CHAPTER 7

Luke Jacobs is back, and has grown since the last time I saw him. A lot. I stopped growing the year after I got my period, seventh grade, with my breasts stalling out somewhere around freshman year. I didn't even realize they were as large as they were compared to my smaller stature until a woman in the Kohl's lingerie department (mind you, just some random woman and not an actual Kohl's employee) blatantly guffawed when I held up a flimsy bandeau bra and asked my mom if I had the correct size. "Honey, maybe for a headband," the guffawer said. It's a wonder I order my bras online.

Luke Jacobs's growth was just as unanticipated as that of my breasts, but a whole lot more exciting (to me, at least. I'm pretty sure my breasts are rather exciting to quite a number of people). His height over the past couple of summers had hovered somewhere in the average range. It wouldn't have been something I'd mention when describing him to someone, like, for instance, my best friend. "He's got shortish brown hair that gets shaggy toward the end of the summer. Eyes that are sometimes brownish, sometimes greenish, sometimes bluish—"

“That’s called hazel,” Lish would interject.

“Really? I thought maybe his eyes have some magical changeling quality that only happens when I’m around. Like mood eyeballs. Can we pretend he has mood eyeballs?”

Ever the romantic, Lish would inevitably agree.

“He has really fit calves that aren’t overly hairy but just enough so that I might have fantasized about running my fingers through them.”

“Through the calf hairs?”

“Don’t pretend like you’ve never had that daydream. And the dimples . . .”

“On his calves?” Lish loves to interrupt me when I’m overanalyzing a potential beau’s body parts.

“On his cheeks, duh. The ones on his face. I knew what you were thinking. One on each side. They appear only when I’m around,” I assure her.

“How do you know?” She barely holds in her snicker.

“Because I can’t see them when I’m not around, can I?”

“I could analyze them myself, if you ever let me meet the guy,” Lish says.

Lish has never met any of my friends and coworkers from Haunted Hollow. The drive is far enough that she couldn’t randomly drop by while she was busy with summer school last year nor will she be able to this year because of her internship at a local pharmaceutical company. The rides at Haunted Hollow are only suitable for ages ten and under (that’s a prepuberty ten for sure), but anyone over the age of eight is too busy season-passing it at Six Flags to care about a rinky-dink operation like Haunted Hollow. All the reasons keeping Lish away are precisely why I like it. Not that I don't love hanging out with Lish, but sometimes I like to feel that I'm nowhere near my actual life (see also: my desire to move to Australia). Working at Haunted Hollow is akin to going away to summer camp (I would imagine, if my mom ever let me go). You see the same people year after year, eat cotton candy for breakfast, watch little kids have the time of their lives, then go home to your family with a pocketful of tales no one will understand except your fellow campers. Each summer is filled with sunburn, churros, and broken hearts. Why would anyone not want to work here? (*cough* Shitty pay, indigestion after every meal, backwoods locals who put cigarettes out on children's ride seats. *cough*)

I'd be lying a smidge if I said Luke Jacobs wasn't one of my main considerations when coming back to a job that pays significantly less than Lish's internship (not that I have any interest in the world of pharmaceuticals, unless they can do something about turning me into a half human/half unicorn). It's not as though Luke and I ever really had a relationship. Or a date. Or any actual romance, since he's been dating the same person since the two Frankenstein-slow-danced together in eighth grade. Except . . .

. . . none of this stopped us from making out. Once. It probably wasn't even technically making out, since it lasted less than five minutes and there was only minimal tongue involved. His hand did cup one breast, although that might have been due to its colossal size and his hand having nowhere else to go once in its proximity. I am now wondering if it's technically possible to cup something accidentally. The act occurred behind the Wheel of Torture, where most seedy things do, on our last night of work before the park closed for fall. Sam Hain threw a bash for seasonal workers before the park was dismantled by the full-time employees, women and men who work year-round on technical and aesthetic upkeep and who mostly look upon us seasonals with polite disdain. I don't blame them. We are the ones who push the incorrect buttons and hold levers too long, which makes rides malfunction and their jobs more complicated. But without us, what would they do all summer? Eat funnel cakes and drive around in their miniature trucks blasting AC/DC out of the open windows due to lack of air conditioning? They need us, and we need them, and most importantly the kids need all of us.

And that night I really needed to kiss Luke Jacobs.

We were all sugared up on too much Witch's Brew, the park's signature drink of strawberry lemonade mixed with 7Up. I ordered mine with extra maraschino cherries because I knew the kid working concessions, Jerry B., had a crush on me. It was good for some extra cherries anyway.

Luke and I had a pretty fun summer together, using a system of lewd hand gestures we'd devised to communicate across the chasm between our rides. We also wrote out a few paper signs for important occasions, such as LUNCH?, SNACK?, and PEE? for those times we needed someone to cover our ride between break times. Lunchtime was spent with a group of seasonals, the majority of whom attended the same high school, and therefore knew each other in an "I saw you when you had your awkward bowl cut" kind of way. The few of us seasonals not from the immediate area brought with us a bit of intrigue, albeit not as much as the foreign exchangers. The buzz at most lunches varied from pop-culture chat to college applications to advice for the love-lorn, and almost always inevitably turned to Empties. Every summer a crop of seasonals had recently turned eighteen, and like the first kid who figured out Santa was a sham, they loved acting like the ultimate MTB authority.

"Don't let anyone tell you otherwise: It hurts like a bitch."

"He's full of shit. It tickles. Like, in a really good way."

"I didn't even notice when I got mine."

"You were probably too stoned to remember it was your birthday."

And that was just the conversation about the materialization of the Name. When it came to discussing what people believed the Name meant, that polarized the seasonals hardcore.

"Of course I'm skipping college to look for him. What kind of a future wife would I be if I didn't?"

"More like a Stepford wife. He doesn't want to meet you now. He wants more time to, what do they say, sow his wild horses. If he's really your MTB, he'll be around even when you're old and saggy."

"Better than being young and saggy. How many pumps of butter are you adding to your bathtub of popcorn? Do you think your MTB is going to be thrilled when she discovers it's you she's supposed to be in love with?"

"Is that how it works?" That was Luke. "When you meet the person, do you still have to fall in love? Or is there a chemical reaction that feels like love instantly? What if you're in love with someone else at the time? Does that just go away?"

No one had an experience-based answer for that. I didn't want to share my story of humiliation with Jared Mason, especially since I wasn't certain that he was really in love with me to begin with. But I did wonder.

"In that one movie" or "on *Maury*" were the only points of reference we had. *Maury* went from a daytime television show whose paternity tests exposed "you are NOT the father" to a daytime television show whose tagline became "you are NOT the soul mate." They even devised a smock with a sheer panel that fits directly over a guest's chest that can be ripped open with Velcro to reveal their Empty's Name. Keeping it classy, *Maury*.

A few seasonals had left work at Haunted Hollow to find their MTBs, but since they never returned, we were still left wondering. The older full-timers never gave straight answers.

"It feels like you're floating on a cloud of cotton candy, and then you start shitting rainbows."

"It's more of a physical sensation, like when you eat too much Thai food."

"I'll show you what it feels like if you want, sweetheart."

Yeesh. The only person at Haunted Hollow who had anything remotely useful to say about Empties was Mr. Sam Hain himself. "Love is love. It's going to feel good. It's going to feel even better, it's going to hurt like hell, and it's always going to be confusing. . . ."

Cryptic, but at least he (vaguely) answered one of my queries. It's not straight-up cloud-nine perfection all the time. It's still *love.* And if it's still love, then there can still be some mystery to it, some excitement, and, I pray to Chuck, some choice.

As we gathered on the final night of last season and chugged our Witch's Brew, involuntarily scratching our mosquito bites and peeling our sunburn, conversation turned once again to MTBs. Alexander McMahon had recently sold his grandfather's baseball card collection, unbeknownst to his parents, to pay for a Signature Scan. Instead of leaving for college, he was flying to Sweden, where his MTB awaited.

"I accept the intrigue of secretly flying to Sweden to get it on with a presumably gorgeous Scandinavian, but should true love really be about lying to your family? This isn't fucking *Romeo and Juliet*," I argued.

"And what if she isn't gorgeous? What if she's been using a fake photo?" Luke added.

"We Skyped. Her gorgeousness is official," Alexander contended.

"But is that enough to know you want to spend the rest of your life with someone?" Luke prodded.

"It is when her name is on my chest and mine is on hers. You guys will understand when it happens to you. It changes everything." Alexander nodded to everyone with the sophistication of a bobblehead, but at the time I thought maybe he knew something we didn't know.

We seasonals milled out of the food area, hugging goodbyes and promising to keep in touch during the school year. When it was my turn to hug Luke, our hug lingered. He whispered into my ear, "What if Alexander is right?"

I was confused as to which item he might be right about, but I allowed Luke to take my hand and pull me to a shadowy space behind the Wheel of Torture—really just a regular Ferris wheel with torture implements painted on the sides of the buckets. As Luke held my cheek with one hand, my hip with the other, he asked, "What if next year we won't want to do this?" And he kissed me. It was blissful enough that when we were interrupted by the cackles of nearby revelers, I grabbed at a convenient fence to steady myself.

That was the last time I saw Luke until today. Back when he had a girlfriend, before he had the Name of The Girl imprinted on his body. And, damn, his body. All of a sudden he's well above six feet tall, shoulders straining against his fitted fluorescent work shirt, veins roping down his inexplicably tanned forearms. He's a fucking cover model for a

Savannah Merlot novel. His hair is longer than it usually is at the beginning of the summer, longer even than it usually is by the end. The dreamer part of my mind wants to believe he stopped cutting it after our kiss, to freeze some piece of the moment. The thought feels ridiculous, until he smiles at me and those dimples, still deliciously intact, pop out just for me. Now I'm sure of it.

CHAPTER 8

"What the hell happened to you?" I ask Luke, attempting funny but realizing it may have read rude.

His laugh clears my conscience quickly. "Oh, this old thing." He flips his hair dramatically, like he's in on the joke of his newly expanded vessel. "My dad's been training for his first marathon, and he dragged me into it. And I joined the swim team to help get into college." He shrugs, way too modestly.

"All I got when I joined the swim team was a urinary tract infection," I joke. But it doesn't sound like a joke, and I cringe at my tragic attempt at casual. "Kidding! I don't know why I just said that. Your Thor-like makeover is very distracting," I admit.

"You should see him with his shirt off." Adam Callas, Luke's friend who runs the Terror Train, saunters over. Adam has not changed very much physically since last summer: same stocky build, same freckly skin and greasy black hair hidden under the same ratty Haunted Hollow baseball cap he's worn with pride since he started working here.

"Hey, Adam, glad to see you're as stunted as ever," I mock him endearingly as we hug hello.

"Do I get one?" Luke asks. This is one of those moments that I have to place into storage for more dissection later. Does he want a friendly hello hug? Would he have hugged me if Adam didn't? Is he jealous? Is he chill? Is he just doing this out of obligation?

When those superhero-worthy arms wrap around me, and my face lands on the pillow that is his chest, I don't really give a shit what the answer is. What was the question?

The romance-novel moment (which I must remember to describe in detail to Uncle Jim) ends far too quickly as Adam shuffles around us, bragging, "I added a strap to the back of my cap! Look! My head grew!" He shoves his rancid hat in my face, and I'm forced to leave the paradise that is Luke's chest. People should retire there; it's that majestic.

"Perhaps you can celebrate by washing the damn thing. Why does it smell like yeast? You baking a loaf in there, Adam?" Luke grabs the hat from Adam and holds it above his head. "This is my new trick. What do you think?" He winks at me.

Do not wink at me, young man. There could be dire consequences.

"If I can be honest—can I be honest with you?" I ask in mock seriousness. Luke responds with a pensive nod. I continue. "It's a little cheap. You're tall. How tall are you?"

"Six foot four."

Yowza.

"And Adam, you're still a paltry . . ." I leave room for his reply.

"Five six. And a half," he notes.

"We of the five six *and a half*"—I emphasize the importance of the half—"and under club don't really think it's cool or funny to mock our dainty stature."

"I'm not dainty! I'm beefy!" Adam argues. "I wouldn't say you're dainty, either, Aggy." And there it is. The first of countless times Adam will ogle my breasts this summer.

"Hey, man, not cool." Luke whacks Adam in the chest with the putrid cap.

"Careful. This is very delicate material here." Adam adjusts the cap back onto his head. I pass an appreciative smile to Luke.

Lest we manage to catch up on anything more than our changing appearances, Luke adds, "I like your hair. Did you change the color?"

"I added a few red streaks underneath, but they pretty much only show if I wear a ponytail."

"You look good."

Supersexyawkward silence follows. Does he, too, feel the pressure of the Name on his chest? The need to divulge anything and everything about our newly developed marks of soul mate–dom?

Mr. Sam Hain brandishes his impeccable timing and blares, "Pep talk!" over the loudspeakers. We head for the stage, where a weak glee club performs Halloween-themed songs and skits throughout the summer. Sam Hain's shoulders take up nearly half the width of the paltry stage, and his stumpy arms wave robotically as he speaks.

"Seasonals, new and veteran, welcome to the most haunted summer of your life!" This elicits cheers from us old-timers. "Children expect to enjoy themselves here. Parents expect safety, cleanliness, and professionalism. I expect you all not to fuck up." Giggles from the newbies, knowing nods from the vets. "Today we do a run-through. Foods and Retail, you will be tested on your knowledge of your stations and the layout of the park in case patrons ask you questions. Ride operators, you will be observed for following safety procedures to a T and proving you know what the fuck you are doing."

"Sam Hain has really toned down the language this year," Luke bends over to whisper in my ear. His hair tickles my cheek. It's a good thing we don't operate the same ride, or his distractions might cause a lawsuit.

"If you have any questions, ask your team members or supervisors. Try not to bother me with little details. I fucking hate that. Have fun!"

We applaud, some politely, some stupefied, as Sam Hain ambles off to smoke his last in-park cigarette before the season begins.

"How can one man be so intimidating and so comical at the same time?" Luke muses.

"I keep wondering when some poor, naive soul dares to approach him with the fact that Samhain, as in the actual festival of the dead, isn't pronounced like *Sam* or *Hain*."

"I weep for their future," Luke agrees.

"Time to start spreading the rumor that he killed a man and fed him to the piranhas in Loch Mess. Adios, amigos!" Adam doffs his nasty cap and walks away.

"Will you please use your superpowers to dispose of his hat?" I look up at Luke.

"I don't know. I'm afraid his head will fall off if he doesn't have it with him. Like the woman with the—"

I finish his sentence. "—red string tied around her neck!" We nod concurrently and watch Adam strut toward the Terror Train.

"Shall we?" Luke offers me his elbow, and I hook my arm into his. We reach the Devil's Dinghies, the bright red Beelzebub looming over the tunnel entrance gleaming in the summer sunshine. My shoulder is screaming from the height discrepancy. Totally worth it, of course.

"Catch you for lunch? I hear they have veggie burgers at the Hallowed Hamburger now."

"You a vegetarian now that you're Mr. Fitness?" I tease Luke.

"No, but I thought *you* were." He scrunches his forehead in confusion. He has the scrunchiest forehead. How does he make a scrunchy forehead a *thing*?

"I was. Two summers ago, but my mom was afraid I would become anemic like her aunt Rhoda. Plus, I was having wicked corned beef cravings. I'm not great at committing." I laugh.

"Yeah. I get that." Quiet settles between us amid the

rumbles and squeaks of the surrounding rides. "Guess I should test-run the Ghoster. My trainee is waiting." He thumbs toward a guy bobbing his head to the beat of whatever music is blaring from his earbuds. "Can't wait to tell him Sam Hain doesn't allow headphones of any kind around rides."

"You must remain focused at all times. These kids' lives are in your skilled hands." I wag my finger and deepen my voice in imitation of Sam Hain.

"That's pretty good." Luke laughs. "I'm gonna take my skilled hands over there now. See you at lunch?"

"Definitely," I agree, and my eyes follow as Luke walks to the Ghoster.

Did he reference his skilled hands on purpose? How am I supposed to focus on the Devil's Dinghies when a newly sculpted Adonis is one ride over?

More important, what was that cryptic bullshit about committing? Luke, you and your double entendres are going to be the death of me.

CHAPTER 9

Brian, a burly full-time member of the maintenance crew replete with piquant cigarette fragrance, fills up the water for the dinghies. Not that the dinghies are actual vessels in need of water; the bottoms of the small, rainbow-hued boats are slotted into a metal track that powers them at a brisk two-mile-per-hour clip around the ride. Passengers are amused by macabre—yet child-friendly—paintings of devils with whip-sharp tails, cooking up evildoers in cauldrons and stabbing each other's butts with pitchforks. The wow factor (for the under-eight set) comes on the final bend, when you are plunged into the tunnel's blackness (*plunged*, again, at two miles per hour) for a whopping sixty-six seconds. Just so you understand the madness that is Sam Hain's mind, the story goes that when the tunnel was originally created, the length of time spent inside the tunnel was always hitting either sixty-five or sixty-seven seconds, but never sixty-six. Sam Hain would have none of that; 666 *is* the number of the beast, and many of the Haunted Hollow rides are scientifically engineered to hit marks including at least one number six. For example: The Devil's Dinghies has six boats circle at a time, as does the Terror Train. The Carousel of Decline has exactly six of each ghoulish creature: six bats, six black cats, six goblins, six hairy spiders, six werewolves, and six garden gnomes. (Believe me: they're creepy as hell. No one ever chooses to ride on them.) The number-six slot wins the majority of the time in the Crushin' Roulette wheel game. (Kids sit on a spinning contraption as a spongy ball bops around like popcorn. When the ride stops, the ball lands in a hole in front of one kid. That kid wins a prize, in addition to the joy of being socked in the face multiple times by the bouncy ball.) Sam Hain is a math savant, for sure.

When Sam Hain couldn't figure out how to get the Devil's Dinghies to speed up or slow down the precise amount to make the tunnel portion sixty-six seconds long, he ordered maintenance (possibly ol' smoky Brian) to hack off a portion of the tunnel itself. Today you could set your watch by the exactitude of the Devil's Dinghies tunnel. And even if you couldn't, no one would tell Sam Hain that.

I walk up to the control booth, an electronic panel housed underneath a meager fabric cover provided to prevent team members from passing out under the summer sun. The square canopy is approximately three feet by three feet, and with the control panel taking up a hefty portion of space, I consider how little shade Luke will be getting this summer. Can he even fit underneath it?

I have managed to go approximately five, nay, *six* minutes without thinking about Luke.

I run my fingers over the control buttons, but know I

must wait for my supervisor, Carolyn, to go through the standard operating procedures with me before pressing may ensue. Purely a formality for me at this point; each year Carolyn tests the ride operators on their controls, and if we pass we receive a certification to run the ride. As rinky-dink as Haunted Hollow sometimes seems, Sam Hain plays by the rules to keep it open (plus, I figure he's secretly got a storeroom of illegal substances he really would rather not be found due to poor operations practices). Each ride operator is quizzed, and if they fail to answer a certain number of questions correctly they receive a "green slip." Then they attempt a retest. If you get a shit-ton of questions wrong (and really, if you do, you'd be better off drying cars outside the local gas station for tips), you get a pink slip and have to retest on a separate day. It gives you extra time to study and berate yourself that you have failed at button pushing.

While I wait for Carolyn, I lower the wooden plank used as a bridge to cross over the water and access the grassy island within the ride. This is occasionally necessary if a child drops something into the grass or if they get stuck in their seat belts and I can't reach them. Today I step across the wood, twice the width of a balance beam and ten times as flimsy, to view the crumbling devilish paintings on the stone wall encasing the ride. Sam Hain assured me the paintings were to be retouched over the spring, but eye sockets and pitchfork prongs are still peeled away. I sag a little, my pride of three seasons with the Devil's Dinghies tarnished a wee bit.

"Hey, Brian!" I call to the maintenance man, hose in

hand and requisite asscrack on full display. I don't know if he's hard of hearing from so many years surrounded by machinery and screaming kids or if the splash of the filling moat cloaks my voice, but he doesn't acknowledge me. I walk toward him and call his name again. Nothing. I'm two feet behind him now and realize he's wearing can headphones, although I can't tell if there's sound pouring into them or if they are blocking sound out. Either way, I'm going to have to touch the guy if I want his attention.

I've never touched a full-time employee. Truth be told, most of us are scared of them. It takes a certain character to work year-round, life-long, for Mr. Sam Hain.

I opt for a gentle foot tap. That means my skin won't actually touch any part of his body, but with the major crackage happening I have to make certain my foot placement is highly strategic. I take the toe of my gym shoe and lightly tap the side of his hip where there is still fabric from his Dickies pants working hard at covering his love handles. So much hair that I wasn't meant to see.

The instant my foot makes contact with his body, Brian jumps fifteen feet into the air and drops the hose into the moat, where it immediately sinks to the shallow bottom.

"Jesus goddamn Christ, you scared the fuck out of me!" Brian shouts, and I stumble backward onto my butt in the grass. I'm really hoping no one saw this interaction because (a) I looked like a goober and (b) if Brian thinks I did anything to make him look stupid, he can make my life hell for the rest of the summer. There's nothing like waiting an extra half hour on a scorned maintenance guy while fifty whining, shrieking five-year-olds bake in the sun. I listen for laughter and hear none, save for the clown chortles emanating from the nearby bathrooms (Sam Hain's theory is that if kids are too scared to stay in the bathroom very long, the lines move quickly).

"Sorry. Really sorry." I offer a smile through terrified teeth. "I wanted to ask about the walls. If you knew when they were going to be painted."

I believe Brian stares me down through his large, reflective shades, but I only see a disfigured me in the lenses. "Didn't happen this year. Maybe next year." He offers me a leather-gloved hand, and I'm confused until I realize he's helping me up. Reluctantly I take it, and with surprising ease he rights me to my feet.

"Thank you. Well, do you know if we have the paint?" I ask tentatively.

"We got it in the storage shed. But he don't have time to paint this summer." Brian reaches into the nearest edge of the tunnel and unhooks a large net attached to a pole, one of our most useful tools for fishing out dropped paraphernalia.

"I could do it. I mean, when there's downtime. If there's downtime," I blather.

Brian works while he talks. "Don't see why not. I'll run it by Sam. Let you know."

Wow. He calls Sam Hain *Sam.* Respect.

"Cool. Thanks. And sorry about the hose."

• • •

Carolyn is a lifer and a full-timer, meaning she has worked at Haunted Hollow since its inception, and she works at the park year-round. She also happens to be Sam Hain's aunt, but I'm not supposed to know that. She likes me because "You're not some one-season floozy," as she put it. Loyalty means a lot to these people. Carolyn and her husband, Steve, had been celebrating their twentieth wedding anniversary when the Naming took place. Carolyn and Steve had made a commitment to each other, and since they both have a penchant for tattoos (my favorite of Carolyn's appears whenever she bends down to take a lookie-loo at a broken switch: the tramp stamp of CARNY FOR LIFE. Depending on my ultimate career choice, I may be sporting one of those in the future), they became some of the early adopters of the Concealment movement. Concealment is when one either (a) covers up the Empty with a tattoo of sorts, mostly hiding the Name (since it is three-dimensional, you can always still see it in certain light) or (b) the far more disgustingly extreme involves either grafting skin on top of the Empty or essentially carving it off. I throw up every time I get a splinter, so I won't be partaking in any form of Concealment. Maybe with a Sharpie.

It drives me batshit that there have to be terms for everything surrounding MTBs; it makes people feel that as long as someone out there is naming things, it means they're trying to figure it out. I think that they're spending so much time thinking up clever labels for body parts and theories and movements, no one's addressing the fact that we still don't *really* know what any of this means.

Carolyn and Steve have successfully lived their lives as if the Naming never happened, and she is quick to snap whenever she overhears us youngins talking about seeking out our MTBs. I admire her greatly. Except maybe her choice of forgoing dental care for the last thirty years or so.

A strapping woman with sun-weathered skin and blond hair highlighted with gray streaks, Carolyn tugs me in for a quick hug and proceeds to test me on the Devil's Dinghies standard operating procedures. I pass the test with flying colors (even when she quizzes me on all the lyrics to the tune, definitely not in the manual). She slaps me on the back a little too hard, and I stumble forward with pride. Why I choose that moment to look over at the Ghoster, I have no idea. Maybe it's because I look over there six billion times a day anyway. Or maybe it's because they say when someone is looking at you, something within you can sense that so, in turn, you look at them. Like yawning when someone yawns. Whatever the case, when I do look at the Ghoster, I immediately lock eyes with Luke. He smiles and slow claps at my trip, and I subtly scratch my cheek with my middle finger. We're rudely interrupted when his trainee asks him a question, so I turn my attention to the new seasonal Carolyn delivers to me.

"This is Keely. She is going to be one of the game girls," Carolyn explains.

"Toss your cookies!" Keely enthuses.

"And she's going to be your backup for breaks. If you can train her on the Devil's Dinghies, I'll be back later to test her." Carolyn walks away, leaving me with the new kid.

And, damn, does she look like a kid. Not like I'm some sophisticated, mature woman, but even with a good six inches on me Keely has one of those tiny baby faces that will make her look perpetually like a Disney Channel ingenue.

Keely is eager and not too much of an idiot, and she seems to have a handle on the Dinghies by the time I feel a virile tap on my shoulder. Okay, so it's a regular tap, one that could not be distinguished from any other tap, but when Luke is attached to that tapping finger, it's hard not to add a manly adjective.

"I tried to throw the lunch sign up at you, but I couldn't get you to look at me."

Oh, if he only knew how badly I wanted to.

"Yeah. I was busy training Keely here."

"Hi," Keely sighs breathily. I swear bubbly pink hearts flutter out of her mouth.

"Um, yeah. Luke, this is Keely. Keely, Luke." My voice barely hides my irritation at this moment. Luke subtly gives Keely a once-over, and I swear I'm not jealous of her legs (twice as long as mine) or her shiny blond hair.

Before I get in my first-ever brawl, Luke introduces his youngster. "Hey. This is Chaitu. He's first season, too. You guys should have a lot to talk about. You ready for lunch?"

Luke directs this question at me, but he is answered by an overzealous "Yes!" from Keely.

I envy Keely and her pre-Empty possibilities. It seems like just last week I could choose who I liked based on their actual qualities, not on their Name.

Oh yeah. It *was* just last week.

CHAPTER 10

On most workdays, I pack a lunch. Eating carny food on a regular basis turns into a tragic tale of acne, tight jeans, and acid reflux. However, there's nothing like a Beastly Burger, Freaky Fries, and a funnel cake bigger than your head to start out a summer at Haunted Hollow.

Luke and I spot Adam lording over a round table, and I hear him proclaim, "There are two piranhas. You want to jump in and find out?" to a new guy. Chaitu sees some friends from high school at a different table, offers a "Catch you later," and joins them. Keely also sees a group of people she knows, possibly from school or maybe from the Games area, but she forgoes sitting with them in order to not eat her lunch while staring shamelessly at Luke from our table. At one point during our meal, her mouth is in full gape, and I have no choice but to jab her with my elbow and hiss, "Pull yourself together, woman. Have you spent the last fifteen years in a convent?"

"Home schooled," she sighs.

Oh. "Did they at least let you leave the house?" I joke,

but she can't hear me over the cartoon birds flying around her head.

Adam attempts to snap her out of it. "So, Keely, how are you liking your first season at Haunted Hollow?" He chomps on a fry with his mouth open, and I mime at him with a hand to close it. He doesn't get the hint, probably because I look like I'm doing a hand-puppet show without the puppet.

"It's my first day," she says.

"Well, it's all our first day. You like it so far?" Adam continues.

"S'okay, I guesssss. . . ." She snakes her *s* at the end of her word, and we all wait for her to finish. When she doesn't say anything more, Adam turns to me.

"Aggy, you got a Name?" He joggles his eyebrows at me. I'm about to tell him that of course I've got a name, he just said it, when I realize he's asking about *the* Name. My MTB.

Here we go.

"Yep," I answer. The table remains expectantly quiet, but I'm busy ripping apart my funnel cake with a spork. "This is so not the right utensil for a funnel cake," I say in true avoidance fashion.

"So spill," Adam prods.

"The funnel cake?" I know I'm being an asshole, but if being an asshole is what it takes to avoid the Empty chat, then consider this ass-holed.

"Funny, Aggy. Isn't our girl funny?" He looks to Luke. *Our girl?* When was I ever Adam's girl? Or Luke's, for that matter. "Really. What's the guy's name? Or girl's name?" The eyebrows are back in full effect.

"You don't know?" I choke dramatically. "It says Adam Callas! Doesn't yours say Agatha Abrams?"

For a moment, Adam's eyes bulge underneath his skeezy hat, until he figures out I'm kidding.

"Ha-ha. Come on. What does it say? I'll show you mine if you show me yours." If he doesn't stop it with the eyebrows, I might have to spork them off.

"Leave her alone. If she doesn't want to tell us, she doesn't have to," Luke defends me.

"What does yours say?" Keely asks Luke glumly. He looks at me with his crumpled forehead of confusion. I get it, if he's feeling anything like I'm feeling. The more people you tell the Name to, the more tied you feel to the notion that this Name has weight to it. When you say the Name in front of other people it becomes public knowledge. Does it make you and this enigmatic person a couple in most people's eyes?

When Luke doesn't immediately respond to Keely's request, Adam outs him. "Scarlett Dresden! That's Luke's MTB. Hot, right? I can just picture her." Luke leans back and crosses his arms over his chest. He looks down at the table. Adam continues to bulldoze. "Mine is—ready?—Anita Lopez! Latina. My mom shit a brick when she saw it. She was hoping for a nice Greek girl." Adam blathers on a bit about his mom and how he'll have enough money at the end of the summer to scan his signature.

Luke looks up from his pensive place and gives me a

knowing eye roll. I smile and mouth *Scarlett Dresden* with a seductive lift of my shoulder. He shrugs.

"I can't wait to get my MTB. Only two and a half years." Keely begins picking at her food. It's amazing how a crush can be instantly derailed when you learn you're not a person's Empty. It makes me almost wistful for third grade, when I blew kisses in every direction at bedtime to ensure one would hit Scottie Del Ray.

"It really does change everything," Adam muses, sprays of whipped cream flying from his mouth. "I feel like I have a goal now. You know, something to do with the rest of my life?"

I groan, a lot more audibly than I mean to.

"What?" Adam spits.

"A person is not something to do with the rest of your life. Traveling and writing and working and meeting lots of different people—not just one—is how you spend a life."

Adam scoffs. "Yeah, but now I have a person to do all of that with."

"But shouldn't it be part of the excitement of life? Trying to find that person?" I argue.

"Meh. This is easier. Ask Luke. Jenny dumped his ass like a hot tamale when she got her MTB. And they were together for years. Right, Luke?" Nudge nudge.

I hope Anita Lopez isn't a fan of tact.

"Sorry," I offer to Luke for the loss of Jenny, although admittedly it's undoubtedly a sorry-not-sorry kind of offering.

"It's not a big deal. I mean, it was, but it was also kind of a relief. With going off to college and everything. Who knows if we were really meant to be together anyway?"

"You *weren't.* And *you* know that because of the Naming! It's brilliant!" Adam claps.

After lunch, Luke and I walk back to our rides together. "She really dumped you when she got her Name?" I ask.

"Yeah. We talked about it before her birthday. I already had mine, but we said we could try to make it work. But it was like a switch flipped in Jenny's brain. She was able to stop loving me instantly and was so excited to find this guy she didn't even know."

"That really sucks. I had a boyfriend who did the same thing to me. Right after we had sex, too. Or kind of during it, actually."

Ugh, Agatha. Way to make yourself sound both slutty and losery.

"His loss." Luke bumps me with his shoulder.

"Her loss." I bump him back, jabbing him in the ribs. "Scarlett Dresden will hopefully be more committed," I offer.

"I don't know yet if I want to find Scarlett Dresden," he admits. "Going away to college and everything. So many possibilities."

"I get that." I nod.

"I never did get your guy's name," Luke presses.

"Oh yeah. Hendrix Cutter," I divulge.

"Hendrix Cutter," Luke speaks the name aloud. "Sounds like a douche."

"Maybe he should meet Scarlett Dresden," I chide. "They'd make a perfect couple."

"We could introduce them."

"It's a plan," I say.

"It feels like we're still so young not to have a choice." The big bad wolf grins down at me.

"Yeah," I dumbly agree. "We're still so young." I guess that makes me Little Red Riding Hood.

CHAPTER 11

The first night of work is usually the last night of summer I'll be home for dinner. Mom has been in graduate school for social work the past two nights, so we're finally able to celebrate my eighteenth birthday the right way. With cake.

My mom is not a cook. Or a chef. Or a person who likes to make food that requires turning something on. She considers button-pushing the final frontier in the kitchen, so microwave, toaster oven, and coffeemaker were the go-to appliances of my childhood. Not that I drank coffee as a kid. Or even now. I do love the smell of coffee beans, but somewhere between the process of grinding the beans and pouring hot water through them, coffee pretty much tastes like tomorrow's garbage smells. Maybe because it was my job to take out the garbage, and I was usually remiss in doing so in a timely fashion. My dad was such a cliché stereotype of a man; I don't know how my mom found him attractive in the first place. He actually sat around on Sundays and watched football. Who does that? (I mean, besides the millions of other people who do.) It is mind-numbing. They stop every five seconds, the game lasts for twelve thousand hours, and the cheerleaders are such a throwback to an era that should be obsolete but disturbingly isn't. It felt like the whole reason he watched football was for an excuse to eat nachos and cheese ("like the good Lord intended," he would say) and sit on his ass all day. My dad was very good about things being dropped in his lap, as opposed to actually putting a little effort into making things happen. Example number one: my mom. The two of them were set up by a friend in high school their sophomore year and that was it. He never bothered looking further than high school. Example number two: He went to college to become an accountant and had a job waiting for him the second he graduated. Example number three: Florence Hildebrand, Dad's hoochie MTB who rang our goddamn doorbell six years ago with a bouquet of red roses (trite much?), and that was enough for him to drop everything for her shiny new ass and leave our family.

To recap: I hate coffee, Mom can't cook, and Dad's a dickwad.

Thank God for my uncle Jim.

Uncle Jim, like me, believes in choice, in having control of one's life. Granted, he's a shut-in who people believe to be a bouffanted madam named Savannah Merlot, but at least he's a bouffanted madam on his own terms. He is completely shunning what the new world has set up for him, and he's making a living doing it. Plus, he's a fabulous cook. For my birthday, Uncle Jim prepares a filet mignon dinner (my request because, for some reason I will never be able to explain, *filet mignon* cracks my shit up), complete with garlic mashed potatoes, creamed corn, and creamed spinach (living it up with creamed vegetables). For dessert is a magnificent birthday cake, the likes of which I've never been able to decode. Somehow he intersperses chocolate cake with white cake, turning the inside into a checkerboard pattern. He claims it is merely a special pan, but I hate to ruin the mystery. This year's cake is frosted in regal blue with gold accent balls around the top and bottom. Delicately swirled in frosting is HAPPY 18TH BIRTHDAY, AGGY.

Seeing the number eighteen, the neatly curled handwriting, and my name in one round and delicious place, I am instantly reminded of Hendrix Cutter.

Mom sits down, harried, as has been her permanent state for the last six years, her hair frizzling out of a low ponytail. She spends five days a week as a receptionist for a construction site, a job she found through a temp agency, while she earns her social work degree.

"How was work?" I ask and help myself to an ample serving of creamed goods.

"Not too bad. Busy, but not overly so. Boring, but not mind numbing. I keep telling myself it's only temporary, and soon I'll have an actual career to stress over. I still have time to work on my homework most days and fit in a couple squares of sudoku."

"People still do that?" Uncle Jim asks.

"Sudoku is not a fad, Jim, it's a lifestyle," Mom responds.

"Holy balls, this creamed corn is good."

"I milked the cream directly from an imported French cow," Uncle Jim teases.

"Gross?" I comment. "Don't you have to churn milk or something to get cream?"

"That's butter. Fat French cows secrete cream."

I look to my mother to confirm Uncle Jim's factoid. She shakes her head no.

"You know, someday you're going to tell me something like that, and then I'm going to share the information with someone as though it's true, and they're going to think I'm a total dipwad."

"I thought I would have to stop when you became a teenager, but you stayed so damn gullible. How could I?"

"I'm not gullible," I pout.

"You are, and it's adorable."

"Gotta agree with Jim there," Mom concurs. "You are infinitely adorable."

"You have to say that because you're my mom," I accuse her with a forkful of creamed spinach, the limp, coated concoction dripping onto the table.

"You should use a spoon with that," Uncle Jim advises me.

"Wrong. It's a vegetable. I use a fork."

"It's a creamed vegetable; therefore it is a liquid."

"How can you have created it and be so completely wrong? If I eat it with a spoon it becomes a soup. I don't like creamed soups," I note.

"You are a complicated woman. I can call you that now because you're eighteen."

At the mention of my age, I brace myself for the first family interrogation of my MTB.

"And you know what that means. . . ." Uncle Jim stands up and pads to the counter. He turns to produce the miraculous cake. A glowing 18 candle sits in the center.

"So purty," I marvel.

Mom and Uncle Jim sing "Happy Birthday" and root for me to make a wish. I hastily throw this winner together, "I wish I find love, and that it has nothing to do with a Name on my chest." Of course, I wish this in my head, because everyone knows saying a wish aloud means it won't come true. Plus, it's a pretty goobery wish.

I manage to blow out all two candles (Love, here I come!), and I slice into the cake with my deceased grandma Lil's cake cutter. I never met the woman, but I feel connected to her through various utensils my mom hoarded after her death. In addition, Grandma Lil was once a Ballyhoo Girl at long-gone Riverview Amusement Park in Chicago. I inherited her carny genes.

I dole out the checkered cake slices, avoiding cutting into the portion with my name on it. I feel like there should be a superstition around eating one's name. Just as there should be one involving eating one's face on a photo cake.

My mom, Uncle Jim, and I have our way with the cake, until only my name and the number eighteen remain. A questioning silence fills the chocolate-scented air, and I know my mom and Uncle Jim are dying to ask about my MTB. How could they not be? That's all this world cares about anymore. Finding your one true love, prepackaged and served up expressly for you.

Forks clink. Dishes scrape. Segments of drying creamed vegetables congeal audibly. It's deafening. I can't take the pressure, and I burst out, "Hendrix Cutter!"

My mom drops her fork in shock. Uncle Jim looks at me, annoyed, holding his hand to his chest. "What the hell was that?" he asks.

"His name is Hendrix Cutter. Okay?" I enunciate.

"Whose name?" my mom questions, a look of bewilderment on her face at what I now recognize was a completely random outburst.

"Never mind," I grumble, standing to hastily collect the dishes.

"Did that doctor correctly diagnose you with Tourette's after all?" Uncle Jim asks.

"No! It was a sensory issue. I was six," I defend myself.

"Then why would you blurt out a name like Hendrix Cutter? I may have to steal that for one of my books, by the way."

I sigh loudly, angry at myself for bringing up a conversation that clearly I was the only one having. "Hendrix Cutter is my MTB. The Name on my chest? My eighteenth birthday?" I speak in questions, as though my mom and Uncle Jim need reminding what MTBs are.

"Oh," is all my mom says.

"Hendrix Cutter, huh?" Uncle Jim rolls the syllables around. "Interesting Name. Have you started looking for him yet?" My mom shoots daggers at Uncle Jim, but says nothing.

"No," I quickly assert. "God, no. I don't want to know who he is. I don't want to meet him." I glance at my mom, to assure her.

But as the words leave my mouth, my brain does the most annoying thing. It tells me that I'm not speaking 100 percent truth. That, although minuscule, there is a part of me that wants to know something—anything—about Hendrix Cutter.

Which is why I better fall in love with someone else damn quick.

CHAPTER 12

Opening day at Haunted Hollow is complete madness. It's like kids have discovered the joy of summer freedom for the first time, exploding with sugar from cotton candy and ice cream and licorice yards. Parents are thrilled to have other adults to talk to while they push their children onto rides. I'm crazy busy, ushering kids into boats, checking safety harnesses, yelling for them to sit down, the occasional E-Stop when something is dropped into the water. It's fun, electric almost, to be around so much youthful energy. Not like I'm old, but turning eighteen truly makes me feel like I've lost that childhood sense of innocence. More so than getting my period. More so than losing my virginity. More so than trying my first cigarette and promptly throwing up into a Sonic's drive-through garbage can.

Kids don't know how good they have it. Say you're a second grader, and you have a crush on a boy so you name your little ceramic Dalmatian *Mikey* after him (speaking hypothetically, of course). You toddle after Mikey (the boy, not the ceramic Dalmatian) on the playground, leave notes on his desk, sit next to him at the lunch table. It's all very sweet.

Fast forward to junior high. Your first slow dance with Danny Eastman, Frankenstein-style. He cops a feel of your butt, and you manage to rest your head on his shoulder before a teacher ix-nays the situation. Adorbs. Next up: sophomore year. You're making out with Corey O'Dell in the front seat of his car (the backseat was the undesirable home to his pet husky's favorite blanket and the piles of magnetic hair that came with it). You didn't think that much about the future then. About the potential and the *what if?* It was all about the moment and good feelings and keeping curfews so all those delicious things could happen again.

Now it feels like all of that was just a dead end.

How can something considered pure romance by a significant chunk of our population feel completely stifling to me?

I'm going to say it right now: I want to have a meaningless summer fling. Like I've read about in older books and watched in movies made more than six years ago. Like in *Before Sunrise,* where an American boy and a French girl spend one dreamy night together in Vienna. In the end they plan to meet up again in six months. If that movie were made today, would they even bother hooking up at all? Has it become fruitless to try and connect with someone because their name isn't the one scribbled on your chest?

As much happiness as I felt most of the day, I feel disheartened. Because when Luke Jacobs smiles at me from his booth and my insides tug on one another with the need to be near him, I can only think about Scarlett Dresden and how damn lucky she is.

• • •

After work, I hang at Lish's house as she prepares for Travis's arrival. If not for the MTB factor, would her parents really let a guy she barely knows from the Internet stay at her house for a summer? It's mind-boggling the trust people put in this thing.

Subconsciously I run my fingers over the bumpy script on my chest. It's so strange. Through my shirt it feels like a loop-de-loop scar, which I suppose it is. But actual scars are usually the result of something traumatic. The scar should be the end result of the trauma, not the beginning.

Hendrix Cutter. Hendrix Cutter. Hendrix Cutter.

The Name skitters across my brain. My willpower not to look him up online has dropped a notch in the past couple of days. Seeing Luke again is bringing up all kinds of confusion. He certainly is flirty. And lovely. And fun to be around. But he is not the Name on my chest. Does he even remember our lip lockage behind the Wheel of Torture? What if he does that all the time, and I was the nearest female body with whom to smash faces? Does he think about us on random occasions while he's trying to fall asleep with his hand in his undies, too?

Lish manages to distract me. "I have narrowed it down to seven outfits. I shall now highlight the merits of each outfit, while you write down your score, ice-skating style." Lish gestures to the clothing neatly splayed across her double bed. I grip the dry-erase board and marker she handed me upon my arrival.

"Ice-skating scoring is ridiculously complicated now. I would have no idea how to average all my categories together," I say.

"What categories?"

"Fit, maturity level, color scheme, appropriateness, flava . . ." I drone.

"Flavor? Like what it tastes like?" Lish raises a seductive eyebrow.

"Um, no. Flava. With an *a* at the end. It's a word the kids used to use. I'm bringing it back."

"How about you just score them from one to ten?" Lish suggests.

"If you want to sell yourself short on my classically trained outfit judging, then one to ten is fine by me."

"Seeing as you're still wearing a fluorescent orange t-shirt from your place of employment, one to ten should be sufficient."

"You can borrow it if you want. This thing's got flava for days."

"Thanks, but I don't know how Travis feels about that color orange. Or any color for that matter. What if he's color blind? This is so exciting! So many questions." Lish practically squees as she shivers in delighted anticipation. And I'm happy for her. I think. I've been happy for her in the past when she's gone out with guys she's liked. But this is beyond like. This is straight-up old-fashioned setup with a new-jack twist. What if Travis is a serial killer? Seriously, what if the magical force that brought on the Naming is maniacally evil?

I don't even know what to believe about why or how the Names are here: religion, magic, chemistry. It's all so arbitrary and abstract. And it still doesn't explain a damn thing.

Not that any of this matters to Lish. She looks adorable in every outfit she tries on, glowing with impending servitude—not quite what I mean, but what *do* I mean exactly? "Hey, Lish? I understand that you're excited to meet Travis and get to know him, but what exactly do you see as the final frontier of this summer?" I ask.

"Well, marriage, natch. Eventually. Not at the end of the summer or anything. But the goal is, you know, forever."

The word *forever* rings in my head with a cavernous echo, a flashing neon sign. My skin bristles at this prospect. For Lish. For me. I want to run out of her house screaming, steal a car, and drive across the nearest border to escape this insanity. But it would be no use because it is everywhere. Every state. Every country. Every continent. I could hide in a bubble kingdom on the bottom of the ocean and the Naming would still find me. It already has.

And it seems to be taking my best friend.

CHAPTER 13

I didn't bother telling Lish about the happenings—or nonhappenings—with Luke. One of my favorite qualities of Lish is how comically judgmental she can be about the smallest things—toenail shape, nose-hair volume, the distance between piercings in earlobes. And yet it is this same trait that's preventing me from talking to my best friend about a guy I like. Because now the potential is there for judgment, size grande. If Lish firmly believes Hendrix Cutter is my meant-to-be-forever, tie-me-to-his-wall-with-a-chain-and-throw-away-the-key soul mate, then liking anyone else will seem to her like cheating. *Ballistic* is a gentle way to describe her reaction to my dad and Florence Hildebrand (I had to talk her down from a road trip. Destination: egg his new house).

Besides, Luke only seems vaguely interested in me on the occasions we've been near enough to talk and make physical contact, but our Empties are the big black cloud in the *possibility* of our lust-filled summer.

Or so I thought.

Following our opening weekend, Monday is far less crowded. Luke and I even manage to throw up our handy-dandy signs at each other, once for me to take a pee break and once to signify lunch together. The morning passes slowly, with short enough lines that I allow several kids to remain in their boats over multiple go-arounds. The temperature is annoyingly chilly for a summer day, and the clouds aren't helping the matter. I snuggle into my Haunted Hollow hoodie. While the awning offers shade on hot and sunny days, on cooler ones it feels like it drops the temperature another ten degrees. Or maybe it's all the standing still I'm doing. I'm dreaming of the leftover pizza I packed for lunch when I feel a tap on my left shoulder. It's Keely from Games, here to take over during my break. The nice thing about Keely being my lunch replacement, aside from the obvious saving me from the brink of starvation, is that it means Keely won't be at lunch with me and Luke. It's no fun having drool on cold pizza.

I leave Keely with the controls and head over to pick up Luke. Keith, a second-season concessions worker, chats with him. "Hey, hey, Aggy. How goes it?"

Keith just finished his junior year at Luke's high school, and I've never gotten a very good read on him. He seems nice enough, and I was nearly prepared to hook up with him last summer. There were times when he climbed his fingers up my back, a spot where I'm incredibly ticklish, and I recall one day where we held hands underneath the lunch table. All very innocent and leading nowhere, but I would have been open to it. Besides, last summer I could have been with anyone I wanted and not worried about whether or not we had a future together.

I want so badly to live this summer the same way.

And why can't I? Hendrix Cutter isn't here to stop me. Why is that? Maybe Hendrix Cutter is sleeping with an entire cheerleading squad, laughing in the face of Empties. God, I hope my MTB wouldn't sleep with an entire cheerleading squad. Not that he can't sleep with whomever he wants, but really—cheerleaders? I'd prefer he sleep with the girls' hockey team. Or the Science Olympiad.

Ugh. At least get out of my brain, Hendrix Cutter, if I can't get you off my body!

That sounds pervy no matter how you slice it.

"Catch you later, Keith," Luke says as he drapes his arm over my shoulder. It feels very marking-his-territory to do it in front of Keith. I'm glad he doesn't pee on me. For various reasons.

I consider reaching my right hand up to hold Luke's hand on my shoulder, but I decide against it. I'm so confused by the message he's sending that I don't want to encourage the hope that's growing in the pit of my stomach.

Or maybe that's hunger.

I wish I knew what Luke is thinking. What if Luke wants to shun the constraints of Empties altogether, combine our Haunted Hollow earnings, and run away to Australia together at the end of the summer? What if Scarlett Dresden has already made contact, and he's merely biding his time until she gets here? What if he's just resting his arm on my shoulder because I'm the perfect height for an armrest?

We enter the employee cafeteria, and Luke walks to the counter to buy a hot lunch. I place my pizza in the microwave because, as much as I love cold pizza, I'm too chilled to eat it. I damn myself for not wearing jeans today, but I hate those days when I put on jeans in the morning, the temperature rises, and by the time the afternoon arrives I've got sweat rings under my fluorescent orange armpits and a fine line trickling down my butt crack.

When we've retrieved our food, Luke and I meet at a table for two in a far corner of the cafeteria.

I really do love the way his longer hair frames his face. I love it even more when he tucks it behind his ears to eat his salad.

"You're putting me to shame with your salad," I note, blowing on the overheated pizza slice in my hand.

"I have chicken tenders, too." He nods his fork to the fried chicken strips on his tray.

"What's the difference between chicken tenders and chicken fingers?"

He considers. "The meat inside? *Tenders* sounds tasty, while *fingers* sounds like you're eating a body part."

"Which you are," I point out.

"True, but not that one. Chickens don't really have fingers, right? And there's no meat on the ones they do have."

"Okay. So what's a nugget, then?"

"Is that a trademark? Like technically a McDonald's thing only? Or can any small ball of fried chicken be called a nugget?"

"I don't know. I'll have to do some research. And then there's the mysterious popcorn chicken. . . ."

"Definitely add that to your study. Take notes, and write a full report for me tomorrow," Luke assigns.

"Will I be graded on this?" I ask.

"Pass/fail." He laughs. "Speaking of research," Luke awkwardly segues, "have you looked up your MTB online? What was his name? Morrison?"

I'm not thrilled to have a conversation with Luke about my Empty, although I do enjoy that he attempted to remember his name. "Hendrix." I look to the side coyly, acknowledging the uniqueness of the name.

"Right. Like Jimi." Luke dips a chicken tender in mustard.

"I guess. I mean, I'd assume. Maybe his parents were big music fans." I have tried not to think too much on the origin of the name Hendrix Cutter, yet here I am having that exact conversation with a guy who could make most girls forget they even have an Empty. "And, no, I haven't looked him up."

"Not at all? Not even, like, a Google search?"

"No. I don't want to know who he is because I don't want

my love life to be dictated by some bizarre skin irritation," I spit out a tad too aggressively.

Luke breathes out a laugh through his nose as he chews. "It is pretty weird, isn't it? My mom looked up mine."

"Scarlett," I say, and immediately kick myself for remembering her first name. And her last name. But at least I only acknowledged the first.

"Yeah. There aren't many. The one closest to my age, at least according to Facebook, lives in Idaho. Mom says she's cute," he says tentatively. Just what I want to hear. "But . . ." I like hearing that more. "I didn't want to see her just because her name is scratched into my chest." My eyes scrutinize his chest, clearly defined through his orange t-shirt, but no sign of Scarlett's name. God, I hate that name.

"How would I even meet her without making the effort to travel to Idaho? Or for her to come to me. It's not like I've heard from her." Do I detect a hint of disappointment? "If we're so 'meant to be' why don't we live near each other? Seems like a lot of work for someone I don't know. I'm going to college in Wisconsin." Luke rocks back in his chair, running his hand through his hair. Brown strands fall over his eyes. I note they're gray today.

I want to tell him that he doesn't *have* to meet her, that he, we all, have a choice. But he goes first. "Agatha, it's probably our last summer here, and I have no idea what the future holds."

"We can head over to Madame Grizelda's tent after

lunch," I joke. Luke's dead-serious expression makes me wish I could take back a dorky joke about a psychic.

"What I'm trying to say is: What do you think of me and you together? Like, for the summer? One last go before . . ." He trails off into the unknown.

I'm dumbstruck. I want to stick my napkin in my ears and clean them out so they make a squeaky cartoon sound. Luke is saying exactly what I'm feeling, what I've fantasized coming out of someone else's mouth, particularly one as tempting as Luke's. When I take some time to think, he says, "I'm a tool. I know it sucks to hook up with someone when you know it can never last, and I don't want to put you in an awkward position."

"Yes!" I interrupt with a probably too enthusiastic high-pitched cry. "I will absolutely be your noncommitted girl person." Please put me in whatever awkward position you deem fit.

Luke's gray eyes glint naughtily. "Just for the summer, right? And pretend like the future doesn't exist?"

"What's the future?" I snicker. Why is it he sounds like someone from a John Hughes movie, and I sound like a snorting *Full House* character?

Who the hell cares? He wants to be with me. Time to stop asking questions.

"All right, then." Luke grins. I melt at those dimples. He looks at the clock. "Lunch is over."

"I wouldn't want to keep Keely waiting. I'm sure she's dying to eat her Ring Pop for lunch."

“And then an entire bag of cotton candy for dessert. I’ve seen her do it.”

“Ah, the spoils of youth,” I say as we walk back to our rides. This time, when Luke hangs his arm over my shoulder, I hold his hand and lean in. Future be damned.

CHAPTER 14

Besides texting and/or messaging through any of seven different apps on my phone, my social media site of choice (for the last six months, so you know it must be good) is Chapbook. Embarrassingly enough, my mom got me into it. In her teens she created and sent real paper minibooks of poetry, pictures, questionnaires, comics—some pages meant only for reading, other pages with quizzes and multiple-choice surveys, some pages even left blank. She and her friends, whom she mostly met in the backs of teen magazines (that really used to exist. People would list their addresses in magazines so they could find pen pals with similar hobbies and obsessions. Seems like the perfect recipe for stalking and kidnapping, but my mom swears it was different back then. Don't remind me), traded these "chapbooks" with each other so that they could, I guess, delve into one another's minds and get the answers to pertinent questions like, "Would you rather drink a bottle of Tabasco sauce or your own pee?"*

Since no one has time anymore to make and trade paper chapbooks (I don't think. They for sure aren't splaying out

**actual page from one of my mom's chapbooks*

their home addresses in magazines for every Tom, Dick, and Scary to see), a brilliant woman of my mom's generation invented Chapbook.com. The format is so gloriously old school, with each entry looking like a crappily photocopied book, and it offers a multitude of page formats for everything from a daily journal to a photo album to a survey where I, too, can ask my friends (and mild acquaintances, plus friends of mild acquaintances) if they would rather drink Tabasco or their own pee. (My own pee, by the way. Tabasco is gross.)

What I like the most about Chapbook, aside from the creative slant as opposed to the complete "Look at me" parade of most social media sites, is that I don't have to see anyone else's crap unless I click on their icon. A list of Chapbook friends lines the side of the screen, and the only way I'll see what they're doing is by clicking on them. I much prefer it to looking at puffed-lip selfies and grammatically abhorrent updates.

I click on Lish's face, a picture that I took of her pretending to sun herself with a reflective panel (really a disposable turkey pan). I flip through the pages of her Chapbook, mostly filled with doodles about graduating high school and the start of summer. What begins as a smattering of posts about MTBs turns into a full-on assault by the end of her Chapbook. She obviously has Travis on the brain. I stop on a page with a quote: *"We do not choose. He chooses it for us, and we are guided by our hearts." —Susan Lobel.*

Huh? I know Lish is enamored with the idea of Travis, that he is *The One*, but is she seriously drinking the True

Lover Kool-Aid? I don't know who Susan Lobel is, and technically the *He* in reference may not be God, but why am I finding out such revelatory information on my best friend's Chapbook?

Or am I reading too much into it? Did she merely repost a quote about love because she's feeling lovey-dovey?

I close Lish's book and flip through a few other friends' Chapbooks. The themes of many are the same: true love, destiny, The One. Am I really in the minority here? I guess I've always known that I am, but here is solid Internet proof that even the people with whom I'm closest don't share the same ideals as I do. If that's the case, then maybe it'll be infinitesimally more difficult to find partners who want to explore the world with me without the constraints of an Empty. What if I'm alone, and I don't want to be alone, and therefore I am forced to find the one man who, based on my FLESH, is meant to be my man? What if I'm bullied into falling in love with Hendrix Cutter because there is no one left?

My phone cackles at me, a sound byte from *Hocus Pocus*, and it's Lish over Viddle, our video chat app of choice. Reluctantly I answer. "Travis will be here tomorrow!" I've never seen her so giddy. Well, maybe when she discovered the flippy-haired, gap-toothed beauty that was Zac Efron in *High School Musical* at age nine. And I don't care what angle you're shooting from—Travis is no Zac Efron.

I wonder who Zac Efron's MTB is. Seems the paparazzi never catch him with his shirt off anymore, even at the beach. Shame.

While I'm thinking of something supportive to say, Lish carries on. I don't think she'd notice if I hung up the phone. Or walked away to make a sandwich. I kind of want a sandwich.

"We chatted for two hours today. Two hours! We have so much in common. How did my body pick the perfect guy for me? It's insane."

Insane is one way to view it. "Maybe you shouldn't be talking for such long chunks of time. What if you run out of things to say? What if you've already run out, and he arrives tomorrow and all you can say is hello?"

Damn, I'm being a shitty friend. I try to reel in my cynicism for Empties. "But probably not. I'm sure you'll have lots to talk about. And if not, you can watch a movie and discuss it. Or read a book. You could start a book group!" I enthuse. "But remember: Don't invite me. Because if there's one thing that stops me from reading a book, it's the accountability of a book group."

I'm blathering about book groups.

"Which outfit did you choose?" I ask, hoping I sound genuinely interested, which I would totally be under normal circumstances. Lish and I have dressed over the phone for countless bar mitzvahs, birthday parties, school dances, and first dates. But dressing for her Empty, for *Travis* (will I ever be able to say his name without disdain?), gives me that icky tummy knot you get when the seat belt light pings mid-pee in an airplane bathroom.

My discomfort is not necessarily with Travis proper. For

all I know, he's a great guy and a suitable match (I refuse to use the word *perfect*) for Lish. But for frak's sake, does it have to happen now? When we're only eighteen? Why couldn't the Names appear when we're twenty-five instead? When we've had time to percolate, mature, explore, experience, graduate college . . . for those who want to do that. Or travel the world seeking out new and unusual amusement parks, if that's what floats our boats. Finding your partner for life at eighteen is putting an expiration date on youth.

Lish and I have been partners for a solid fifteen years. When we were little, we played Star Wars and My Little Ponies and Teenage Mutant Ninja Turtles. We made them fight and fall in love and fly on airplanes. I had the travel fantasy even then, and none of our story lines were impeded by a lack of free will. Then the Naming happened, and even though we were getting too old to technically play with toys, we still did so, on occasion, holed up in Lish's bedroom. The story arcs began to morph. Princess Leia knew from the get-go she was looking for Han Solo. There was never an uncomfortable kiss with her twin brother, Luke. Instead of looking for help to save the galaxy, she was seeking her MTB.

And it wasn't just me and Lish who changed history with the Naming. Pop culture jumped on that shit quicker than me flying out of my bed when I spot an earwig. Existential art films examining the pull of destiny versus choice, of old loves broken, became award-season fodder. Big-budget romance flicks of lovers overcoming great obstacles to find their MTB. Reality TV following young men and women on their searches. Follow-up reality programs about life with the newlywed MTBs. Science-fiction novels about futuristic MTB technology, where scientists can synthesize the proteins involved in creating the Name at birth so you can actually start dating at one week old. Pop stars crooning about serendipity; indie rockers warbling over love lost when Empties are found; clothing lines specifically designed to showcase the Names.

If I didn't see it on my own skin, I would dare to say the whole thing was a complete scam devised by mass media corporations.

Lish, while more enamored with the concept of an MTB than I, still managed to share a relatively normal high school existence with me. There were giggles and boys and curfews and fights and fencing club and after-school jobs and good-enough grades that we both aspired to go to college.

I guess we both changed a bit on that front.

Not that either of us doesn't want to go to college. Sort of. Someday. Lish is all forward momentum, choosing a local university with a promising chemistry program. I'm technically still registered at another nearby school (until the Wizard gives me some courage and I tell my mom my actual plans) with a decent art history program as well as graphic design. Not that I necessarily want to pursue careers in either of those fields. How am I supposed to know what I want to do for the rest of my life? And to top that off, the universe decided it also needed to throw who I'm going to spend the rest of my life with into the mix?

I can only hope having Travis around doesn't change things too much between me and Lish. I don't know if I could take that.

"So I have a little guy news myself," I segue, hoping my prior fears about Lish's judgment go unfounded.

"Hendrix found you! I knew it!" Lish bounces on her bed.

"Calm down, Lish. Sorry to disappoint you, but I'm talking about Luke."

"From work?" I detect an air of skepticism. Or maybe I'm projecting.

"Yes. He doesn't have a girlfriend anymore, and he looks ten times more tasty than he ever has, which is saying a lot because he was already a six or whatever on your fancy ice-skating scale. He kind of asked me to go out for the summer."

Her face reads mom-level concerned, and I watch as she deep breathes herself down a couple of notches. "Just for the summer?"

"That's what I said. For the summer. But it would be perfectly okay if it lasted longer. I mean, what if we really like each other?" I don't know who I'm trying to convince more, me or Lish.

"That would be . . . nice?" I give Lish friend points for her attempt at supporting me. Not that there's anything to support. Luke and I said we're together for the summer, and that's that.

But what if it's not?

How does one casually date when the future has been vehemently laid out in dissenting directions?

I don't want Lish to hear the confusion in my voice. "Don't worry, my little Lish loaf. One fun summer is not going to kill my romantic future. Enjoy your Travis dreams. I can't wait to hear all about your first day together. I'm sure it is meant-to-be perfect." I chuckle.

We hang up, and instead of feeling happy for Lish's big day or for my destiny-free summer, I merely feel aimless.

Isn't that what I wanted?

CHAPTER 15

I wake nursing a strange combination of anticipation and dread. My aim is to suppress the negativity over Travis's arrival by focusing on the newly established relationship with Luke. *Relationship* might be the wrong word. Is he technically my boyfriend? Do people have "boyfriends" once they grow their MTBs? Am I theoretically cheating on Hendrix Cutter? I wonder how that would make him feel. I wonder if Hendrix Cutter wonders how I feel. I wonder why I can't stop myself from wondering about Hendrix Cutter.

"Luke Jacobs," I say his name aloud as I brush my teeth in my underwear. *Spit.* See. That wasn't so hard. Well, it wouldn't be if Hendrix Cutter's name wasn't staring at me from above my bra. So rude.

I slide a clean Haunted Hollow shirt over my head. I made sure to wash it last night, seeing as it might be in close proximity to Luke. I wouldn't want the daily rank of working nearby a funnel cake stand to overshadow our freshly formed . . .

There it is again. What are Luke and I if we're not each other's MTB?

I am already bored of postulating, and the monstrosity only blossomed on my chest days ago. Is this why people get together with their Empties? Because they are driven mad by the constant reminder? It's like, "Fine! I don't want to meet this person, but I can't stop thinking about him and I would like to presume he can't stop thinking about me so let's get it over with and fall the fuck in love already."

Bloody romantic.

I sit next to Uncle Jim on the couch. He watches DVR'd episodes of *Maury* every morning before he writes. Some days I join him, even though the monotony of the show's theme annoys the shit out of me. Particularly over the last week.

Maury looks into the camera and says a string of words he has spoken countless times over the last six years. "We have three sets of eighteen-year-old friends. Some are certain they are each other's MTBs. They have yet to reveal the Names on their chests and have come to us today to find out the truth."

"Ugh," I groan, sitting down with a piece of raisin toast. "The biggest morons go on this show. Seriously, you can't just ask the other person? Peek down their shirts? Bust in on them 'by accident' in the shower?"

"They want the drama. They want to be on TV." Uncle Jim sips his coffee knowingly.

"Do they think looking like a dumbass on a show only watched by total weirdos—present company completely included—is going to lead to fame?" I sound worked up, but I love that shows—and people—like this exist. Because then

I get to watch and laugh at them. They get their fifteen minutes of *Maury* fame, and I get to feel superior to a subset of my fellow Americans.

This at least makes sense to me.

Plus, Uncle Jim and I have this conversation once, maybe twice a week.

Back on *Maury*, the first couple has donned their "soul mate suits," a ludicrous creation that looks like a set of scrubs with a plastic window sewn into the chest area. Concealing the window is a patch of fabric, clinging for dear life with Velcro and covered with clever question marks, as though the Riddler designed the ensemble.

The slow reveal is expertly dragged out by Maury, honed through years of practice back when his catchphrase was "You are NOT the father!"

When the young man and woman finally rip their Velcro veils from their shirts, Maury yells out, "You are NOT the soul mate!"

The young woman on the television sobs, while her anticipated beau jumps onto his pleather chair to celebrate. "I told you! I told you!"

"Romance never looked quite so beautiful." I shake my head, wiping away a fake tear. "Time to go to work," I announce and peel myself off the couch. Before I leave the house, I feel the need to glean my uncle's opinion on the Luke state of affairs.

"Uncle Jim," I call from the front door. He looks up from his WHAT WOULD BUFFY DO? coffee mug and crooks an eyebrow at me. "Remember that guy I told you about from work? Luke?" Uncle Jim switches eyebrows. A gift. "Well, we're kind of going to go out this summer. Like, date, I guess. I don't quite know what it means, since we both have MTBs now and it's supposed to just be for the summer, but he's really cute and funny and I've always liked him and . . ."

Uncle Jim finally puts the eyebrows to rest and speaks. "Aggy, you do what you want. Don't let any letters on your chest dictate your life. Go have fun. Ask yourself what Savannah Merlot would do," he offers. "Just don't tell me too many details." He grants me a coy smile and returns to sipping his coffee.

Feeling puffed up by the advice, I open the door to leave. As I shut it behind me, I hear Uncle Jim shout, "Wear a condom!"

Is this happening?

It's not like I haven't had a boyfriend before or been in a relationship or hooked up or whatever. But this is a new era.

And it is Luke Jacobs.

He of the newly expanded shoulders and shaggy, grab-able hair and mysterious mood-ring eyes. And I have not forgotten every delectable moment of last summer's kiss. What if that's all he wants? A summer booty call? Would I be okay with that?

He is überlovely, but I also kind of like him. Enough that when I'm alone in my bed on a lazy Saturday morning, it's him that I think about. That when I eat a caramel apple during the fall, long after the gates of Haunted Hollow have closed for the season, I reminisce about the time Luke and I were practically attacked by bees as we attempted to eat candy apples during one of our breaks. And I like him enough right now that I don't want to admit to myself that the anticipation of seeing him is probably the reason I have to poo when I get to work.

I wonder if love equals poo in anyone else's world.

Not that I *love* Luke. I don't know him well enough to go that far. So let's just say I like him and I better stop getting red lights or I'm going to have to call in sick as a result of not making it to a bathroom in time.

This conversation in my head has been brought to you by the Irritable Bowel Syndrome Society.

After a quick pit stop in the nearest kiddie bathroom (I'm not leaving any aromatic evidence in the staff room), I make my way to the Devil's Dinghies. I check today's schedule and see, annoyingly, that Luke is off for the day. Kind of a shitty start to our not-exactly-relationship, no?

I sluggishly walk toward the ride, and upon arrival am surprised to see cans of paint and paintbrushes lining the wall near the mural. I'm not sure when Sam Hain expects me to do the painting, but I'm excited by the prospect. Even though I'm no great artist, I took art classes all through high school and would love to be able to continue doing something creative in my daily life. It's daunting to think of creative pursuits outside of class assignments. Some people write or draw or play music in their spare time, and I envy them. Me? I've never found the motivation to do more than read fan fiction, watch TV, and go for the occasional run when my industrial-strength sports bra is clean. How do I become inspired enough to create unless someone else is forcing me to do so? Is Sam Hain forcing me to do this? I wouldn't want to tell him no now that he's bought the paint.

I'm glad that I have the assignment. Especially since today Travis arrives, and I can assume that my nights, once filled with vintage sitcoms or Viddles with Lish, may start to become significantly freed up.

CHAPTER 16

One of the many perks of working at a kiddie amusement park versus an all-ages park is that Haunted Hollow closes at six o'clock. That means I still have nighttime to do . . .

. . . what exactly am I going to do tonight? Employees aren't allowed cell phones at their ride areas, so if I want to communicate with the non-Haunted world (some days I do, when I'm particularly bored or annoyed with belligerent parents or excited about a hangout later in the day; some days I don't, when the kids are excruciatingly adorable, the parents polite, and Luke is decidedly charming) I have to wait until I can access my locker at lunchtime or the end of the day.

At the beginning of lunch, I assume I'll have fifteen texts from Lish detailing every moment of her long awaited rendezvous with Travis.

Nada.

Not a text or emoji or any message on any one of my six thousand options for cellular communication.

Must be busy.

There is, however, a message from Luke.

Anyone fall into the Dinghies abyss today?

I smile a secret smile as I reread the message sixteen times. Adam eats his tuna surprise (they add raisins. Surprise!), oblivious to the newly blooming pinkness on my cheeks.

Only a Buzz Lightyear toy. It was like the horror Toy Story sequel the world has dreamed about.

I slowly chew my peanut butter and banana chips sandwich, awaiting a reply. Some days Uncle Jim decides he wants to be parental and packs me a lunch. That's how I end up with chunky peanut butter and dried banana chips in the same sandwich, which sounds gross but is insanely delicious and crunchy and I think Elvis would have approved.

My phone cackles in my lap, and I eagerly read the next message from Luke.

Come over tonight?

Ugh and swoon and melt. Could that have been written any more perfectly? Let us dissect:

- He skips the formalities of the "Can you," almost as though he desperately needs to see me.
- There is something nonchalant yet seductive about the word *come*. Or maybe I'm looking too much into that one.
- By not saying "to my house," he is already adopting a casual familiarity, like, of course I know where "over" is (even though I have never been to his house before and have no idea where he lives).

- My absolute favorite piece of this is the question mark. Without it, Luke would have sounded like a dominant asshole. But the question mark turns him into a pleading puppy dog.

My fingers are itching to type a resounding YES into my phone, but I allow myself to take two more bites of my PB&B sandwich to feign coolness. Before I can enter the letter *y*, another message chimes. This time from Lish.

Travis is here and he is everything. Come meet him after work!

Analysis:

This text bothers me for a slew of reasons.

- Why does the first word have to be *Travis*? No greeting? No *I* statements?
- He is Everything? Like, fucking EVERY-THING? How is that possible? What does that even mean? Everything she ever dreamed of? Everything he presented to her on his online profile? Everything to her, and, if so, everything she'll ever need from now on, which does not include me?
- Her usage of the word *come* is very bossy.
- Why doesn't she ask if I want to meet him? Why must she demand that I do so?
- Exclamation point=Order me around much?

- Why does she assume I have nothing to do after work? Maybe I'm tired after a hard day of pushing buttons and helping kids after they've had a *guest illness* (ie, ride barf). Maybe I'm going to hang out with other friends from school. Or work friends. Or one work friend in particular who is over a foot taller than me and writes magnificent messages to me instead of this dictatorial drivel and wants me to *come over*, if you know what I'm saying.

Before I can stop myself, I type:

Sorry—made plans.

And send it to Lish.

But then I feel a little guilty. Because this is Lish. And it's not like she's telling me to come over and clean her toilets or take a physics exam or go to college when I don't want to. And it *is* like she's including me on what could possibly be one of the most important thresholds of her life.

I type another message.

Tomorrow? I can't wait to meet him.

It may not be true, but at least my conscience won't berate me the rest of the day.

Lunch break is almost up, which I am made fully aware of when Adam asks, "If you're not going to finish, I'll take that oatmeal scotchie off your hands."

I shove the entirety of the cookie into my mouth before

he helps himself, and he pouts accordingly. Then he proceeds to eat the slice of cafeteria cake he already had on his tray.

"How do you eat with that hat on?" I crinkle my nose at the tangy stank drifting off certain angles.

"I'm immune at this point." Adam's lips are framed with frosting. My cue to return to work. I type a hasty but cool *Sure. What's your address?* to Luke and stow the phone in my locker, then spend the rest of the afternoon in my head's fantasyland that's probably too PG-13 for a kids' amusement park. Maybe R. Although it's pretty hard to be too pervy in my daydreams when I have to seat-belt flailing five-year-olds into tiny boats as their moms apathetically pacify them from the queue.

A busy afternoon fast forwards my shift quickly, and by the time six o'clock rolls around and the stragglers are ushered out the front gates, I'm a bundle of nerves.

It's not as though Luke invited me to his house to have butt-naked sex. And it's not like I haven't had sex before (albeit somewhat mediocre, kind-of-ending-in-emotional-trauma sex). I've had boyfriends, boys who were friends, gropey friend–acquaintance things, and we didn't do the do. What am I getting so bunged up about? Maybe it's because Luke and I have known each other awhile, so there's already an established relationship of sorts. But never with a label (as non-labely as our label is) and never when he didn't have a girlfriend (note: this didn't stop us that one time). Do I want to have sex with him tonight? Theoretically, I've wanted to have sex with Luke Jacobs since the first time I saw him. The way you do that in your head, to your best friend, you say, *Oh my god, I want to sleep with Luke Jacobs*, where you don't actually envision you will ever really be taking your clothes off and seeing his penis and then, you know, the whole condom thing and the crinkly wrapper and then rolling it on down and then him actually inserting his penis into your vagina and . . .

OH MY GOD I just made sex sound like the least sexy thing imaginable. I should fucking teach sex ed because kids would be all, *If that's what it's like, why bother?*

How am I even related to my bodice-ripping writer uncle? Maybe I should get some pointers from him the next time I attempt to pontificate on the fantasy world of a teenage girl's brain.

What I was getting at, before I rudely interrupted myself with the words *penis* and *vagina*, is that the *idea* of sex with Luke Jacobs is hot. The *possibility* of sex with Luke Jacobs is slightly trauma-inducing.

It is, however, only June.

CHAPTER 17

I casually sprint to my locker to check my phone. As I hustle along, I faintly hear Adam catcall, "Looking good, Aggy!" Damn you, average-support bra! I remind myself to review the park's sexual harassment policy and race to the staff room at a pace that will get me there quickly without breaking a sweat.

There, standing in front of my locker is one Luke Jacobs, all brawn and silky hair, in a Faith No More t-shirt, shorts, and ragged checked Vans.

"No fair," I quip. "You get to be dapper, and I'm stuck in fluorescent orange."

"I don't know if I'd call this *dapper.* And it would be a lot weirder if I wore my Haunted Hollow shirt on my day off, wouldn't it?"

"I suppose," I concede.

"Besides. You look cute in fluorescent orange." Giggle.

"You kind of have to say that, seeing as you've never actually seen me in another color," I say.

"Well, we're just going to have to change that, aren't we?"

He smiles down at me, warm and gooey like a hot-out-of-the-oven chocolate chip cookie.

I don't have the wherewithal for a clever retort, so I ask, "What are you doing here, exactly? I thought I was going to your house."

"Yeah, well, my mom and her man are home, cuddled up on the couch, and I thought that might take away from our first date."

First date. First date. First date.

"Yeah. Parents. *Pffft.*" If I continue with this enchanting dialogue, there may be no second date.

"You wanna get something to eat? I just have to pick up my sunglasses at the Ghoster. I left them yesterday."

"Sounds good," I reply, and reach into my locker to grab my stuff.

The two of us walk toward the Ghoster, periodically bumping arms due to our close, but-not-too-close strides. His skin feels warm, and the light hair on his arm tickles my own.

We pass the Terror Train, and Adam whistles at us, the *swit-swoo* sound from antiquated cartoons. "Does he understand that what he's doing makes people uncomfortable?" I ponder.

"He's definitely socially stunted. Did that make you uncomfortable?" Luke asks, concerned.

"Not that, per se, although kind of dorky, no? Mostly it's when he's staring at and/or commentating on my boobs," I say, and immediately realize I am practically begging Luke to look at them. Or maybe daring him not to look at them?

Luke glances down, and I'm not sure if it's directly at my breasts or not. He has to look in that general direction anyway since his eyes are much higher than any part of my body. Plus, he's allowed to look at my boobs. The way I like the ropy muscles of his forearms. An even trade.

"Adam's harmless. I mean, I can see why it would bother you. The thought of my boobs being anywhere near his hat—"

"Good save," I note.

"Thanks." Luke considers something for a moment. "I can talk to him if you want."

"That could be all kinds of awkward. I don't want him to know I said anything to you about it."

"I could come at it from a different angle. Like, stop looking at my woman's body," he says in a gruff, assertive voice that makes me blush.

"I'll let you know," I say, and tingle at the *my woman* detail.

Luke picks up his sunglasses from under the control booth console. Together we decide on pizza for dinner, and he recommends a local place called Bill's since I don't know the area well.

We pass the Devil's Dinghies, and Luke spies the paint cans along the wall.

"Is someone finally repainting the mural? That project is way overdue."

"I agree, and actually, that someone is me. Although I don't really know when. I was considering starting tonight before I heard from you."

"I could help," Luke suggests. "I worked stage crew freshman year. Painted the *Fiddler on the Roof* set," he tells me with a modicum of pride.

"Just freshman year? Why'd you quit?" I ask.

"Too intense. It was like a cult."

"I've heard that about the theater department. I considered joining, but I'm too lazy."

"A fine quality in a woman." Luke winks. I don't think I've ever been referred to as a woman so many times in one day.

We walk to the parking lot, and Luke leads me to his gray Ford Focus. He moves to the passenger side, I presume for purposes of chivalry, but proceeds to lean in and throw crumpled fast food wrappers into the backseat. "I have a confession to make." He draws his lengthy torso out of the doorway. "I am a junk food addict. And a total slob. Can we still be lovers?" he asks.

"Lovers?" I cringe.

"Bad choice of word. Friends? With benefits? Possible benefits, I mean. I don't want to assume."

"Because then you'd make an ass out of you and me," I volunteer.

"Exactly," he concurs.

We avoid the answers and drive with music loud and windows open. I'm glad I don't hate the songs he chooses.

It would be tragic for our nonrelationship to end so soon based on musical incompatibility. I once had a crush on this adorable band geek until I realized he was a hard-core country fan. Not like good, old country music, but new country that's all 'MERICA and drinking out of plastic cups.

When we arrive at Bill's I let myself out of the car, a gesture that feels perfectly natural to me but is a point deducter on Lish's list. Luke soon rectifies any potential dating gaffe by meeting me at the front of the car and lacing his fingers through mine. His hand is slightly steering-wheel sticky, but the size discrepancy negates anything bad about this situation.

Bill's Pizza is an institution of hunting and stuffed animals. There is a dead duck mounted directly above our booth. They also have baskets of peanuts on the table, and you're encouraged to throw the shells on the tiled floor. A restaurant deadly to both animals and anyone with peanut allergies.

We order a half-sausage, half-cheese pizza and munch from a basket of peanuts as we make small talk about our senior years. Luke has a million stories about everything from overstretched swimsuit elastic mishaps on the swim team (not his) to spending most of prom in a hotel bathroom throwing up due to a wonky shrimp salad. I share tales of Uncle Jim's romance novels and the time Lish and I went to a late-night Harry Potter movie marathon where I fell asleep during *Sorcerer's Stone* and didn't wake until Harry, Ron, and

Hermione sent their own kids to Hogwarts. Luke tells me he's never seen or read Harry Potter, and I act like this isn't a huge kick in the gut. Not everyone can like the same things, I convince myself. Even soul mates. I wonder what his thoughts are on *Doctor Who*. (Best not ask. That could be a deal breaker.) I consider how I'd feel if Hendrix Cutter didn't like Harry Potter or the Doctor, and quickly reprimand myself for even thinking about Hendrix Cutter at such a time. Then I can't stop myself, and I break out in a light sweat at the prospect of Hendrix Cutter busting through the double doors of Bill's Pizza holding a limp bouquet of daffodils, calling out desperately, "Agatha Abrams! Where are you?"

Luke keeps talking as though I'm not insane, and the voice in my head eventually shuts up. Conversation is relatively funny and easy and does not once fall into the trappings of MTBs or college or The Future. I imagine this is what dates were like before the Naming.

The pizza arrives, and I stick with the all-cheese side. I failed to tell Luke that sausages gross me out due to the tiny fat globules inside. Luke doesn't notice, and he manages to polish off the entire sausage side himself. Not without offering me the last piece, of course.

The one thing that would make this date better is if I were not wearing my work clothes, but seeing as Luke didn't seem to care (maybe he is one of the chosen few who is turned on by fluorescent orange), I try not to let it bother me.

When the check comes, Luke pays it with a wave of his

hand and "I got this." Hendrix Cutter is nowhere to be seen. I'd say this date is going quite well.

As we walk back to the car, Luke rubbing circles on his unnoticeably distended belly, he hooks his arm over my shoulder. It's heavy but welcome, and I decide to make the move of linking my fingers through his. He pulls me in closer, and I lean into his t-shirt, trying not to be too obvious as I inhale his soapy scent.

This time he does open the door for me, not just for fast-food evacuation, and I slide into the seat. Take that, Lish! We drive back to Haunted Hollow and park in the employee lot. The back gate remains open, as maintenance and Sam Hain stay late some nights. We enter the park and stroll past Sam Hain's office. Mr. Hain looks out the window at us, and I attempt an international symbol for painting (gleaned from *The Karate Kid*—up, down, up, down). It seems to satisfy him, and Luke and I travel to the Devil's Dinghies.

I lower the wooden plank from the park side to the grassy island inside the ride, considering for a moment that Luke may be too large for the flimsy plank. He deftly crosses, and we survey the mural to select which devil wins the first face-lift. I choose my favorite image, that of a red devil boiling three humans in a cauldron, stirring around their rope-restrained bodies with glee. Much of the red on the devil and the black on the cauldron have eroded, and the terrified expressions on the people's faces are barely recognizable.

"Let's start here," I say to Luke.

"Ooh. That one's my favorites." He grins. How are we not a match made in heaven? Or science? Or wherever Empties come from? I try not to dwell on the elephant in everyone's room and attempt to open the black paint canister. The lid won't budge.

"I got it," Luke offers, and with the tip of his keys manages to pop off the paint lid effortlessly.

"Thank you, Gaston," I chide.

We dip our brushes into the inky liquid and delicately dab strokes of color back onto the wall. Our bodies are in near-constant contact, a shoulder here, an elbow there, an occasional lean on Luke's back for leverage.

"If this were a cheesy movie, you and I would start playfully paint-fighting each other right now," Luke notes.

"But it's not, so don't you dare," I threaten.

We work in comfortable silence. As great as it is to be able to talk with someone for hours on end, it's just as valuable to be content in silence. My mom told me that once, and I recognize it in my relationship with Lish. Sometimes I'm so comfy with her, I fall asleep while we're in the middle of a conversation. And she doesn't mind. Now here I am with Luke, feeling pretty content without speaking. This is what things are supposed to feel like, right? It's not that we've already run out of things to say?

The sun begins its late descent, closing in on the longest day of the year. "I guess we'll have to stop soon," I say, wondering what's next for our night or if it ends when the sky turns dark.

"Then I better take the time to do this," Luke replies, and I feel a paintbrush stroke across my back.

"You didn't!" I yell, and turn around violently to wrestle the brush out of his hand. Our fingers become locked in death grips, and with some effort, I manage to knock him over, pinning him to the ground while straddling him.

I am straddling Luke Jacobs.

And he is laughing hysterically.

"There wasn't any paint on it," he gasps through guffaws.

I remain on top of him, holding hands, and our fingers relax into one another's. My hands are dwarfed by his, and the size differential is a bit daunting. In a good way. A protective, this-guy-is-really-strong-but-would-never-hurt-me way. A but-what-will-he-do-to-me kind of way. Luke stops laughing, and he lightly pulls my hands to bring my face closer to his. I let go with my right hand and drop it to the grass next to his head to steady myself. He cradles the back of my head and draws me in for a kiss. I try to ignore the sausage flavor on his lips because everything else about him is so damn delicious. He's a gentle kisser, slow, deliberate. I lean in farther, dropping our other handhold to rest my fingers on his chest. It feels so cliché, but the solid, muscular build of this guy is completely turning me on. I have never been with a guy so sturdy, and I find myself essentially feeling him up. He totally has man boobs, but, like, the really good kind. I get a sense of what guys must enjoy from groping me.

Luke's newly freed hand clasps around my waist, then

slides its way down to cup my butt. He grinds me against him, and I am made aware of how much he is enjoying all of this through his shorts.

The kissing continues with added tongue bonus. Extra sausage flavor surfaces, but I don't let it deter me. Smoothly and effortlessly, Luke rolls me to my back and holds himself above me, balancing on his arms to avoid crushing me. I really think he *could* crush me. Again—way too turned on by the thought.

It's his turn to feel me up. His enormous hand on my enormous breast. Perfectly matched. He is being gentlemanly in his groping, keeping his touching above my clothing. Through my blazing orange t-shirt and my industrial-strength bra, my senses aren't adequately engaged. I take his hand and ease it toward the hem of my shirt. Luke slides his fingers up my stomach and manages to dig his way into the top of my bra cup, not an easy feat for a mere mortal man. Now Luke Jacobs's actual hand is touching my actual breast, and the skin-to-skin contact is so exquisite I think I may lose all control of the rest of my body.

My mind, however, kicks into overdrive. "What if someone catches us?" Without losing contact, Luke scoops a hand underneath my back and shimmies the two of us to a slightly more private locale behind the Dinghies tunnel. I laugh at the absurdity of what he just did, what we are doing now. His dimples make being this clothed unbearable, and my fingers tug at the bottom of Luke's shirt to raise it over his head. We break from each other for the painful amount of time it takes to remove the clothing, first his shirt then mine, then we hurriedly reattach at the lips, his hand back underneath my bra.

The sun is nearly set, and in a startling instant the bright evening security lights burst on like police searchlights. The beams illuminate our bodies, and there they are: *Scarlett Dresden* and *Hendrix Cutter.* Are they taunting us, or are we mocking them? Luke's large hand must have felt Hendrix Cutter above my breast. Is he able to ignore it?

I am now completely aware that I am on the grass at the Devil's Dinghies at Haunted Hollow with my glaring white bra on full display.

"Luke," I mumble into his mouth. He takes it as encouragement and kisses my neck. I let out a pained sigh. "Luke." This time I press my hands against his chest. He lifts off me to look dazedly at my face.

"Yeah?"

"We should probably stop here. Security lights mean Sam Hain is going to be walking around the park soon and—"

"And neither of us is wearing a shirt." He looks down at himself, then me, and smirks. He sits up, offers me his hand to help me sit, finds our shirts, and we dress ourselves. We stand up and survey our work on the mural, as though we weren't close to naked mere moments ago.

"We actually accomplished quite a bit tonight," I say.

He nods and says, "I'd have to agree with you there." He

rests his palm on my lower back. "More than you thought would happen tonight."

"What do you mean?" I ask.

"I actually did get to see you in something besides your orange work shirt."

CHAPTER 18

I step out of the shower after replaying last night's tryst, solo-style. It's my day off, and I have the rest of the day to fret about tonight's introduction to Travis. What if I genuinely dislike him? Do I have to feign interest because he's Lish's MTB? The stakes are so high. It's like my best friend has a fiancé that I somehow never met. Except *she's* barely met him.

Why did I have to wake up at eight a.m. on a day with the potential for sleeping in? I could have avoided several more hours of overthinking.

Here I am in front of the bathroom mirror with way too much time on my hands. Hendrix Cutter is looking at me.

"What?" I snap at him. "What do you want? Do you want to contact me so we can enjoy hours of get-to-know-you Viddles?" I stop myself when I realize, "Why *haven't* you contacted me, Hendrix Cutter?"

It's absurd that I'm somehow offended by this. I haven't contacted Hendrix Cutter, nor do I want to, nor do I want him to be the type of person who even gives a shit about Empties.

Except his Empty is me.

And it would be just a little nice to know he gives a shit.

Damn you, Hendrix Cutter, and all that you stand for!

I shrug a shirt over his name and attempt to waste the day by playing Halo.

Uncle Jim slides into the kitchen around lunchtime. Our kitchen opens directly onto our family room, so on nights when we don't want to speak, we all sit on one side of the table and watch TV. It also gives Uncle Jim a clear view of my game.

"Back in my day, we jumped over mushrooms instead of killing people in video games." He opens the fridge.

"I'm not killing people. I'm killing aliens," I correct him.

"A shame. People aren't all that great," he muses.

It's comments like that that make me sad all over again for Uncle Jim. I get the whole introvert thing, not needing to go out and be around a lot of people to make you content. But Uncle Jim doesn't seem very contented holed up inside our attic all the time, either. "You want to go out for lunch? I've got Subway coupons," I offer.

"Ick. All their sandwiches taste exactly the same. No thank you."

"We could go somewhere else. Jimmy John's? Free smells," I attempt to entice him with sandwiches.

"Sounds like you need a sub. We have some rolls, actually, the pretzel kind." Uncle Jim rifles through plastic bags on the counter.

"You sure you don't want to go out? We don't have to get sandwiches. Sushi?" I ask, making a huge concession, seeing as I can't stand sushi. But even that doesn't sway him.

"No, I'm sure. I'm on a deadline. Savannah Merlot waits for no man. Or should I say, no woman waits for Savannah Merlot?"

I give up and allow Uncle Jim to make me the most amazing sub sandwich I've ever tasted. "What's on this?" I inquire at the kitchen table, taking a break from my game.

"Rémoulade. A fan sent it to Savannah at her PO box from New Orleans."

I stop chewing and ask, "How do you know it's not poisoned?"

"People love Savannah Merlot too much to kill her. They send New Orleans stuff all the time, since the books are based there."

I resume chewing and figure death by tasty sandwich wouldn't be the worst way to die. "When was the last time you went to New Orleans for research?" I realize the load in the question.

"Fifteen years ago. I know a lot has changed. That's what books and the interweb are for."

"I thought you didn't like the 'interweb,'" I air quote Uncle Jim's word.

"For communication. Too many assholes who can say awful things in real time from the safety of their anonymous lairs. Research is another story. When I can get the blueprints for a church or see a live image of a street corner without leaving my house, why bother?"

I want to tell him, *Um, I don't know . . . because actual people can be kind of interesting*, but recognize I'm pressuring Uncle

Jim in a way I would hate to be pressured. The way I already do hate: having someone telling me how I should do things because that's how things are supposed to be done.

Fuck that.

I switch gears. "So, things are getting interesting with Luke Jacobs at work."

"Is that the tall kid?"

"Yes. Very tall. And he's not so kidlike anymore."

Uncle Jim stands to run his empty plate under the faucet.

"Promise me two things: You won't get pregnant, and you won't fall in love."

"Uncle Jim!" I bumble over his response.

"That's Wise Ol' Uncle Jim to you, Agatha."

After lunch I attempt to shake the heebies that having your uncle discuss your sex life creates. Shooting buffed-out aliens isn't doing it for me, so I flip through my worn copy of *Abandoned Amusement Parks*, the book that began my love affair with carnival history when I checked it out from my school library in fourth grade. In gory detail, the book explores amusement parks once in their full glory, now rusted and shrouded in plants. Then-and-now pictures reveal each park's twisted history and why it closed forever. The juxtaposition of happy kids and gruesome casualties was a combination I couldn't resist. So much so that I pretended to lose the book and had my mom write a check to pay for it. If pictures of Ferris wheels devoured by weeds weren't scary enough, the true stories of deaths on rides were pure catnip. Darkness and light, danger in a place of seat belts and safety harnesses, smiling children and dead bodies, are all metaphors for life itself, really. It is why I love to work at Haunted Hollow, why I want to travel the world and see other places like it. Life should be unpredictable. It should keep you in suspense. We shouldn't always know what's coming next.

My phone buzzes on my desk.

Luke: *Come over tonight? (Part 2)*

Instantly I'm hit in the loins (do I have more than one loin? Do I even have one?) at the thought of seeing—and touching—Luke again, but I can't punk out on Lish two nights in a row.

Me: *Meeting best friend's MTB. Wish me luck.*

Luke: *Good luck. See you at work tomorrow?*

Me: *Yup*

I scold myself for the unenthusiastic reply, but it was either that or *YES I CAN'T WAIT UNTIL YOU TOUCH MY BOOBS AGAIN.*

There are still three hours until I meet Lish and Travis at Casa Louisa for dinner, so even though I already showered, I go for a run.

I try to focus only on the music, on the pounding of my feet on the concrete, on my raggedy, only slightly in-shape breathing. It's been a while, and I slump into a walk. I pass house after familiar house, the same streets I've lived near my entire life. I don't want to go to college here. I don't particularly want to be in school anywhere right now, sitting at desks or in fancy auditorium chairs with tiny flip-up writing trays (Lish is especially excited about those). I don't know what kind of classes I don't want to take. I don't want to do homework anymore or get graded, and for what? A future job I have no idea what it should be? Paying tens of thousands of dollars to do something I don't want feels wasteful.

So what do you want, Agatha?

"What do I want?" I talk to myself, my heart rate steadying.

An old song hits my player, a 1970s singer named Jim Croce singing about making a phone call using a dime. There once was a time when people used pay phones. Talked to operators. Paid ten cents for something. A time when he could make that call to any woman or man he wanted, and no one had the added complication of an MTB to screw up the already overly stressful concept of *future.*

What if I'm not meant to go to college? What if I'm meant to go to Australia, to work in amusement parks across the globe? What if finding a creepy library book all those years ago was my destiny? People call these fucking Names *meant-to-bes.* Are they the only things in our lives that are truly meant to be? Or is it just more obvious when they're staring back at us in the mirror every day?

Why did it have to be a name? Why not advice?

Be a carny

Wait on college

Fall in love with Luke Jacobs if you want

Exhausted and frustrated, I pick up my pace again into a jog. I manage to shuffle about a mile, then allow myself to walk the rest of the loop back to my house. Exercise isn't so bad. Aside from the change of clothes, sweating, and general exertion of it all.

I have time for a second shower (Luke Jacobs daydream, part 2) and select a casual army-green skirt and plain black t-shirt for the occasion. The outfit reads, "Look, I made the effort to put on a skirt and a t-shirt without an ironic statement on it. Points for me!" I shove on my fanciest flip-flops (the ones without the erosion in the shape of my foot) and sit in my car. Three deep breaths later and I'm backing out of the driveway. Ten minutes later and I'm at Casa Louisa. I recognize Lish's car in the parking lot and scan the front of the restaurant to see if Lish and Travis are waiting outside. They are not, so I park and take the opportunity to look at myself in the rearview mirror.

My hair is still damp, and I sweep it up into a loose bun so I don't look quite as bedraggled. I roll red-tinted gloss over my lips to give me a hint of color, check my nose for boogers, and I'm ready.

But I'm not ready. Because the second I cross the threshold of Casa Louisa and meet Travis, this whole MTB thing becomes real. Lish is on a path to the rest of her life while I'm flailing around at a haunted amusement park trying to avoid reality with the boy of my dreams who is not technically my soul mate.

I'm about to turn around to check for a lurking booger again when the Casa Louisa doors open and Lish barrels out to grab me. "We saw you through the windows, and I couldn't wait anymore for you to come in! What? Were you farting outside before you entered the building?" she jokes loudly. Now she's giving away my trade secrets?

I chuckle awkwardly and see Travis, who is not, per my imagination, wearing a cowboy hat, cowboy boots, and an NRA belt buckle. He's medium tall (not Luke tall by any proportion) and has sandy brown hair cropped neatly into a slightly-longer-than-buzz cut. He sports a blue t-shirt with an Adidas logo on the front, and his cargo shorts hover over fluffy, hairy legs. On his feet are gray running shoes, the kind I would only wear while running, providing little insight into whether or not he does, indeed, have a style. Travis looks like a guy Lish and I would pass in the halls and not look twice in his general direction, nor would he look in ours. MTBs don't have a clause somewhere about being stylistically compatible?

Travis juts out a hand, a hand that will someday grope Lish. Why is that the first thing that comes to my mind? Oh, I don't know, Agatha, because you're a total perv? No, I'm not. I'm merely trying to make light of a dire situation. See? My brain is injecting visions of Travis's hand on my best friend's butt to avoid imagining a wedding band on said hand when he marries her and moves away to Kentucky to have sixteen babies and film a reality show about their lives.

"Hi, I'm Travis. Nice to meet you. I've heard so much about you." He smiles genuinely, and I feel a twinge of guilt for the mockery my brain made of his outfit.

"Wow. That's so nice. I've heard a lot about you, too." That's what I'm supposed to say, right?

Lish bounces up to the hostess and informs her, "Our entire party is here!" She is very loud and springy. Part of me loves seeing Lish in this blissed-out state, and the other part questions whether or not Travis has ever seen the real Lish or only this hyperpleasing version.

At our table, Lish sits next to Travis and I sit across from Lish. Immediately she busts into cheery conversation. "How is work? Were you with Luke last night?"

I look at Travis uncomfortably. What must he think about me cavorting with a man who is not my Empty? "Yeah," I start, "but we don't have to talk about that now."

"It's okay! I've told Travis all about you guys!"

"Really?" I raise one eyebrow at Lish, and Travis interjects.

"She said you two have flirted the last couple summers, and now that his girlfriend is gone and you two haven't met your MTBs yet, you're having a summer fling."

When he says it, it sounds so unsexy. Also, *haven't met our MTBs yet*? Who says that is part of the equation? I mean, maybe I did, but not to him. And it's none of his business anyway. But if he thinks he's so chummy with me by proxy because of Lish, then why hold back?

"We made out last night." I lay my napkin on my lap triumphantly. "After work. At the Devil's Dinghies, the ride where I'm stationed, although I'm sure you already know that."

Lish isn't sure what to make of my forwardness, so she continues with her bubbly banter. "Oooh. Sounds romantic."

Who is this person? The old Lish would have asked for every tongue position and lewd sound. I realize there is another human next to her, and I don't know him, even though he apparently knows a hell of a lot about me, but she brought Luke up in the first place.

The waitress appears, and I'm calmed a bit after ordering a burrito. Naturally, I judge Travis for ordering the chicken fajitas because that's pretty much the lamest thing you can order at a Mexican restaurant, but I bite my tongue.

In fact, by the end of the dinner I have bitten my tongue so much that it may have a permanent indentation.

Dinner conversation steers away from me and toward every minute detail of Travis and Lish's first twenty-four hours together. I consider myself lucky that Lish didn't text the entire thing to me like I had previously expected.

The story is very meet-cute, with occasional asides of "I'll tell you more about that later," accompanied by a wink from Lish.

The question is: When? Travis is staying at Lish's house. They will be together twenty-four hours a day, seven days a week, subtract their day jobs. When exactly will there be a later for Lish and me to speak privately?

At the end of dinner, Travis refuses to let either of us pay the bill. "My treat," he oozes. Or maybe that was a kind gesture.

I know my face is incapable of hiding things. I'm a blusher and a pouter and a sneerer. Currently, I'm trying desperately to look pleasant and grateful, but my face feels like that of an alien disguised as a human trying to emulate a smile.

Lish sees it.

"Will you excuse us, Travis? Ladies' room." Lish pulls me by the arm all the way into the little señoritas' room.

"What?" I pout.

"You are being a total butt," she says.

"*You* are being a total butt," I counter.

"How am I being a butt? I'm being as nice as I can possibly be."

"That's the problem! This isn't you! If you have to be fake for Travis, is this it for the rest of your life? New, improved, wholesome Lish? No thank you." I cross my arms.

"Aggy, I know you are prepared to not like Travis. If you suddenly found someone you wanted to be with all the time instead of me, I'd be upset, too."

"Who said that? And who *says* that? First off, how can you possibly know you want to be with this guy all the time? And second, how could you choose him over me?" I shout.

There it is.

Lish, instead of looking loving and sympathetic as she should, purses her lips. "Aggy, we are both going off to college—or elsewhere," she corrects herself. When she senses I'm about to stop her, she says, "Like it or not, Travis is my MTB. Whether or not that means he is truly meant to be, I don't know. But I am really curious to find out. Can't you support me in this?"

I jiggle my leg up and down impatiently. "Fine," I

concede. But that's all I'll give her. Lish hugs me, and I hug her back best I can from my currently arm-crossed position.

"I really do want to hear more about Luke. Maybe we can chat later?" she offers.

"Sure." I nod.

We leave the restaurant, me alone in my car, Lish together with Travis.

Her future.

I pray he doesn't make her my past.

CHAPTER 19

A rainy day makes time drag at Haunted Hollow. Or at least it used to. I spend a good portion of my time hiding underneath the three-by-three-foot awning that covers the ride controls, a bar stool, and a place to rest my legs until my butt falls asleep. Occasionally a bedraggled family wants a ride on the Devil's Dinghies, but there is nowhere to protect the parents from the droplets while they wait in line. I make the offer that the child can ride as long as she wants, but by the time the boat completes its loop the parents are ready to move on to shelter.

I am hypnotized by the patter and plunk of raindrops into the ride's water. It's almost enough to put me to sleep. A cool summer rain, the drops feel downright chilly after eighty-degree days. The air today hasn't pushed past seventy, and I snuggle into the Haunted Hollow hoodie I stow underneath the console for such an occasion. I shook it out before I put it on, checking for stray spiders or beetles that may have moved in. The hoodie smells of sunscreen and musty water, and I'd consider holding it under the falling rain if I thought it would imbue it with the tranquil smell.

Looking at the barely touched mural, I sigh at the recognition that I won't have the opportunity to paint today. It was something cathartic I was looking forward to after a confusing night.

The rain switches from a light tapping to a full-on downpour. The torrent pounds the Devil's Dinghies water angrily. Raindrops turn to hail, a few pea-size balls at first, then amassing into pellets the size of quarters. The din they create makes me flinch as they *ping* and *plod* onto the boats. I practically jump out of the booth when I feel two large arms engulf me from behind. Luke pants in my ear. "Holy shit! I was not expecting that when I ran over here."

I turn around, his arms loosening just enough to allow me to move while remaining on my hips. His hair drips onto his already-soaked t-shirt, and now directly onto me.

"Sorry." He backs up a little and looks around for something with which to dry himself. I offer him a backup t-shirt I find hidden crumpled behind where my hoodie was. I imagine it smells mustier than the hoodie, but Luke doesn't seem to notice as he wipes his face and arms with the orange fabric. He rubs his hair vigorously, leaving it tousled with hunks sticking up in random directions. On a mere mortal, this look might detract from one's attractiveness. But Luke looks positively divine. I don't know if his intention was to hang out and talk to pass the time until the rains dissipate and we have to actually work, but my lips are on his before I can find out his true intentions.

He doesn't seem to mind.

Luke grips my face in his gigantic palms, clammy from the rain. I wrap my arms around his neck, pulling myself up on tiptoe while he crouches to meet me halfway. I can feel his soaked shirt against my neck and chin, and I shudder at the chill. He pulls away from our lip-lock to ask, "You cold?"

"It's just . . . your shirt is really wet," I point out, recognizing how lame it sounds when he's the one actually wearing it.

The hail surrounding us slows its assault, and the racket is replaced by the symphony of rain. My body relaxes some; I wasn't aware of how tense the machine gun–like blast on the Dinghies made me. I want to resume kissing, cognizant that when the rain dies down Luke will have to return to duty at the Ghoster.

Luke begins peeling his wet shirt over his head, like an HBO movie my mom wouldn't let me watch as a kid. I want to protest, to tell him we're at work: No shirts, no shoes = no dice, but he's back onto me in an instant—and who can argue with a shirtless Luke Jacobs?

My hands travel over his shoulders, my hoodie acting as a towel for his torso.

I love kissing Luke, who seems so immediate when our lips are touching. How does he do that? Lose himself so easily, where I'm reflecting on every flick of my tongue and clack of our teeth? Or maybe he's the same way and thinks I'm the cool one.

The dumping rain slows to a drizzle, which I'm only aware of when the sound on the shelter becomes deafeningly quiet. I press my hands to his chest to back myself away, inadvertently brushing Scarlett Dresden with my fingertips. I shudder again, this time from the reality and not the cold. Taking off clothing will never have the same sexiness as it did in the time before the Naming.

Maybe we should implement a shirts-on policy for make-out situations.

"The rain is stopping," I pout, pretending I'm not completely distracted by the ladylike autograph on his chest. I try not to let my brain get carried away with jealousy at this girl's fragile signature. "And you're not wearing a shirt," I remind Luke.

"True on both counts. I'm going to run to my locker for a dry one before the kids come back." Luke hastily kisses my lips, and I barely have a chance to return the kiss before he's sprinting topless toward the staff room.

I run a finger over my bottom lip, swollen from the encounter. I'm trying so hard to live in these moments, to enjoy them for what they are and not worry about what may or may not happen in the future.

Scarlett Dresden, like Hendrix Cutter, has an annoying way of popping up to remind me that I may not have a choice.

CHAPTER 20

My mom has to know I'm not going to college. She's got to. But she doesn't.

"I bought you this." She reaches into a college bookstore bag and brandishes a t-shirt emblazed with a college mascot.

"What is that?" I ask, not that I don't know what a tiger is, nor don't I know that it is, indeed, the mascot for the team of the college to which I was accepted. I say *What is that?* in the same way one might question a syringe produced at a doctor's appointment when you expected a shot-free check-up. I don't want to see it, and I don't know what the hell it's doing here.

"I know it wasn't your style to have school spirit in high school, but college is different. You chose the school, and you're paying up the wazoo to go there, so I damn well hope you have the spirit." She nudges Uncle Jim, who is cooking risotto on the stove, in a conspiratorial way, and he hums a noncommitted "Mmmm" to appease my mom.

My mom really thinks I'm still going to college. I haven't yet found the right time to smash her dream to smithereens.

She wants me to be independent, to not have to rely on anyone for financial and emotional stability, which to her means getting a college degree in something sensible, leading to a lucrative career that allows my life autonomy. And I totally agree with her. Except about the college degree. Because I think that maybe my future career lies somewhere out in the world, and if I tether myself to a college program now I may completely miss the opportunity to find the career that I was destined to have.

Do I believe in destiny? I did before the MTBs appeared, but now they've fucked everything up. Before the Naming, I wanted to go to college. Lish and I would, of course, attend the same school, her getting a degree in chemistry while I earned mine in veterinary medicine. No matter that I'm terrified of dogs. Even back then a spark of a dream to visit Australia propelled me. I could treat their unique animals, like dingoes instead of dogs, which are wild dogs so they're not as scary. Or more scary. But how will I know if that's what I want to do if I never meet a dingo or a wombat or a Tasmanian devil?

Right around the time of SAT score mailings, my mom and I sat down to pore over a book of college listings. Well, she pored over it. I left about sixteen times to go to the bathroom because it made me so panicked. Mom thought that was normal. Who isn't a little nervous about leaving home? But it's not leaving home that worried me; I *want* to leave this home. There are too many memories of our family here, the one made up of me, Mom, and Dad. Australia contains not an iota of Abrams family memories. I can make my own memories, my own life.

After appeasing Mom with three college applications, bullshit essays about my dream to become a veterinarian (totally inspired by an episode of *Supernatural* where Sam hits a dog with his car, and he falls in love with the bland yet curly-haired vet who saves it), I built up the nerve to tell her my deferment plan. I used the word *deferment* because it sounded official but also like there is a possibility that I am merely putting off college for an unspecified amount of time. To sweeten the deal, I presented my deferment plan as only one year, although I knew in my heart there was no definitive time frame. The beauty of my plan is that there is no plan. That's the whole point.

Needless to say, Mom did not go for the plan-that-is-not-a-plan. At all. To the point where she stopped the discussion with a hand, left the room, and told my uncle to inform me that dreams are fine but that they are merely dreams. Reality is the shit we don't want to do but we have to.

And that was it.

Bleak as fuck.

Completely my mom's outlook on life, which I get. For her. I want to change that for me, especially so I don't end up alone in a house purchased with an ex-husband and occupied by my shut-in brother.

I want to escape, to fly away figuratively and literally on

a big ol' airplane for twenty terrifying hours until I'm on the other side of the world with only possibility guiding my way. And carnival rides.

Think my mom would be cool if I just sent her a text with all that once I get there?

CHAPTER 21

Another day off from work. I know days off are normally appreciated, even coveted, by most people, but being at work means sexy time with my not-really boyfriend and being home means way too much time to think about these heated topics:

a) How to tell my mom officially that I really would rather move to Australia than go to college.
b) My best friend may or may not be on the road to marriage and a future that does not involve us backpacking through exotic countries where we may or may not ingest toasted insects.
c) My computer and phone are fully accessible, nearby, and seem to have the disturbing ability to taunt me about searching for Hendrix Cutter.
d) As long as I'm wearing a tank top, I can see my Empty. I may have to start wearing turtlenecks in the summer.

Ugh. The Name's itchy. Maybe. I can't tell if it's actually itchy or if it's like when you hear your friend's little sister has lice and your scalp starts to crawl. That's how my Empty feels, so I yank on a crew-neck t-shirt. I consider the new college shirt my mom procured for me but decide that would be sending the wrong message. See point *a* for actual message.

What do I want to do today? Making out with Luke is high on my list. But since Luke is working, and I don't have a jet, cake, or pizza, I consider messaging Sahana Patel, a friend more from proximity than from having much in common. We grew up on the same block and attended many of each other's birthday parties, but lost the playdate factor in junior high when she fast-tracked it to the highest-level classes and I hovered at next-to-highest. My dad used to chide me about wasted potential, but I wasn't about to let homework get in the way of finding out what kind of baby my human Sim and vampire Sim would make.

Maybe I'll play the Sims today. It's been a long time since I interacted with a bunch of pretend people.

I grab a tub of dried apricots (a snack that I only partake in when I know I'm going to be spending a lot of time alone. Toot toot) and a glass of water, and head to my bedroom.

Being an only child, my bedroom is on the larger side. What once was my dad's but is now my mom's office (why did he get the original office in the first place? It's not like he worked at home) is the smallest bedroom, with Mom getting the master and Uncle Jim residing in the finished basement. Technically, Uncle Jim has the largest bedroom, and with the attic as his workspace, the largest office. With my mom always at work or school, I don't think she cares. When my dad originally left, my mom's first inclination was to sell the house and move into an apartment. Uncle Jim saved us from having to pack up our lives (so many boxes filled with memories that are better left taped closed) when he moved in and helped share costs. Uncle Jim also helped with a modicum of redecorating, encouraging my mom to paint the walls and buy a new bedroom set and comforter. He took the renovations a bit too far when he sold my parents' wedding dishes (apparently a discontinued pattern that sold for a shitload on eBay) without my mom knowing and surprised her with a newer, more modern line. She cried for three days after that. Who knew dishes could mean so much to someone?

My room hasn't changed much since I was a kid. At age eight, my parents let me choose a paint color. I chose a lavender that looked too light to me on the tiny paint sample card, so I insisted on a darker shade of the color. The man at the paint store suggested I stick with the lighter shade, since large amounts of any color will appear darker. I wasn't going to be swayed by this man who obviously had a vendetta against the color purple, so somehow I convinced my dad to not only go with the darker shade but to actually go with the very darkest splotch at the bottom of the card. Ten years later, and I still refuse to admit that my walls are not anywhere near the color lavender and veer dangerously close to eggplant.

I don't mind, and the darkness makes it the perfect room in which to sleep and/or zone out to simulation computer games. I'm still a sucker for classics like Zoo Tycoon and RollerCoaster Tycoon, but the Sims, where you basically create and control people, will always remain my number one. The beauty of the Sims is it's almost social, but you can build walls around people you hate and make them pee themselves if you're in that kind of mood.

The most recent edition of the Sims came with the annoying feature of MTBs, so any Sim you made automatically wasn't ever 100 percent satisfied until they found their computer-generated soul mate. The feature annoyed players so much, kindred spirits of mine who didn't want their computer-created humans to have their love lives dictated any more than they wanted their real love lives dictated, that the game's production company released a second version of the same edition that did not include the MTB feature. I wasn't about to shell out another fifty bucks, so I stayed content by playing older, pre-MTB editions of the game.

Today I settle in with the classic Sims 3, which doesn't have as many fun expansion packs as Sims 2, but does have much better graphics. Plus, no MTB to spoil the Sim-humping bits.

I sit down at my desk, painted green by my mom and me after the dad exodus. It was originally supposed to be a place where I could write in my journal or draw comics, but once my laptop settled here the creative endeavors fell by the wayside. Unless you count my single foray into writing *Doctor Who* fan fiction. (Tenth Doctor, obviously.)

I touch the track pad, and my desktop glows to life. I am so tempted to spend time on the Internet, reading Tumblr pages analyzing Chris Evans's beard or Norman Reedus's haircut, but the more time I spend on the infinity of the web, the stronger the lure is to Google the hell out of Hendrix Cutter. He is plaguing my brain. Already he has defiled my body; what more can I give him? I double-click the Sims 3 icon before I go into searching territory I cannot unsee.

My Sim, Hermione Stranger, busies herself striving to become a rock star. In between jobs, sleeping, and eating, she woo-hoos her way around town with any Sim I deem attractive. Sometimes she woo-hoos with a really old Sim, sometimes with girls, and sometimes with boys who look like girls. Then she goes shopping for groceries.

My stomach grumbles, and I realize that six hours have passed and all I've eaten is the entire tub of dried apricots. I curse myself for what I know will be the dire consequence of an entire tub of dried apricots. I stagger into the kitchen in search of any food my mom has labeled "binding" (her word for foods that have chemical properties to stop the unpleasantries of, shall we say, *loose stool.* Although that really didn't sound all that much less pleasant than *diarrhea*). A serving of Uncle Ben's white rice and two bananas later, and I'm pretty sure I may never leave the house again.

The couch looks deliriously inviting, and I curl up into a ball and fall asleep.

An hour later I'm awoken by the doorbell. My body tells me to ignore it, but the bell rings again. From my vantage point, I see a face pressed to the glass pane along the side of our front door. Lish peers into the living room, and I'm pretty sure she recognizes my blobuous shape on the couch.

Standing up, I expel gas, the odor of which can only be described as apricots with a hint of Satan's butthole. It's toxic, and I graciously offer it up to Lish as I open the front door.

"Jesus Christ." She steps inside. "Did someone forget to take out the garbage?" She attempts to cover her nose with her hand, then a light of recognition shines in her eyes. "You were eating apricots, weren't you?"

Who but my best friend would know what I ate based on the smell of my farts?

"You have a delicate palate," I tell Lish.

"And you have a nasty digestive system," Lish replies.

"Touché."

"Tushy," Lish responds with our classic and clever touché/tushy one-two combo.

Maybe things won't be so different.

"What are you doing here?" I ask in a way that says *I'm glad you're here, but I'm surprised.*

"I was on my way home from work, and I saw your car in the driveway." *Sweet,* I think. "Plus, Travis won't be home for another two hours, so I thought you and I could catch up." Ignore the backhandedness of that, Aggy. Focus on the fart identification.

"Cool. Come on in."

Lish walks to the kitchen and helps herself to a Coke. "You want one?" she asks. "Don't tell Travis."

"Sure," I say, seeing as it is on my mom's list of food items deemed okay for consumption during turbulent tummy times. I also like this hint at Lish's dark side.

It feels like the first time in forever we've been on the couch together, *Sanford and Son* on in the background, but if memory serves it was only last week. Still, we have a lot of catching up to do. "Luke and I made out!" I explode at the exact time my best friend yells, "Travis and I had sex!"

Um, you win?

"You go first," she prods, but a story about kissing and a minuscule amount of grinding seems like a pathetic warm-up act for her full-on penetration tale.

"No, you go. Your story sounds way more interesting."

"You sure?"

Hell to the no, but what kind of asshole would I be if I didn't say, "Definitely."

Lish spends the next ten minutes expounding on every last gory detail of sexual intercourse with Travis. I tune out at the mention of his "lithe fingers" . . . and only tune back in when she mentions how they didn't use a condom.

"What? What the fuck, Lish? Since when are you a total moron?" I crack.

"Harsh, Agatha. Part of the website we used to find each other requires a full blood workup and physical exam."

"A website? You trust a website? How do you know he gave accurate results? Or what if he had sex with someone between the results and when you two met?"

"He's not like that, Aggy. He's honest and kind, and I love him," Lish insists.

"You love him? Really? Already? Because he put his penis inside your vagina?" I reprimand myself internally for once again sounding like a junior high health teacher.

"That's not why I love him, but, yes, technically *because* I love him I let him put his penis in my vagina. God, Aggy! I thought I could tell you this without you going all Mother Superior on me."

"So you love him, and he is supposedly disease-free. Are you ready to just jump in and be a mom at eighteen? 'Cause last I checked, his semen inside you is how babies are made." Lord help me and my sexual language disease.

"I'm on the pill," she sneers.

Lish actually *sneers* at me. And she's on the pill. "Since when?"

"Since last week. I haven't had a chance to tell you. You've been busy at work, and I've been busy with Travis—"

"So I hear," I grumble, albeit in an attempt at humor. "Well," I concede, "as long as you think you're being safe."

"We are," she assures me. This conversation isn't complete, the *I love him* still dangling in the air, but I'm not ready to hear more on the topic. She asks me to tell her about Luke, but what I have to say sounds silly and frivolous. Still, she is currently my best friend. I want to be able to tell Lish everything. I want Lish to be able to tell me everything. I just wish everything wasn't what she just told me.

CHAPTER 22

That night I text Sahana to see if she wants to hang out. It's better than being alone with my thoughts or, god forbid, my computer or phone. Unfortunately Sahana has family over and can't escape. I seem to remember this being a common theme in our friendship of yore: She'd often miss events outside of school due to familial obligations. I wonder how super-tight-knit families deal with MTBs; people whose parents are completely devoted to each other, like Lish's. Her parents chose to ignore their Empties and even renewed their wedding vows as a symbol of their commitment.

But there has to be a tiny twinge for both of them, perhaps on those days when Lish's dad is chewing too loudly or Lish's mom criticizes her dad for leaving the toilet seat up for the 7,562nd time, an occasional tug of *what if?* It sucks for my generation, not having any say in who we choose for love, but it sucked even more for my parents' generation. Thinking you've already figured it out, then having your own body slap you right in the face.

I swear Hendrix Cutter is making me itchy.

How can someone I know not even a modicum about have a physical effect on me? It's disturbing to say the least.

I walk into the bathroom to see if I'm imagining things. Maybe the itch is nowhere near Hendrix Cutter's signature. Lifting my shirt, I instantly spot the blotch of redness from me scratching myself through my shirt. It is located directly over Hendrix Cutter's name, like a pink cloud from hell highlighting this bane of my forever.

I send Luke a message.

Busy?

He doesn't respond right away, so I take that as my cue to research international amusement parks. Fuji-Q Highland in Osaka, Japan, looks enticing, with both an attraction called Mizuki Shigeru's Ge-Ge-Ge Haunted Mansion (the third *Ge* is the kicker) and a Super Scary Labyrinth of Fear. Who wouldn't love visiting an attraction offering the Third Operating Room (I love the enigma of numbers one and two) plus the beguiling Bacteria Lab.

I add the park to my "Amusement Parks" Chapbook page, but being on Chapbook almost leads to some dangerous Internet searching. Willpower tested, I wrestle my laptop closed and begin the arduous task of digging through my underwear drawer to rid myself of any pair that has a hole or period stain. I turn on some music and divide my undies into three piles:

1) Keep.
2) Wear only when I know no one will see my underwear.
3) Throw to the dogs.

I consider donating my substantial pile of throw-to-the-dogs to a charity, but I question whether anyone wants used underwear let alone holey and/or stainy ones. I make a mental note to buy some new underwear for the next holiday clothing drive.

Drawer successfully weeded, I pick up my phone to make sure I didn't somehow miss the cackle of a message.

Nope.

On to the sock drawer.

My sock collection hasn't been culled in so long, I actually find a sock with rubber lettering on the bottom reading "3–4 years." Naturally I try it on. In a way it still fits, if I don't mind the heel of the sock bunching up underneath my foot. A shame. The turtles around the top are so cute.

Still no message. I resist the urge to turn my phone on and off, lest it's merely a problem with my phone and not Luke Jacobs ignoring me. Instead, I succumb to the call of my computer. A note from Lish is waiting on my Chapbook.

Are you mad at me?

She included a pouty face emoji, which is irritating to look at but means that she's asking in a cutesy way instead of an angry way.

I type:

Because of the penis-in-your-vagina thing? It's forgotten. Really. What is this penis I speak of? I'm not mad. I'm happy you're happy. I just care about you and want you to be careful. That is all.

I click on the return to sender button, and the note folds itself with basic computer animation and whisks off as though being delivered by owl. Admittedly one of my favorite Chapbook features. You can even choose the silly sound the letter makes when it flies away, my selection a chuggy old-fashioned car sound with an *ah-ROO-ga* horn.

As long as I'm sitting here at my computer with my Chapbook open, my chest itching, and no one named Luke Jacobs calling me . . . I click on the space labeled FIND A CHAPFRIEND.

H-E-N-D-R-I-X

I start with the first name. Maybe I'll find out there are a lot of people named Hendrix Cutter, and that way I won't have to worry about finding the actual one with only a single search. Multiple people's Chapbook covers pop up, some with photos, some with artwork, and some with simply a typed name. All the ones I see are people with the last name Hendrix. I casually scroll, proving to myself how much I really don't care.

I care so little, what the hell, why not type *Cutter*?

So I do.

And there is only one Chapbook cover that pops up.

Shitshitshitshit.

I click on the *x* to close my browser as quickly as if I accidentally stumbled on a porn site just as my dad walked into my bedroom (which may or may not have happened when I was twelve. I can still remember the uncomfortable look on the woman's face).

I didn't see anything.

But I did see something.

It wasn't a picture of him, so I didn't actually see Hendrix Cutter. What I saw was his name. My brain recognized the arrangement of letters instantly, possibly because the same arrangement is permanently taking up precious real estate above my boobs. What I wish I didn't see was the extremely cool way the name was hand-drawn, in full color, on a piece of notebook paper. Creepy-looking characters hooked together to form *Hendrix Cutter.*

I only saw it for a split second, a guilty porn second, but my stupid brain photographed the letters perfectly to store alongside my suddenly evolving collection of Hendrix Cutter memorabilia.

Is Hendrix Cutter an artist? A pretty good one at that?

I don't want to care. I don't want the urge to open the screen back up, to type those letters again, to stare at something created by an actual human being who is connected to me by—what? Fate? Faith? A cruel intergalactic practical joke?

I wish seeing his name, his art, in something other than my flesh didn't stir something inside me. It almost feels like there's a candle in my belly, one that sat unlit until this moment. Now a small flame clings to the wick. It's not enough to brighten a room or warm anyone, but there is a faint glow.

I'm disgusted at myself for feeling anything for this person forced upon me. I don't touch my laptop for the rest of the night, and instead lie on my bed and read a book written pre-Naming, so I'm not reminded of my recent indiscretion.

As I close my eyes to go to sleep, my phone pings. It's Luke.

Sorry. Was at my great-uncle's wake. See you tomorrow at H.H. Wear something revealing. Or orange.

I smile at the cuteness and the fact that he did not ditch me, making sure to take a moment to feel sad about his great-uncle. The gushiness of a message from Luke is almost enough to eclipse the memory of Hendrix Cutter's drawing. Until I tell myself that thinking of Luke will eclipse it. Then Hendrix's drawing is all I can think about.

CHAPTER 23

I stride into work with a purpose: to take back control of my body. My life. Yes, I cannot change the fact that there is a ridiculously cool, or possibly dorky (leaning toward the former) Name on my chest, and now that Name has even more dimension after seeing it drawn in Hendrix Cutter's hand (which, technically, I don't even know is true. Maybe he had a friend draw it or ordered it on Etsy or paid an artist at a carnival. My vote is the carny. Although my gut says it was Hendrix Cutter himself. Why you gotta play me like that, gut?).

I'm ready to fight this. Hendrix Cutter has done enough damage to my body. I know Luke and I said what we have wasn't going to be anything, but if I convince myself that I truly don't care about Hendrix Cutter maybe I can turn this nothing into a something. With a spring in my step and my brown ponytail wagging high on my head, I skip over to the Ghoster to kibitz with Luke before the park opens. Keely is virtually rubbing her scent onto Luke, she's standing so close. He looks engaged, but does not exhibit any body language that screams, "I want to touch that underaged hussy."

As a matter of fact, the second my orange torso fills Luke's peripheral vision, he extends his arm to gather me into a hug.

Perhaps he got the memo?

"I guess that's my cue to go back to Games. See ya." Keely slinks away while I attempt to find my breath against Luke's expansive chest. I manage to tilt my chin up and use my palms to press away from his firm embrace.

"Sorry." He looks down at me. "I needed an out." I suppress a slump at the notion that he didn't hug me just for the delightful physical contact until he says, "Plus, you know, we get to hug." Luke Jacobs, can you do any wrong? I make a mental note to write this anecdote in the journal that I shall someday keep about the summer Luke and I fell in love and knocked this Empty bullshit on its ass.

I'm riled up.

This becomes more evident at lunchtime when Adam expounds upon the pluses of finding his MTB, Anita Lopez, online over the weekend. "She didn't even need to see me, and she's already interested in me!"

"So you're saying that seeing you used to work to your advantage?" I muse.

"Shut up, Jugsy," Adam shoots at me.

"Excuse me?" I stand up. "What the fuck did you just say?" Our lunch table becomes pin-drop quiet.

"What, you're allowed to throw digs at me, but I can't throw one at you?" he asks.

I'm about to spew some venom when I realize he is kind

of right. I did just make fun of the way he looks. Still, his obsession with my breasts is only slightly less unnerving than his commitment to the janky hat he's worn for three years straight.

"What do Anita Lopez's 'jugs' look like?" I air-quote the word, as it is not particularly one of my favorite breast epithets.

He looks appalled. "I don't know! I just started talking with her this weekend. She lives two states over!"

"How would Anita Lopez feel if she knew that every conversation you have with a particular coworker had to include, subconsciously or not, allusions to her larger-than-average-size breasts?"

I hear snickers from some of my colleagues, but I refuse to feel self-conscious because Adam has a dick for brains.

"She doesn't get to know about it." He looks around as if trying to solicit breast-ogling team members.

"What if Anita Lopez has size-A cups? What if Anita Lopez doesn't even have A cups, just tiny bumps like newly formed mosquito bites?"

The table chitters at the thought of this. "What if she is breastless, and yet she is supposed to be your MTB? How will you handle that?" My voice is louder than I planned, but I'm done. Maybe it's that, once again, I'm focusing on my body instead of my life. Maybe it's because Adam is sleazy, and it makes me sad that Anita Lopez was slapped with an MTB who will probably spend the rest of his life subscribing to Internet porn. Or maybe I'm mad that another eighteen-year-old has fallen into the clutches of the Empty. Whatever the reason, I surprise even myself when I say, "I give you permission to temporarily ogle my boobs."

Gasps and guffaws resonate from the table. Luke, sitting next to me, attempts to quell me with an "Aggy," and his hand on my shoulder.

"It's fine," I dismiss him.

"You want me to look at your tits?" Adam grins.

"You are not allowed to refer to my breasts as tits. Breasts or boobs, but not tits. Certainly not jugs. Or hooters. Whoever named that restaurant chain is a fucking dickhole," I aside. "And I'd like this on record," I address the audience of the lunch table. "I do not *want* you to look at me in any way, shape, or form. The thought of your beady eyes coveting any part of my body makes me want to bathe in acid. However, I really am tired of you talking about my breasts no matter how casual you think it is. Referencing a woman's body part, unless you and this poor woman are, or plan on, becoming intimate, is grounds for a sexual harassment lawsuit. And, frankly, it defines you as a perverted loser."

"But I can still look at them?" Adam questions.

"Lord. Yes. But here's how it's going to go down: You get five seconds. I am not removing any of my clothes, and you are only to view them over both my bra and t-shirt. Once your eyes are on my breasts—or singular breast, your choice—the clock starts. After five seconds is up, you must avert your eyeballs immediately, lest I stab you in the nutsack with a spork. And after that: nothing. You don't look at my breasts, talk about my breasts, or make any sort of casual reference to them bouncing or jiggling or slapping me in the eye while I'm jogging. If you mention my breasts to anyone at this table and I get word of it, my compensation is one—or more, *my* choice—punch in your face. Do you agree?"

I can see the gears in Adam's head cranking away: Eyes on breast=good, punch in face=bad, spork in nutsack=really bad.

"So, what you're saying is: I get to stare at your ti—" he starts in with *tits* but is immediately halted by my death stare. ". . . *breasts* for five seconds?" I wait for him to reiterate the rest of what I said, but he seems finished.

"You did hear all that about punching you and how from here on out you leave my breasts—and let's add every other woman you ever meet's—breasts alone. Unless, perish the thought, they actually want that kind of attention from you. God help Anita Lopez."

Adam pauses in thought, then enthusiastically announces, "I accept the challenge!"

I turn to Luke with a look of disgust on my face. "Do you think he heard me?"

"It's hard to say. I think you might have broken him with the prospect of being invited to ogle you."

I detect a note of discomfort in Luke's voice, so I assure

him, "I'm not offering up my naked body to him, Luke. I'm wearing clothes. And it's not sexual because I'm not going to let him do anything more than rest his eyes there for five seconds. Don't worry. It'll be like getting a shot: over quickly and not quite as awful as you thought."

The end of lunchtime is nigh, so I speed things along. Scooting back my chair, I walk to the other side of the table where Adam sits. "Well," I say, "here they are. Live the dream."

"Now?" he asks, less confident about things now that my breasts are practically in his face.

"You want me to pencil it into your date book? Yes, now. I want your ogling to be done with. Plus, if you and Anita Lopez get serious, you can't go around staring down another girl's boobs, can you? Here, I'll help." Before Adam can resist (although I'm guessing he would not) I grip his head on both sides, careful to avoid his hat, and aim it so his eyes have nowhere to look but at my chest of glory. "One, two, three, four, five," I count. I remove my tainted hands from his clammy face before I think Adam can actually register what has transpired. "Would you look at the time? Lunch is over. Remember our deal, Adam. I will honor it, and I did take self-defense lessons last summer at the JCC."

I stride away confidently, laughing to myself as I pat my bravado on the back. Luke trots up next to me as I walk. I'm smiling, but his dimples are nowhere in sight. "I didn't exactly appreciate what you just did," Luke offers.

I'm taken aback that he didn't think it was as hilarious

as I did, albeit I am charmed by his forthrightness. "The boob thing?" I clarify.

"Yeah," he says, as though it's obvious.

I say, "It's not exactly yours to appreciate, is it? I did it for me."

Luke takes my arm to stop me from walking, and we stand facing each other. I squint at the sun as I look up to his face.

"How would you feel if I put, say, Keely's hands here?" He grabs my wrist and places my hand on his pectoral muscle. I know I should be focusing on the seriousness of his tone, but I'm distracted by the comforting feel of his body. God, I'm such a hypocrite.

"I don't know. I wouldn't particularly like the action, but if the intentions were good, like, say, it would stop her from objectifying you and making you feel like a big-breasted monster, then, yeah, I'd be okay with it."

"You feel like a big-breasted monster?" Boys are so simple.

"No. However, I would like to be able to run to the bathroom without having to make sure someone isn't watching my body parts flop around when all I want to do is take a pee."

"Do I have to feel bad that I really, really like your breasts?" It's amazing how one person can make me feel so icky and another person, this person, can make my entire body rigid and liquefied at the same time.

I clear my throat. "Only if I have to feel bad that while

you're talking to me, all I can think about is how badly I want to kiss you."

The cheesiness of that remark is gloriously washed away by the plushness of Luke's lips against mine. Maybe I have some control over my life after all.

CHAPTER 24

Before the park closes at six, I hold up a piece of paper to Luke reading, PAINT? He takes a minute to scribble something that, when held up from Luke's distant location, looks like an eye exam I was destined to fail. I throw my hands up in a "huh?" position. He signals with a "one second" finger. During that time, the Devil's Dinghies come to a stop, and I spend several minutes unhinging seat belts and hoisting children out of the boats. After that, I load another crew into their dinghies, check their seat belts, give the all-clear ride signal to the nonexistent person who doesn't work with me, and I hit the start button in my booth. Once all this is over, I look to Luke's position at the Ghoster. He is busy with his own job (the nerve!), so I lean against my booth and hum along to the Devil's Dinghies ditty. It truly never gets old.

I feel a nagging tap on my shoulder, and I turn around to find Chaitu, Luke's right-hand boy. He presents me with a folded-up piece of paper and walks away without a word. Good old Chaitu. I think that's his name.

As the Devil's Dinghies song tootles in the background,

I gingerly unfold the note. This must be how kids felt back in the days when they had to pass actual notes in school instead of texts. Like that scene in *Sixteen Candles.* I love the crinkly sound of the paper.

Hey Aggy,

I can only stay an hour. Lots of family still in town for the uncle. Painting sounds fun. I'll meet you at the cauldron.

Luke

Is it my imagination, or did my body react to seeing Luke's name in print? Like when you think you might be having a heart attack, but it's more in your elbow so then you realize it's probably gas although why there'd be gas in your elbow you'll never understand. Or is that just me? Whatever the feeling, something in my pestering gut is telling me that the feeling was a direct response to the visage of Luke's name in his own handwriting.

Or not.

The annoying part of it all is that instead of being stoked that I will be spending one whole hour in the presence of Luke and his subtly pheromonal man musk, I am now thinking about signatures and Names and, dammit, why is my chestal region itching?

The Devil's Dinghies round their final curve out of the terrifying tunnel, and I am able to shake off the mystical weirdness of the last two minutes. Aside from this pestering itch. Seriously, am I the only one who has it this long after the damn thing sprouts?

I consider inventing a cream specifically for the MTB. I'll call it Soul Mate Salve. Genius.

Six o'clock comes relatively quickly, but by the time all the straggling families are ushered out of the park it's closer to six thirty. This wouldn't be a big deal except that it cuts my Luke time in half. After I secure the boats underneath the tunnel (that way if it rains, they don't fill with water) and lock the ride starter, I cross the river to the grassy area with the mural. Very little has changed, what with Luke and I distracting each other last time. I assume tonight will be strictly painting business, as the park still has a lot of team members milling about. I remove the blue plastic tarp Brian provided for the paint cans and pry open the red. After touching up one of the devil's faces, arms, and hands, I brighten the frothing concoction bubbling over the sides of the cauldron (I like to think it's a tomato-based stew in which the devils cook the people, not their actual blood. This is a kids' park, after all). Satisfied with my work, I pop open the cans of black and white. Using a lid as a palette, I mix the two noncolors together to make a gray, brushing it around the base of the cauldron to add depth. If only I had some glitter, I would sprinkle it strategically to spruce up the pitchfork. I make a note to bring some.

By the time the scene is completed, it's ten minutes to seven. I was so focused on the painting, I didn't even notice

Luke isn't here. I'm about to worry that this has something to do with his Empty arriving in an unexpected romantic maneuver when I get a text from Luke.

Have to leave but want to see you. Meet me at my car?

Before I overthink it, I type:

Be right there.

The paintbrushes resting in the grass, I practically skip all the way to the employee lot.

Luke leans against his car with the swagger of a 1970s vice cop, and I'm on his lips in a second, standing on full tiptoe. After a beat, Luke leans away and, if I see this correctly, *blushes.* "That was unexpected."

"I thought you wanted me to come to your car," I note.

"I did, but because I really have to get going and I didn't have time to meet you at the Dinghies."

I shrink back to my flat-footed size, but Luke doesn't allow for it. "Hey," he soothes, squeezing me against him with an arm around my waist. "I didn't mean it that way. It's just that my cousins won't stop texting, and my mom keeps calling. Twenty-five people all need to agree on a restaurant, apparently."

"Yeah." I blandly nod, still slightly embarrassed about my aggressive entrance.

Luke hugs me, and I lean in while kicking a peeling rubber piece dangling from my gym shoe.

"Fuck it," he declares, and somehow my shoes are being lifted off the ground as Luke boosts me into his arms, bridal-style. "Can you reach the door?" he asks, and I grasp at air until I find the handle. Once open, Luke tosses me inside like I'm a bag of feathers and dives in next to me.

"Are you kidnapping me?" I grin.

"For five minutes. Or until my mom calls. Whichever comes first."

I'm horizontal on the front seat, the gear shift jabbing into my back. Luke balances on his elbows above me as we frantically kiss and grab at each other. I wrap my legs around his torso, pulling him toward me. We're overeager, not knowing what to touch or take off before our time dwindles down. There's not enough room, in the car or between us, to easily remove clothes, so we resign ourselves to shimmying hands into each other's waistbands. It's a lot of messy stroking and groping, sloppy kisses and missed reaches. I want to suggest the backseat when a tinkling tune plays from Luke's pocket. He rests on his forearm to tug his phone out of his shorts.

"It's my mom," he tells me, and we separate like we've been caught. "Hello?" he answers. I adjust my clothes and place my hands neatly in my lap. Luke's short call consists of mostly "uh-huhs" and "okays," and he ends it with "See you in a few minutes. Love you, too."

A boy who loves his mother and could bench-press me if the occasion ever arose? How are we not meant-to-be?

Luke bids me good-bye with two slow kisses and one even longer, lingering kiss. His eyes are hooded when he pulls away. "I wish I didn't have to go. What are you doing tomorrow after work?" he asks.

Playing Halo and trying not to open my Chapbook, I think. "Probably nothing. Why?" I look at him coyly.

"Maybe we can get something to eat and then do the painting I was supposed to help with today."

"Sounds fun," I agree. One last quick kiss, and I exit the car to head back to the Dinghies.

I spend a few minutes cleaning off brushes and closing paint cans, then I walk to my locker and gather my belongings. Three texts on my phone.

From Lish:

Come meet us for dinner tonight! I miss you!

Us? Ugh.

From Sahana:

Board games with the fam tonight if you want to join.

Maybe . . .

From Lish again:

We're at the Pie House at 7 if you want to meet us. I have a coupon!

Board games at Sahana's house could be fun, if it weren't for her ultracompetitive twin brothers. Imagine the Weasley twins, but Indian American, and instead of pranksters they're hard-core studiers who have to out-know every other human on the planet about every subject ever invented.

Pass.

It's hard to deny Lish and her coupon.

I text her:

I'm just leaving H.H. Be at the Pie House at 7:30.

When I get to the Pie House, it's packed. I forgot it's Wide

Wedge Wednesday, when you get double the amount of pie for the price of a single slice. I spot Lish and Travis sitting side by side at a booth and slide in across from them. Lish whispers, "We had to tell them we weren't expecting anyone else, or they wouldn't have seated us." Then she says loudly, "Agatha! I can't believe you're eating here, too! What a surprise! Why don't you join us?" Lish is so adorable when she's being a dork.

I humor her and reply boisterously, "Yes! I was in the neighborhood and thought, *I could really use some wide pie!* Who would have thought I would run into my best friend, plus guest!"

No way in hell I'm calling him her boyfriend in my Pie House theater show.

The waitress takes my order, a tuna melt and fries, and then it's time for dinner conversation. I wish it didn't feel like Dinner Conversation; having dinner with one's best friend should be the easiest, most comfy dining experience available, aside from toast in bed on a sick day off from school. But even that has crumbs. With Travis here, I feel so stunted in my topics of conversation. Talking about Empties is moot because they are obviously never going to side with a person who doesn't want to believe in the concept of meant-to-be. Talking about Luke is awkward, since he is not my MTB but is certainly more than a boy-slash-friend. I opt for conversation C: "I made a guy at work gawk at my boobs today." Totally acceptable, right?

As dinner progresses, I'm pleasantly surprised by how affable Travis is. While initially shocked, he enjoys the boob-leering story (and I don't get the sense that he enjoyed it *too* much, if you know what I mean). We were even able to have a real conversation concerning talking to my mom about Australia.

"As unhappy as she may be at first, you're an adult, you've earned your own money, and you have the right to go where you want," Travis logically advises.

"Plus, it's not like you're staying out of college forever. It's temporary. Focus on that, and maybe she won't freak," Lish adds.

"But what if it's not temporary? What if I fall in love with the country? The *continent*? And I don't want to leave?"

"You could go to college there," Travis suggests.

"Tell your mom that! She's so obsessed with college, maybe that will sell her," Lish adds.

"These are good ideas, but I don't know. I'm still not ready."

After dinner, Lish and Travis invite me to see a movie with them, but I decline. I don't know if I can stomach their hand-holding through the popcorn bucket. Plus, I want to be bright and shiny for work tomorrow. Or more importantly, after work.

At home Uncle Jim has classical music blasting (if that's a thing) from the attic, and there's a note on the kitchen table from my mom.

Out with work friends. If I don't see you before bed, hope you had a nice day at work. Good night! College mail on the table.

Glurg. Damn college and their ever-present mail.

I shuck off my clothes and put on my jammies. The lure of my laptop is strong, but I resist it by throwing on my ear cans and listening to the Monks. They're fast and poppy and punky, but somehow I manage to fall asleep relatively quickly.

I wake up in the morning with a cord imprinted on my face.

After my shower, I check my phone. A text from Lish:

Don't get grossed out, but sex with someone you love is so amazing!!!

Followed by seven hundred emojis, from hearts to fireworks to pieces of pie (I don't want to know).

Does Lish think tormenting me about her sex life is helpful? Does she think it will inspire me to look for Hendrix Cutter so I can have MTB sex with him? I don't need Hendrix Cutter to have great sex.

My stomach flips.

Is this a challenge? I accept!

I rummage through a shoe box in my closet until I find the condoms supplied in our sex-ed packet in health class. I tuck them into my backpack and gnaw on my cuticles in nervous anticipation.

Oh yes. Tonight I will have sex with someone I don't love! Or someone I could possibly love but isn't my MTB! Take that, Hendrix Cutter!

Get ready for a flurry of emojis, Lish.

CHAPTER 25

Rubber band wrapped around my fingers, I sling my hair into a high ponytail. Not because I think it looks phenomenal, although it does have a slightly seductive *I Dream of Jeannie* bend to it, but because it's hella hot. I don't know why summers take so long to get like this. The first week of summer is always so lovely, I almost forget to wear sunblock. Too quickly the humidity hovers near 100 percent and the temperature comes close to triple digits, and there ends up being no point to wearing sunblock since you're just going to sweat it off anyway. It's days like this I make sure to pack at least one back-up Haunted Hollow shirt. Nothing screams, "You want to have sex with me later, don't you?" like the shadow of pit rings.

On days that are this hot, crowds are usually thinner but extra-obnoxious. Kids are cranky, parents are short-tempered, and breaks with air-conditioning are scarce. The only departments of the park that benefit are (a) the ice cream and drink concession stands, (b) the store at the front of the park that everyone is forced to walk through on their way out (tired parents fork over the cash for all kinds of crap just to get their kids out of there faster), and (c) the Squalid Squirters. The title explains exactly what they are: pump-powered squirt guns mounted on swivel pedestals, each painted to look decayed, rundown, and like whatever liquid comes out of them would require one to seek a tetanus shot and some stiff antibiotics. Naturally, it's the same water that runs through the taps and drinking fountains. You'd be surprised how many kids stand directly in front of the squirters, mouths open, for a free drink. Or maybe you wouldn't. Kids are pretty gross. On hot days little kids may not have the same armpit stank we get once puberty hits, but there's still something pungent about a sweaty kid. Almost akin to a wet dog.

On these extra-hot days, I make frequent stops by concessions for ice water and take the long way back for a quick spritz by the Squalid Squirters. Kids love to think they're getting away with something when they spray me, but I'm grateful for the temporarily cool sensation. It takes less than five minutes to dry under these climatic circumstances.

Today as I take my second stroll through the Squirters, I notice Adam walking toward me from the opposite direction. The instance he sees me coming his way, I recognize the painful effort it takes for him to pull his eyes away from my chest. I kind of forgot about the whole wet-t-shirt aspect of my temperature-control system. Thankfully the Haunted Hollow t-shirts are a relatively thick material, and I subtly glance down to make sure it's opaque, pretending I needed to rub the back of my neck. All clear for sheerness. We might be talking a tiny hint of nipple. Still, I must commend Adam for managing to look away. I'm not in the face-punching mood today anyway.

My ponytail bobs as I sashay past Luke's ride and offer a friendly wave.

"Get caught in a rainstorm?" he chides.

"Yeah. Didn't you?" I ask curiously.

"We still hanging out later?" Luke asks with a sly smile, and most of me is really happy I went with the whole wet-t-shirt look. The other piece of me is quivering and trying to remember what it feels like to have actual sex and if I have any idea what I'm doing.

The afternoon sun blazes on, and I take shelter underneath the shade of the tunnel while the boats run. Something about the cold water flowing through the concrete walls makes it at least ten degrees cooler in here. Plus, it's really fun to scare the shit out of the kids as they round the corner.

The repetitive drone of the Devil's Dinghies is almost enough to drown out my escalating nervousness about having sex with Luke. While I'm not a virgin, sex with one dude who was also a virgin before we got together doesn't offer me loads of experience. According to Lish, who now has two more notches on her belt than I, plus a very advice-doling older brother, Archer, it's pretty hard for a girl to be bad at sex this early in the game. Teenage boys can get an erection if their underwear is bunching up in the wrong way. Archer also expounded upon the joys of oral sex, both giving and receiving, and it was at that point in his sex-ed talk that I locked myself in the bathroom and sat on the toilet for thirty minutes. It was a lot to take in at twelve.

What is it about sex that scares me? I make a mental list (because God help me if I write it down and someone finds it):

1) See the whole "What if I'm doing it wrong?" fear above, even though I attempted to talk myself out of it.
2) What if Luke doesn't actually want to have sex with me? That's a possibility, right? Maybe he's the type of guy who merely enjoys removing clothes from the upper half of the body.
3) What if he's a dick and doesn't want to wear a condom? Then he's a dick, and I move on. I'm not messing with the loss of my future due to baby and/or disease just to out-sex my best friend.
4) What if I don't have an orgasm? Judy Blume made it seem so easy in *Forever*, but I've never managed one while doing the deed. If I counted correctly, I've really only had two orgasms at the hands of someone other than myself. Would it be horrible if I didn't with Luke? I wouldn't get the emoji satisfaction with Lish. Or, you know, the actual satisfaction.
5) Are we moving too fast? Is there time to move slower? Do I want to move slower? Plus I need

> to have sex so I can one-up my best friend on her emojis.

That is a really stupid reason to have sex.

I guess the question is, do I like Luke Jacobs enough to have sex with him?

Is "I think so" a satisfactory answer?

Maybe I'm overthinking this. Luke and I will hang out tonight, get something to eat, and paint. Who knows what that will lead to . . . but, really, I'm cool with whatever happens.

Cool as a cucumber . . . that's been left out in the sun and is now wilting and actually Broasting™ on the sidewalk.

That's how fucking cool I am.

The park closes at six, and the obligatory wait for the crowd to leave commences. I head to my locker, change into a black tank top with red stars on it, then do an armpit check.

Could be better.

I rinse my armpits with wet paper towels then reapply deodorant with my secret locker stash, readjust my ponytail, and apply lip balm with a tinge of color (so I don't seem like I'm trying too hard). I look at myself in the mirror and realize I haven't worn this tank top since I turned eighteen. The top of my Empty peeks over the edge of my shirt. I consider changing, but all I have with me are extra Haunted Hollow shirts and Luke has seen me in enough orange. "Screw you," I say to Hendrix Cutter in the mirror. "You can watch."

It feels brazen to go on a date with my MTB showing. Who cares if the world thinks this is who I'm supposed to be with? I make my own choices, and tonight I choose Luke Jacobs. I'm fueled by this rebellion, enough to stride right up to Luke, who's chatting with Adam outside the staff locker room, and pull him in for a kiss. He "mmmms" into my mouth. "Hey there." Luke loops a finger into the top of my shorts, not in a manner where he's touching anything dirty but definitely in a way that implies these things are coming off at some point.

My breath catches. Coolness plummeting quickly.

"I'll just be going now." Adam waves good-bye with two fingers. "Luke, Agatha," and he's gone.

"Wow." I watch him leave. "He won't even talk to me now."

"He'll get over it. He's probably going to the bathroom to relieve himself." I smack Luke on the shoulder. "I'm kidding! Or not? It is Adam we're talking about."

"Yuck. So let's stop talking about him, please."

"Fine by me. You hungry?" Luke asks. We discuss dinner options. I veto Mexican (no need to be gassy), Italian (garlic breath), and sushi (not a fan). We settle on an Indian restaurant Luke and his family frequent.

As Luke drives, I tell him, "After my dad left, my mom

started taking us to a lot of restaurants that we were never able to try when he was around. The man wasn't very adventurous."

"Where'd he go?"

"Atlanta. He left my mom to be with his MTB." I futz with the edge of my shorts. This shouldn't bother me. I tolerate the man at this point, and my mom's better off with her independence. There's still something a little painful, a little embarrassing, when I say it aloud. "What about your parents?"

"They were divorced before the Naming. My mom met her MTB, Rick, on the Internet a few years ago. They took it really slowly, since they both already went through failed marriages. But he's living with us now. Seems okay."

Luke's indifference about his mom and MTBs surprises me. I presumed his situation was similar to mine, or maybe I merely wished it were. "What about your dad?" I ask, hoping to remedy the discrepancy through a loathing-of-dads commiseration.

"He found his MTB right away. I have three half-brothers already." He looks over at me and smiles as though this is cute news. It is not.

We arrive at the restaurant, Indian Garden, and the decision to order Palaak Paneer and Aloo Gobhi takes enough concentration that we are able to move along from the previously disappointing parental MTB conversation.

Luke sits across from me and periodically holds one of my hands to play with my fingers while we talk about movies and games. The difference in our hand sizes is mesmerizing.

After some time, the waiter rolls a small metal cart up to our table and produces several ceramic troughs of curries and plates of rice and naan. We pass our dishes to each other and sample different chutneys. I try not to eat too much, not wanting to have to poo at any point during the date. Fortunately for me, I'm a quick number two-er, so I could probably pass it off as a number one if necessary.

I wish bodily functions weren't such a source of strife for me.

As we leave the restaurant (Luke pays, even though I offer. I compromise with a promise of dessert later), he wraps his arm around me and pulls me close to his side. We walk to the car as one, a three-legged race we have no intention of winning. At the passenger door, Luke cups my chin and kisses me adoringly while I smile into the kisses. He opens the door for me and closes it once I'm comfortably inside. Throwing himself into the car, I jerk at the weight shift. After he starts the car and moves onto the road, Luke reaches over to hold my hand. I'm pretty blissed out.

The Haunted Hallow employee lot is virtually empty, save for a few vehicles including Sam Hain's black minivan with the license plate HH 666. Speak of the devil, we run into Sam Hain near the gate. I feel mildly conspicuous, as though Mr. Hain can see the condoms in my backpack with his carny vision.

"You guys are a little early for work," he jests.

"We thought we could work on the mural," I offer.

Instantly I recognize Sam Hain's chest puff with pride. Anything to improve his beloved park. "Well then, here," he says, slipping a key off a large ring attached to his belt. "Lock up when you're done."

"You won't need this to get in tomorrow?" Luke asks.

"It's a spare. Keep it until the end of the summer. Good night, you two. Don't do anything I wouldn't do," he advises, arching a wicked eyebrow.

As we walk away from him, Luke whispers, "So that probably means we could sacrifice a goat if we wanted to."

"Or pray to a dark lord for better sales figures," I add.

"Or eat sixty hot dogs in one sitting. Adam swears he saw Sam do it once."

Hand in hand, we walk through the park. With the many thousand carnival bulbs shut off, the setting sun provides a blush-hued glow before the impending flood of security lights.

The evening is clear, and the temperature hovers above eighty degrees. Nary a breeze passes through Haunted Hollow, and the adorable wisps of hair once cascading from my ponytail are now clinging to my moist neck. Luke sports visible sweat rings on his gray t-shirt. Our walk through the park becomes a stroll, then a trudge, and by the time we reach the Devil's Dinghies we're both dripping with sweat.

"Damn, it's hot," Luke states the obvious.

"Uh-huh," is all I can muster.

We stumble across the plank onto the grass, where we collapse next to each other. Luke feels around for a second until he finds my hand, then he links pinkies. "It's too hot to hold hands."

"Too hot to paint," I add unmoving. We enjoy the coolness the grass provides. A breeze picks up, and the hair sticking to my face and neck chills. Goose bumps spring up on my arms.

Senses reawakened, Luke asks, "Is it too hot for this?" His fore- and middle fingers act as legs, sneaking across my belly.

"Depends," I answer lazily. "Do I have to move?"

"Well,"—he props himself up onto his elbow—"you don't have to. But usually it helps." His walking fingers find the hem of my tank top and gingerly lift it to the base of my bra. The barely-there pressure of his touch causes me to shiver, as does the wind.

"Mmmm," I hum unconsciously. The total relaxation of not having somewhere to be on a summer night, lying in a blanket of grass, and being caressed by a beautiful boy is a moment I want to pack away in my long-term memory. For a second I think, *This would be enough for the night. This would satisfy me.* But Luke is ready for more, as is evident by the languid circles his once-walking fingers are now swirling over my nipple. There is no denying the pleasure it gives me. Luke's fingers read me like Braille, and he takes his cue to remove my shirt. The air over my skin feels extra cool now against the quickly drying sweat. I need more, so instead of waiting for Luke to pick the lock of my bra hooks, I save him from the puzzle and remove it myself. I sit up for a moment to toss the bra to the side, then lie back down in the soft grass. How does Sam Hain get the grass to stay so soft? Our lawn at home is so crunchy, even when healthy and green. I would never lie on my back completely topless in it. Here at Haunted Hollow, the wind whipping at my nakedness, I think about how I should do this more often.

Luke is quick to recover his contact on my breasts. My back arches into the touch, my legs clench around Luke's strong body, and my hands grasp at anything to hold on. In one way, it's disconcerting to lose control of myself like this, to not know what my body will do but merely react. But in another way it is liberating to not have to make a choice, to think through every expression or sound I'm making and wonder *am I doing it right?* Because when it feels this good, how could I possibly be doing it wrong?

Luke's kisses are grand and luscious and intoxicating. He kisses down my cheek, my neck, and then his mouth is upon my chest. For the briefest second, I envision him licking Hendrix Cutter's Name, but as he devours me I lose all thought of Empties. Luke feels so good I manage to close my eyes to Scarlett Dresden's Name.

I think maybe this is going to be it, naked chests and mouths rubbing against each other but nothing below the belt. With the friction from our clothes and deliciously wet contact with Luke's mouth, I am feeling the familiar building in my gut and below. I rut against Luke as he smothers me with his lips, his tongue, and anticipate the climax.

Too soon Luke backs off, and I sigh at the loss of contact. He kneels to unbutton my shorts, and in one yank pulls off both my shorts and undies. I am completely naked outside the Devil's Dinghies.

Luke doesn't wait for me to help with his pants, and without a fumble he is completely naked, too.

The sky has darkened significantly since our grassy tryst began, but the lights have yet to kick on. I'd rather not be exposed having sex on the lawn of a ride, and it feels sexier to see each other by the glow of the setting sun, colors reflecting in the sweat on Luke's chest, his hazel eyes settling on a golden hue.

Luke kneels closer to me, and he whispers, "Is this okay?" I ask myself, too: *Am I ready for this? Is this really going to happen?* The answer is that if I'm going to see how great sex can be with a non-MTB, then I have to have sex. It's as (nerve-rackingly, not even remotely) simple as that. "I have condoms in my backpack," I say, wondering if he recognized the nerves in my voice that I heard. Together we crawl, naked asses in the air, bare knees pressing circles into the grass, until I find my backpack in the shadows. The crinkle of the condom packet reverberates comically off the wall of demons. I turn away so it doesn't feel quite as much like they're watching. At least now we are less out in the open than a second ago. I pray Sam Hain doesn't have security cameras hiding behind the devils' eyes.

The moment of condom application is a strange one. Am I supposed to do it? Is Luke? Does he want me to? Were we supposed to discuss this beforehand? Are we supposed to stop and discuss this now?

Something tells me that Luke is not in the mood for discussion. And that something is the way he grabs the condom from my hand and rips the wrapper open with his teeth. I watch him roll it on, pinching the tip like they taught us in health class (would I have been comfortable enough to remind him to do so if he didn't?). Is everyone's head a cacophony of questions before sex? Luke leans over me, and I lie back into the welcoming cushion of grass.

Sex with Luke happens.

One minute his penis is outside me, and the next it's inside me, and instead of being the hot, orgasmic experience pontificated about in my junior-year diary, it's faster and clumsier than required to be pleasurable, like when a crowd of people starts clapping along to a musical performance and the clapping speeds up but isn't in sync with the music and it's really disconcerting. Sex with Luke is also disconcerting while at the same time not all that gratifying. At least for me. Luke comes in a flash. I'm left with grass-stained butt cheeks.

As Luke and his ginormous body lie panting on top of me, the security lights find the least opportune time to blink on and blind us. Luke, in his state of release, doesn't notice, so I not-so-delicately hoist him off me (using strength reserved for lifting a car off a crash victim) and scramble around for my clothes. I'm fully dressed before Luke has one leg through his boxer briefs. I watch him curiously. He really is beautiful to look at, and it wasn't that what he did wasn't enjoyable. But it wasn't *that* enjoyable.

Luke lethargically stretches his shirt over his head. His shaggy hair, previously wet from heat, blows dry in the wind. He looks like a Roman warrior posing for a marble statue.

So why the hell wasn't he mere chivalrous?

Luke's satisfied expression tells me he has no idea he left something extra special to be desired.

What do I do? How awkward would it be to say to him, "Luke, I love what you did early on in our groping session. You may have even noticed I was *thisclose* to letting go, if you catch my drift. But once you hit this zone"—I gesture to my groin with a circular motion—"what happened, buddy?"

You can't say that shit to someone you just had sex with. What's he going to do, rewind? If I tell Luke that I didn't come (although how could he not have noticed?), will he feel embarrassed? Offended? Confused? Maybe he doesn't know what a female orgasm looks like. Maybe his ex-girlfriend faked it for the last three years. Maybe it's up to me to help him help me.

I try to think of a subtle yet clever way to imply that, yes, we will do this again, but with some adjustments, when the windy, dark sky opens up and torrential rains burst down. We bolt to the parking lot, my short legs keeping pace. Before we part Luke attempts to pull me in for a passionate, rainy kiss, but I'm over it and appease him with a rushed peck before I dive into my car, soaked.

I drive home, confused, half-satisfied, and frankly disappointed. I want to call Lish to sort it all out, but she's probably having ridiculous sex with the love of her life.

Is there an emoji for *meh*?

CHAPTER 26

The rain dumps onto my car the entire ride home. I do believe the cloud is following me, hovering above my roof to make me extra-introspective.

Why does it bother me so much that Luke and I didn't have mind-blowing sex? The obvs of it is that Lish claims she did have great sex, which happened to be sex with her MTB. She also claims to be in love with her MTB. Luke, whom I have known for three years, who is the physical embodiment of a teenage wet dream and is fun (enough) to be around, didn't quite do it for me.

This isn't merely about the orgasm or lack thereof.

I park the car in my driveway and click the garage door opener, giving me the shortest route from car to dryness. Not that it matters. I'm still soaked from half an hour ago, thanks to the complete saturation of my clothes mixed with the 100 percent humidity level in my car. It was too hot to leave off the air-conditioning, but the air blowing on my wet shirt had me in perpetual shakes. Half of my drive was spent flipping the AC button on and off.

When the garage door opens, I see both my uncle Jim's

(barely driven) car and my mom's. I brace myself for the downpour, and dash inside. Dripping but home, I walk into my house.

"Hey!" I call. "I'm home!" I untie my sopping gym shoes and peel off my socks. I'd like to strip off everything as long as I'm in the laundry room, but I'm too old for a naked walk in front of my mom, let alone my uncle.

I slide my way into the kitchen where Uncle Jim is cooking something that better taste as good as it smells. "Mmmm. Smells yummy. What are you making?" I sidle up to Jim at the stove.

"You're dripping onto my slippers." He points a spatula at me.

"Sorry." I scooch away. I find it always best not to anger the chef.

"It's paella. You like shrimp, right?"

I do not. Their faces are far too conspicuous for something I would eat, but I don't tell that to Uncle Jim. "Sure," I answer noncommittally.

"Well, you can eat around them. Or give them to me. They were expensive. Well, they would have been if your mom didn't get the sexy lady's discount."

"Jim!" my mom shouts playfully at her brother as she enters the kitchen. "How was your day, honey?" she asks me, kissing the side of my head. "Ew. Go get a towel."

"After you tell me about your sexy lady's shrimp discount," I press.

"Your uncle is exaggerating. There's a nice guy who

works the fish counter at the grocery store. He's been there for years, so we kibitz a lot. Today he gave me a special on the shrimp. It's no big deal," she says, although it's a big enough deal that she tucks her hair behind her ears playfully. And is that a slight blush on her cheeks?

"You are adorable, Mom," I note.

"And you are forming a puddle on my kitchen floor. Go change."

I squelch my way up to my bedroom, stopping in the bathroom for a towel. I sit on the toilet and delicately wipe when I'm finished. My vagina is exhausted.

In my room I undress with the window open and lights off. I heard that a person looking into my room would only be able to see me if it were lighter inside than it is outside. I've never tested that theory and, truthfully, there has always been something safely titillating about someone watching me undress. Of course, in my mind, that someone is the gorgeous Ukrainian exchange student who imaginarily lives in the house behind ours and is most decidedly not the divorced dad who picks the kids up once a month. Or the kids themselves. Maybe I should start closing my shades just in case.

I slide on a pair of leggings covered in sprinkled donuts and a Haunted Hollow t-shirt from two years ago. Then I take the t-shirt off and trade it for a plain black one, lest I be reminded of my earlier choice to get buck naked on Haunted Hollow turf and bone a coworker.

Did I really do that?

I chuckle to myself at the recollection of recklessness and

the choice to bare it all in a public place and do the deed with Luke Jacobs.

It wasn't so bad. I did derive some enjoyment from it, and Luke certainly had a good time. So what if we're not in love yet? At least we both put ourselves out there and didn't fall prey to society's plans for us and our MTBs. Next time we do it, I'm sure it will be a billion times better. I'll be explicit about my needs, and he won't be quite as eager to get to completion. (It'll be hotter than that sounded.)

I have talked myself into believing that Luke Jacobs and I still have a future together of love and hot sex, so much so that I stupidly log on to Chapbook to see if he's written anything about me. The quick answer is no, he has not written anything. In fact, there are no newly created pages by Luke or even a log-in from him recently. There is, however, a page posted on Luke's Chapbook from one Adam Callas. It reads:

You better hope there weren't any hidden security cameras

Followed by a delightful winking, tongue-sticking-out emoji.

This can mean one of two things:

Either Luke Jacobs robbed a bank and Adam is being a good friend in wishing Luke doesn't get caught, or LUKE JACOBS TOLD ADAM WE HAD SEX.

If any part of my body remained wet a moment ago, the anger steaming out through my pores ensures that I am dry now.

How could he? We *just* had sex, and Adam already

knows? That guy is such a perv. He didn't need any more ammo to stare at me salaciously. Was it a total brag for Luke? A conquest? Did he even like me as a human being, or was all his charming hand-holding and dinner-buying a lead-up to this? Do guys actually do that? It's like sleazeball-movie-character bullshit, not something that would happen to me.

What a dick. I feel like this is a test. I'm supposed to roll over and go, "Oh, Lish has sex and love and it's all because of her MTB, and I have no love and iffy sex with a douche-hog who tells a total degenerate about us. If I had merely found my MTB and settled, none of this would have happened."

Well, fuck you, fate! I had mediocre sex, so what? At least I chose to. And it wasn't with Hendrix Cutter? Who says sex with Hendrix Cutter will be amazing? Who says Hendrix Cutter and I will even like each other?

I refuse to let this derail my life. My course is set for chaos. I don't need a higher power or scientific anomaly or whatever it is to tell me what to do. Hell, I may go have bad sex with whomever I want! Because it is my choice, and that's what matters.

I close my laptop and bound down the stairs, fueled by Internet rage and my naggingly stubborn brain.

"Mom," I sputter, "I need to talk to you." She sits at the table in her reading glasses completing the daily Jumble.

"Do I need to leave the room?" Uncle Jim checks.

"No. You can hear this."

"Do I need to worry?" My mom removes her eyeglasses.

"No. Probably not. Just hear me out." I burst right into it so I don't chicken out. "Mom, you know I don't want to go to college. Not yet anyway. There's nothing I really I want to study—"

Mom tries to interrupt with, "You don't have to know right away—" but I cut her off.

"Please let me finish, Ma. I've been thinking about this for a long time. All I want to do right now is go to Australia. I want to backpack around and meet people from different countries and get a job working at Luna Park running the Ghost Train. I don't want to be stuck here anymore in the same place with the same people." I take a breath, and my mom seizes the opportunity to interject.

"Ag, you can do all that after college. And you'll meet lots of new friends at school."

"Mom! I didn't want to play this card, but here it is: It's my money. I'm the one who worked summers and baby-sat during the school year, and I would be the one taking out loans and paying them back. I'd rather use the money for something I want to do. I'm following your lead, Ma! You decided not to subscribe to this MTB bullshit, and that's so cool! I want to explore the world and not have to find Hendrix Cutter and settle. I want to find real love, not arranged marriage!"

"Agatha!" Mom stands violently, cutting me off. I shut up when I see her welling up with tears. Shit. I didn't mean to make her cry. Mom, never one to let tears flow freely, composes herself and speaks more calmly. "Agatha." She clears her throat. "I'm not going to stop you from going to Australia. You're right: It is your money and your choice. I hope to God that you'll figure it all out and get yourself a college degree after you sow your wild oats or whatever it is you think is going to happen on the other side of the world. But you need to know something: I did not, per se, choose to be alone." My mom sits and swallows. "After your dad left, I was so angry at all men and MTBs that there was a period of time when I believed never looking for love again was best. But it's hard when you've been in a relationship for twenty-five years to be out of one. So I had my MTB's signature scanned. I paid some idiot too much money, and this is what I learned: John Taylor, my John Taylor, was listed in the signature database. Because my John Taylor was a marine. And ten years ago he was killed in Iraq." I do the math and gulp, holding in tears and words. My mom remains stoic. "I didn't, nor do I, know how to feel. So the man I'm supposed to be with was dead before I was ever supposed to be with him? What kind of fate is that besides cruel? So, yes, I'm not pursuing my MTB because I have no MTB to pursue." My brain whirs, livid at the brutality of having a dead man's Name on my mom's chest, a dead man she never had the chance to discover. And yet, I feel stupid for how callous I've been toward MTBs for years around my mom, oblivious to her story.

"Why didn't you tell me, Mom?"

"I was ashamed, I guess. For scanning the Name, for caring more than I let on about the preposterous Naming. I don't know what to tell you to do, Agatha. All I want is happiness for my daughter. What if your MTB is happiness?"

"How can it be the only route to happiness, Mom? If it is, where does that leave you?" I walk over to where my mom sits and wrap my arms around her. "You deserve happiness, too, Mom. I love you so much." I squeeze her tightly. "There's always the shrimp guy," I nudge. Mom laughs.

"*You* make me happy, sweetie." She squeezes me back. "Even if you're torturing me by moving twelve million miles away."

"Mom!" I whine. "Do you want me to stay?" I ask, praying she doesn't say yes.

"I want you to find happiness, Agatha. If something is telling you to travel all the way to Australia to find it, then go hug a koala and throw a shrimp on the barbie."

"Shrimp are gross, Mom." I release my embrace, relieved.

"I knew it!" snaps Uncle Jim.

We laugh together and sit down as a family to eat, air cleared, mind blown.

The events of the day make it veritably impossible to fall asleep. My mind is a ticker tape of thought.

Luke Jacobs and I had sex.

John Taylor is dead.

I can go to Australia.

One thought in particular is nagging me.

"If something is telling you to travel all the way to Australia to find it, then go. . . ."

Do I want to go, or is something bigger than me telling me to go?

If the latter is the case, then now must I make the conscious choice *not* to go?

Why don't choices ever bother to make themselves?

Brain maxed out, my phone pings. It's Luke.

Doing the happy dance before bed because of you. Good night.

The image of giant Luke Jacobs dancing around like Snoopy almost outweighs the disgust I feel about him telling Adam. It is, after all, another day. I cannot imagine what bizarre thing might happen next.

Hasn't that been my goal?

CHAPTER 27

I walk into work with a bit of trepidation and a whole lot of chutzpah. It's definitely bothering me that Luke told Adam about us having sex. And not the fireworks-in-my-crotch kind of sex, either. Would that have made this better? Probably not, although I have heard a theory that some sort of chemical reaction happens within a woman's brain after she has sex that makes her feel obsessively attached to a person. Is that only true if she has an orgasm? Is it true at all? How could something like that even be proven? I envision the scientists:

[After watching two people have sex]

Scientist #1: Hmmm, yes.
Scientist #2: Quite.
Scientist #1 to Subject #1 (male): How do you feel?
Subject #1: Sleepy.
Scientist #2: And how do you feel about her?
Subject #1: Who?
Scientist #1: The person with whom you just had intercourse.

Subject #1: [snickers] Intercourse.

Scientist #2: Answer the question, please.

Subject #1: I . . . I like her? Can I go to sleep now?

Scientist #1 to Subject #2 (female): How do you feel?

Subject #2: Pretty great. Can I pee now?

Scientist #2: In a minute. And how do you feel about him?

Subject #2: That guy sleeping over there?

Scientist #1: Yes, that's the one.

Subject #2: I just fell madly in love with him and want to have seven thousand babies together. After he wakes up, of course.

Scientist #1: I think we've proven our hypothesis.

Scientist #2: Quite.

Do scientists really watch people have sex for "research"? I wonder if those people feel pressure to make the sex extra-impressive. What a weird job.

As I contemplate finding work in the field of scientific sex (does one need a degree for that?), I round a corner and am face-to-lascivious-face with Adam. His expression changes from annoyance at someone being in his way to panic that it is me to realization that it is *me* who just had sex with his friend. He's not ogling any part of me, but am I still allowed to punch him?

"Hello, Agatha," he purrs, a sound no one wants to hear from a squatty guy with a crusty baseball hat.

"Hey, Adam." I try to sound confident, nonchalant,

like I either don't know that he knows or I don't care. It's wonderfully powerful to look directly into his eyes and catch the strain as they try desperately not to look downward. Especially since I'm certain he has envisioned me naked at the Devil's Dinghies.

I can't believe I was naked at the Devil's Dinghies.

"Have a nice day," I offer, since we don't seem to be moving.

"Um, yeah. You, too." He smirks and runs off. I hope it's not to the Ghoster because I'm ready to confront Luke. If there is one thing I've learned from Savannah Merlot, aside from fifteen unique ways to describe an erection, it's that one must never let her feelings fester. Yes, I'm pissed that Luke told Adam about us, but I'm not going to sit on it and wait to see if he notices that I'm pissed. Guys are never that observant. Well, maybe some are, but I have yet to be mad at any of the observant ones.

Lucky for me, Adam is nowhere in sight as I approach the Ghoster. Luke's hair looks particularly tousled this morning, no doubt as a result of the magical properties of hooking up with me. Do I look any different? Aside from the pattern of hickeys I discovered on my stomach in the mirror this morning (I hope they fade before my interview at the sex science center). I would be annoyed by their tackiness, but no one else can see them and I did enjoy the process by which they were created.

Focus, Aggy. You're mad, remember?

Inside his booth, Luke leans over to pick something up, and I am compelled to think *datass*, which is offensive and lewd and totally hypocritical. I try to ask the Savannah Merlot in my brain what I should do, but she keeps going on about beignets and has no time to help me.

"Hey," I greet Luke, trying to sound stern but not motherly. He stands up from his bent position and flips his hair out of his eyes. How does he do that in slow motion?

The instant he sees me, a magnificent grin spreads across his lips, dimples as dimply as ever. He steps forward, grips my face in his mondo hands, and kisses me so powerfully I stumble backward. With little effort, he moves one hand from my cheek to my hip to steady me.

I could *not* kiss him back. I could freeze my lips in protest and wait for Luke to feel my displeasure. But it is very hard to feel displeasure when my whole body reacts in complete meltiness. His kisses are strong and sweet, and the delicate rhythm of tongue is goading my mouth into kissing him back.

Let us not forget that I have liked Luke for years. Let us not forget that I liked Luke enough to willingly let him into my pants last night. Let us not forget that Luke told Adam "Super Perv" Callas we did it.

I pull away from Luke's lip enchantment. "Why did you tell Adam we had sex?" I ask bluntly.

Luke's hands encircle my hips while he looks down at me. "How do you know? Did he say something?" He sounds both guilty and peeved, looking around as if the culprit is nearby.

I grab his chin to focus his eyes on me. "You have no right to be pissed. *I* have every right." I am calm and forthright, and I may have slipped into a tiny Savannah Merlot southern accent for a second while holding back the urge to call Luke "sugar."

"I know. I shouldn't have told Adam. But he called me, and I was excited." He shrugs charmingly. "He may be a douchetool, but he's my friend, the douchetool."

"Tell me more about this being-excited part." I attempt to hide the smile growing on my lips and the warmth sprouting in my belly. There is something sweet about a boy being excited about me.

"I don't know." Luke steps back shyly, rubbing his hand along the base of his neck. "I like you," he states dopily, and he looks so heartfelt, his eyes embodying his gray/blue sincerity, it's hard to hate him too much.

"Okay." I nod my head in vague agreement.

Luke looks relieved, his large shoulders visibly releasing the tension they held.

"Good," he says. "I'm glad you're not mad. I'll kick Adam's ass, though, if you want me to," Luke offers.

"Nah. As long as you didn't go into graphic detail and he starts talking about my other body parts." I laugh.

"God, you're cute," Luke pants, and kisses me so compellingly I feel a flush between my legs.

I stumble to my booth in a daze and untether the boats from beneath the tunnel.

Maybe my summer of love is still a possibility. A violent prickliness erupts from the space occupied by Hendrix Cutter's Name, and I angrily scratch it.

When does this thing fully heal?

As a result of last night's rain, the temperature today is far more bearable than yesterday. Instead of sitting inside at lunch (and bristling every time Adam speaks, for fear of innuendo), I grab a quick sandwich and take it to the wall of the Devil's Dinghies for a painting lunch. Keely works the ride as I add fresh color to some naked devil butts. Halfway through my break, Luke joins me on the grass. "Seems like just yesterday. . . ." He stares at the grass wistfully. I smack him playfully on the arm.

"Speaking of yesterday," I begin, dipping my paintbrush in white to add a glint to the round devil buttocks, "I talked to my mom—"

"About us?" he asks, disbelieving.

"No." I'm annoyed by his fixation with us and sex, but I persevere because I miss talking to someone on a daily basis now that Lish is tied down. "About me moving to Australia."

Luke looks confused. "I thought you were going to college." He finds a paintbrush and starts painting a pitchfork.

"I am. Maybe. Someday." I realize that our avoidance of talking about the "future" means he has no idea about my plans. "But I really want to go to Australia first. And I thought my mom was totally against it, but she was actually semicool about it. It was a huge relief. Then she told me this really sad story about her MTB, but I won't go into that."

I wait for Luke, my boyfriend-ish-but-not-labeled person to congratulate me or commiserate with me on choosing my path for the future or ask more about my mom, but his forehead crinkles and his mouth remains closed.

"Hello?" I press. "Great big life things happening here."

"I don't know." He shrugs. "It's just that Australia's really far away." He paints, speaking to but not looking at me.

"One of its finest selling points, one might argue."

"I guess." Luke does not seem to be sharing my enthusiasm.

"What's up?" I ask.

"Nothing," he answers. Luke has obviously not read the Savannah Merlot novels.

"Tell me," I prod, with an affectionate nudge to his shoulder.

"It's just . . . don't you want to see where this goes? You know . . . us?"

Us? The concept has crossed and crisscrossed my mind over the years, and certainly over the last month, but . . . us?

My chest itches again, and I smack Hendrix Cutter's Name hard. It's annoying how the scar acts up at the most inopportune times.

Keely yells from the booth, "Break's over! My turn!" I've never been so grateful for her presence.

"Can we talk about this later?" I smile caringly so as not to bruise his gigantic heart. It's not that I don't want an Us. For whatever reason, that chemical reaction in my brain is not fusing like it should with Luke Jacobs.

It's not because I have another boy's name on my body. Is it?

CHAPTER 28

This is stupid.

I have crushed upon Luke Jacobs for years. He even has this new and enlarged physique that should be catapulting my crush status into complete dominating obsession. Hell, I've slept with the guy. I have seen him naked. He has seen me naked.

He is funny and cute and apologizes and pays for food, and he has those kaleidoscope eyes and floppy hair.

I should totally be head over heels, heart, and mind burning with desire for him.

Then why aren't I?

Maybe I'm trying too hard. You can't force love. It has to happen naturally, like aging wine and moldy cheese and those disgusting sprouty things that pop out of the eyes on potatoes. Just because I crave Lish's MTB-level passion with Luke Jacobs doesn't mean it'll automatically happen. Maybe I need to get to know him better. Love isn't merely about being attracted to someone and laughing when they joke about the size of meatballs at a restaurant. No, love is . . . hell, I have no idea. I've never actually been in love. I thought

I loved Jared Mason, but looking back it was just simple high school crushing. I am much older and wiser now and, yes, still technically a teenager. But I can vote and by many state laws already be married, so it's different now. Or it should be. Why am I not in love?

Maybe it's not that I'm trying too hard. Maybe I'm not trying hard enough. Luke has sent me sweet texts and paid for my dinners, and what have I done for him? Aside from, you know, the sex thing. I will now attempt my hand at romantic poetry. What rhymes with Luke?

Exactly the moment I have this thought, a child stumbling off the nearby Ghoster pukes onto the concrete.

Thank you, vomiting child, for your masterful timing and gift for rhyme.

Forget the poem. I am going to will myself to be in love with Luke. What's not to love about him? After work we'll hang out, have way-better sex, cuddle, and my brain will figure it out and love will ensue.

Damn, I'm romantic.

The day ends, and I mosey up to Luke flirtatiously. It feels unnatural even though I've used the same method numerous times with him in the past. Perhaps it feels redundant to be flirtatious when I know he already likes me, the whole why-buy-the-cow-when-you-get-the-milk-for-free theory. Wait, am I the cow in that theory? Leave it to a cow analogy to make me feel gassy.

"Hey." I provide him with the ubiquitous greeting and slide my arm around his waist so we're side by side. Comfy.

Sturdy. Protective. These are all adjectives I'd use to describe how Luke feels right now. I will not mention how with his arm around my shoulder I am directly in line with his armpit. If I loved him, then this is a feeling I'd enjoy. A scent that draws me in, not repulses me.

Trying to be in love is a lot of work.

"Want to get something to eat?" I ask, maneuvering my way out of the pit. He quickly draws me in for a face-in-his-chest moment and breathes in my ear, "My mom and Rick are at a wedding in the city tonight. Want to order pizza and watch a movie?" He kneads my lower back with his fingertips, and my stomach flutters.

See? I like him. I had a physical reaction to him touching me. Or maybe I'm nervous because ordering pizza and watching a movie is obvious code for that whole penis-in-vagina thing again. Not that that's a bad thing. I just want it to be a really great thing. And to be madly in love with him. That's not asking too much, is it?

Before I overthink the hell out of every nanosecond of our evening, I take a deep breath and try to be cool. "Sounds good." I nod.

We walk hand in hand to our respective cars, the idea being for me to follow him back to his house so I can drive home from there. Luke kisses me slowly and deeply, and I tell my mind to shut up and enjoy the damn kiss. I let out a contented sigh, but I'm not certain if it was genuine or for show.

If I keep this up, I'm going to start monitoring each breath I take. I'm already spent.

Alone in my car, I text my mom to let her know I'll be home late. My foot on the brake, I quickly tap out a text to Lish:

Going to Luke's tonight. We already had sex once. Need to talk to you. I'm off work tomorrow. Are you?

Luke's car begins moving, and I shift my car into drive to follow. Ten minutes of skipped turn signals and speedy yellow-light maneuvers, and we arrive at a white ranch-style house. My phone rings, Luke's number, and I answer.

"Hello?"

"Hey. Park behind my car, in case my mom gets home early."

"Okay."

Luke pulls into a widened section of driveway to the side of the garage, and I pull in after him. My heart races with anticipation, but I don't know what of. We've already eaten together. We've already had sex, in public no less. What left is there to feel nervous about?

The inside of Luke's house is neat and modern with lots of hard surfaces like marble and wood and steel. We walk through the living room to the kitchen, which overlooks a large and wooded backyard. Squirrels scamper up bird feeders, plants bloom heartily in a fenced-off garden, and a compost bin sits in a far corner.

"Nice backyard," I note. Luke slips up from behind to

encase me in his sturdy arms. Watching the squirrels rapidly stuff their cheeks while being held by Luke Jacobs is something I could get used to. It feels normal and reassuring. I congratulate myself on that reaction.

"You hungry?" he asks.

"Yeah. Where do you want to order from?" He begins devouring my neck in kisses, and I realize he wasn't talking about food.

I try to alleviate my brain of all thought, to let the nerve endings encasing my body react to the pleasure of an attractive human being doing sexy things to them. His hands quickly slide up my shirt and knead my breasts, and I melt into the sensation. I lean back into him and reach around to rub the back of his head. Whatever he's doing is working, and a warm and tingly feeling glows between my legs. As I turn around to kiss him, I take off my shirt and bra haphazardly. I know it's fast, but the slower I take things the more time I have to think and ruin it all. Luke rips his t-shirt over his head, and the skin-to-skin contact beneath our frantically kissing lips is delectable.

Luke works at the buttons on my shorts. My brain provides annoying commentary of something my mom once warned me: *Don't have sex right away because once you have sex, that's all you have. All that good stuff that came before gets pushed aside for the final act.*

Not wanting my mom's words to ring true (or, really, be in my head at this moment. Who wants to hear their mom's voice when they're getting naked with someone?), I guide

Luke's hand into my undies. He grins against my lips but doesn't quite get the glaring neon sign of a message: LET'S NOT HAVE SEX YET. EVER HEARD OF FOREPLAY? Oblivious, Luke starts to pull down my shorts with his other hand. I stop him with a hand on his wrist, and then use my other hand to move his fingers inside the thin cotton material of my underwear. He strokes between my legs as we kiss, and I bring my hand to the front of his shorts to rub him over the fabric. There is something about being touched in this way while still wearing clothes that drives me mad. The sensation is so delicious that I am barely able to return his kisses.

Abruptly, Luke pulls his fingers out of my pants and says, "I'll be right back."

He clumsily runs upstairs, and I am left reeling at the kitchen counter. What happened? That was good stuff. Seconds later, Luke is back with a condom packet.

My breasts must be distracting him from the incredulous look on my face because he has no idea I was so close to coming but completely thwarted by his need to get a condom at that precise moment.

I'm about to read him the riot act, or at least shove his hand back into my pants, when he consumes me with his strong chest and arms and murmurs into my ear, "You are beautiful, and I am pudding." Mmmm. Pudding. Luke and I stumble to the couch, entangled and groping as we walk. Our remaining clothes drop off, and soon Luke is inside me once again. It feels good, yet no euphoria builds. He's heavy, but somehow I manage to sit him up. Maybe a different position is what I need. I straddle Luke and try again. The shitty fact is that once my tingling has died down, it's double the work to build it back up. We're clapping again at a soft rock concert, and Luke is pure white boy. I'm frustrated that our bodies aren't working together when I want them to, and that frustration takes over any part of my body or brain that needs to be relaxed enough for an orgasm. Then Luke comes, and pulls out, and leaves to rid himself of the condom in the bathroom. Not quite as speedy as all that, but far too quickly for me to have a grand finale.

Once again I am left orgasmless. I consider relieving myself in the bathroom, but that seems odd with a guy right here and, frankly, I'm not that much in the mood anymore.

We get dressed. We order pizza. We watch a movie. Luke cuddles with me on the couch, and I lean into him, sleepy from the physical activity.

After the movie, I tell him I'm tired and should go.

"You sure you don't want to stay?" He kisses me tenderly, and I reciprocate because his lips are there.

"I told my mom I'd be home by midnight," I lie.

"You're not working tomorrow, right?" he asks.

"Nope. You are, though?" I hope the relief doesn't come through in my voice.

"Maybe we can hang out tomorrow night?"

"I'll see. I might be getting together with Lish. It's been a while."

"Text me," he says. I nod.

In my car, I look at my phone and see a welcome text from Lish.

No work tomorrow! Travis is working, so let's play!

Thank God.

Happy and looking forward to tomorrow as I drive home, I sing along to embarrassing music on the radio that I tell everyone else I hate.

My house is dark when I arrive, so I'm quiet as I step into the shower. As I'm sudsing up, it occurs to me that maybe I can't have orgasms anymore without my MTB. Maybe that's something that happens at eighteen that no one talks about. So I test the theory. An elaborate love story between me and Captain America blossoms in my mind. The hot water, the bubbles, Chris Evans . . . I come quickly and with scant effort, and when I turn off the water I'm worried maybe I may have awoken my mom.

Theory disproved. Maybe I should call the sex scientists. Maybe I'll even get a stipend.

I stretch on a nightshirt and peer over at my laptop. My initial plot was to check Luke's Chapbook page again, to see if there are any new incriminating posts from Adam. But I realize I don't even care, and instead of Luke's page I am involuntarily typing those letters again.

H-e-n-d-r-i-x C-u-t-t-e-r.

Still there is the amazing drawing of his name. My eyes wander over each letter, taking in the shapes of people. I continue to be blown away by this.

On the side I note that Hendrix has several open pages,

those anyone looking at Chapbook can see. One of them is a page entitled WHO I AM.

My hand doesn't wait for my brain to decide and clicks it.

The screen looks like a yearbook signature page, covered in scribbles and doodles. Various words have been written, then scratched over, then written again.

My Work
My Band
My Sister
My Dog
My Hometown

I learn he has a sister named Pippa (which makes me wonder if he's British), his dog's name is Blue, and his hometown is Brunswick East, wherever that is.

The section of the page I'm really drawn to, though, is the bottom right corner. There it reads in scratchy block letters: *My Girl*, with a drawing I assume he did of a lovely blonde with braids and blue eyes.

My head weighs heavy, and my heart aches. I am unable to control the tears that pool and fight to spill over.

Hendrix Cutter has a girlfriend.

CHAPTER 29

A cackle on my phone awakens me from a very bizarre dream the following morning. There were carnival rides and clowns, and everyone was naked except for me in a paisley muumuu and platform shoes. It was very difficult to run, as it often is in dreams, my too-tall shoes sticking to the ground from leftover drips of snow-cone juice. I have heard that very little content in dreams is actually telling of anything, but it's the feeling the dream gives you that has meaning. If I were to look deeply at my dream, I would uncover the sensations of being trapped and out of place. If I merely skim the dream analysis surface, I could say I work too much and probably am a little perverted.

I check the text that I assume is from Lish, and see it's from Luke.

Can't stop thinking about last night. You were incredible.

If I were to analyze my feelings at this moment, words spring to mind like *disenchanted* and *heeby-jeebied* and *Can't delete this from my phone fast enough.* Should I feel this way about someone who's supposed to be my not-really-but-kind-of boyfriend (not to mention a person with whom I've sexed twice)?

I send a message to Lish to get the day moving, and drown myself in the shower to cleanse me of any residue the text from Luke left behind.

Uncle Jim scrambles eggs at the stove as I pop into the kitchen. "Morning," he mumbles. Coffee spits into a pot in the coffeemaker, and I grab two mugs from the cabinet to pour us both a cup. His for drinking, mine for sniffing.

"Morning," I reply, handing him the steaming mug. "What's Savannah doing today?" I sit at the table to watch the master cook.

"Gallivanting with twin bodybuilders," Jim says, then shakes his head with a small laugh at how ridiculous that sounds.

"Of course," I affirm.

"I've been thinking of sending her to Australia," Jim tells me, dividing eggs onto two plates with a spatula. "Savannah Down Under. Think of the trouble she'll get into there." He presents a plate of eggs on the table in front of me. "I thought maybe you could do some research for me. Be my local correspondent. You know, when you go." Uncle Jim sits across from me and looks at me intently.

It's the first time anyone's acknowledged that I will be going to Australia. Hell, I still haven't turned it into reality in my head. I only just got up the courage to get my mom's approval; I'm not quite at the I'm-really-going-to-move-to-another-country stage.

"You're going, you know. You made a decision. A choice. A really good one, by the way, and I admire you for it. That is why I want to give you something." Uncle Jim slurps his coffee and cringes. "This is terrible." He takes another sip. "Where was I? Oh yeah. This is the moment where I should produce an envelope with a plane ticket inside. But seeing as I have no idea when you want to leave or even where you want to land, let's just pretend I'm giving you an envelope."

Uncle Jim theatrically mimes passing an envelope across the table.

"That's a really big envelope," I note.

"It's for dramatic effect. Let's imagine I had a massive plane ticket printed up just for the occasion."

I pretend to read the fake giant envelope.

"I'm serious about buying your ticket, Agatha. Save your money for when you get there."

"Really?" I confirm. "Are you sure?"

"Yes. I'm sitting on a pile of Savannah Merlot money, and what the hell am I going to do with it?"

"You could leave the house. You could go to Australia. Visit me while I'm there? For research?"

"Nah, I couldn't do that. I don't want to impede on your exciting new life. Your uncle Jim will enjoy watching from the sidelines as usual." Jim stands up to clear the table, wearing the same sweatpants, the same Mr. Bubble t-shirt.

"You can choose to do something different, too, Uncle Jim. Why don't you get out? Live a little. You're not that old," I emphasize, knowing I'll hit a nerve.

"I'm not old at all!" Bull's-eye. "It's called being reclusive, and some very unique and fascinating people were infamously reclusive: J. D. Salinger, Howard Hughes, Charles Foster Kane . . ."

"Wasn't he a fictional character?"

"Point being that I have made a choice, and this is it. Yay me. I choose to write romance novels for unfulfilled women, I choose to wear a pair of sweatpants and a t-shirt every day, and I choose to live in a house with my sister and her obnoxious teenage daughter."

"I'm not obnoxious! I care about you and want you to be happy, and it's kind of hard to see how anyone would be happy living the way you do." I wince when I realize how bad that sounds. "I mean, it's just different from what I'd choose and so that makes it hard for me to relate to and I'm just digging my hole deeper here, aren't I?"

"You're lucky we're related," Uncle Jim says coolly. "And that I don't have any other nieces to give my fortune to."

"Thank you." I stand and offer Uncle Jim a peacemaking hug. "I am very grateful I am your only niece, too." He pushes me away, exasperated.

"I'm going to work," he says. "Are you off today? I'm not being blinded at breakfast by your god-awful shirt."

"Hanging out with Lish for the first time alone in forever. Not since Travis came to town."

"Ooh. I like the sound of that. *When Travis Came to Town: A Soft-Core Western with Savannah Merlot*."

"Make sure to dedicate it to your adorable niece."

Lish is deep in a book on her porch swing as I pull into her driveway. She places a bookmark inside the novel, something she does religiously. It makes holiday shopping for her extra-easy, and she has amassed an impressive collection of bookmarks lo these many years. I join her on the swing, currently dangling from a metal base after an unfortunate incident in the middle of her parents' mortifying, chain-breaking makeout session. We spent a lot of time on this swing as kids: pretending we were driving to Greenland, playing endless rounds of Would You Rather?, and discussing plans for the future home we planned to share with our husbands. The last memory makes me sad, both at the idea that we'd want to stay in the same place forever and that we are nowhere near that fantasy becoming reality anymore. Life is so different now. We are so different now. We are so different, period. The world isn't the same world as when we were ten. It's impossible to make sense of it, and yet here is Lish, content with a man she met because of cosmic happenstance. Would I find contentment, too, if I chose to find my Empty?

Would me, Travis, Lish, and Hendrix Cutter all live in the same house?

I blurt out a laugh at this ridiculous thought.

"What?" Lish asks, smiling with me.

"Just remembering things from when we were little," I tell her.

"Like what?" she asks. We spend the next two hours falling down the rabbit hole of childhood reminiscing: the time

Lish's grandma bought her a Barbie McDonald's and we spent an entire day building the set, complete with tiny burger boxes and drive-through headsets. Lish reminds me of our twin stuffed-animal dogs, Chocolate and Peanut Butter (they went so well together) and how neither of us has any idea where the dogs went.

"How is that possible?" I ask. "How could we have loved something so much and have no idea what happened to it?"

"One of life's great mysteries." Lish nods. We avoid any mention of the present, of college, of Travis, of MTBs in general until lunch. "You want a sandwich? Travis has us fully stocked on lunch meat." My first instinct is to make a snarky comment, but what could I possibly have against lunch meat? Aside from the salt and the sulfites and that *meat* is a subjective word. Not that it will stop me from partaking.

We eat at the kitchen counter, standing while we pluck olives and pickles out of jars. Travis also has excellent taste in salty sides.

"How has work been? You haven't mentioned Luke much." Lish waggles her eyebrows and passes me a cheeky smile. Little does she know.

"Yeah, that's a pretty long story. It involves me being naked at the Devil's Dinghies and, oh yeah, his penis being inside me."

"You had sex at work?" Lish practically sprays pickle juice all over the countertop. "Why didn't you tell me?" she demands.

"The timing never seemed right. I didn't want to talk

about it with Travis next to you. And there was so much to say, I didn't know where to start."

"Start pre-penis, and leave out no details from that Devil's Dinghies story. I can't believe you did that, by the way. And yet, you've always had a weird connection with that ride. Maybe it makes sense. Just don't name your first-born Beelzebub."

I start from the beginning, how Luke was extra flirty when work started and how he broke up with his girlfriend. "Luke and I were both open to exploring people other than our Empties. . . ."

"And explore you did!" Lish interjects. It makes me giddy how *Lish* this feels. I was afraid that the silly, pervy, BFF part of Lish was fading.

I told her how the Devil's Dinghies sex went down, but how it wasn't quite as I'd imagined.

"First-time sex never is," she says as though expert. "It's just fact. Sex gets a lot better when you know the person and can tell them what you want."

"Like you and Travis, I'm assuming?"

"It's so cliché, but ever since we said 'I love you,' sex has been explosive. Like, nothing has ever felt that good."

"But is that why? The whole 'I love you' thing? Or could it be something else? Like, maybe he read a guidebook or took lessons or something. Or maybe your bodies are proportionately correct together," I hypothesize.

"Or maybe he's my MTB, and this is part of that," Lish offers.

Frustrated, I pound my fist on the kitchen counter. "I don't want to believe that! I *can't* believe that! It goes against everything I feel about choice and free will. The only good sex I'm ever going to have is with someone named Hendrix Cutter? Who, by the way, has a girlfriend."

"We are definitely coming back to the fact that you know factoids about Hendrix Cutter. And just because his Chapbook page says he has a girlfriend doesn't mean he still does. Maybe it's outdated."

"How the hell did you know that was on his Chapbook page?" I yell.

"I looked once, but then Travis told me that wasn't cool and you should be able to look when you're ready."

"Travis said that?" I'm reluctantly impressed.

"Of course he did," Lish affirms. "But back to sex. I'm not saying the only way to have good sex—or a good relationship with good sex—is necessarily with your MTB. But if your MTB is really your meant-to-be, then why wouldn't it all be great? I would like to believe that whoever or whatever started this Naming thing knew what he or she or it was doing."

"That sounds so bogus! How is this reality now? My life is dictated by a stupid Name on my body that will be there forever—we think! What if it goes away? Or changes? It's only been six years."

"It's possible. I mean, if a Name can suddenly grow on my body, then anything is possible," Lish concurs.

I try to calm myself. "I want to know, Lish, if I'm going

through all this effort to change my destiny, only to find out that my destiny would have made me the happiest. What if the only people in the world who find happiness are those who seek out their Empties? Am I dooming myself to be miserable?"

"No, of course not," Lish answers assuringly, although I detect a note of hesitation. "Look, my life is not going to be candy and roses all the time, I'm sure. It's still life. People suck, cars break down, there's still war, poverty, racism, disease, clogged toilets . . . the world is essentially still a shitty place. But maybe finding true love will make it all more bearable, and gradually even the bad things will get better."

"Do you really believe that?" I ask skeptically.

"Maybe? I sound like a total culty turd, I realize, but perhaps that's the MTB love messing with my brain."

"I still don't know what to do about Luke," I add.

"What does your gut tell you?" Lish asks.

"My gut is very confused. When I'm not near him, I'm kind of over him. When I am near him, I can be swayed."

"I think that's your groin, not your gut talking."

"So now I have a talking groin? Maybe I'd be better off joining the circus."

"You're pretty close with that carny you work at."

"Judge all you like. I bring happiness and joy and, you know, devils to the little children."

"I say stick with Luke for a little while longer. Until Hendrix knocks at your door. Can't hurt, right?"

"I guess not. And if Hendrix wanted to knock at my

door, he would've done it already. Not that I care. Maybe I just need more time with Luke like you said, and then it will get really good," I say not at all convincingly.

"Now tell me about Hendrix Cutter's girlfriend. . . ."

Lish persuades me to sit at her computer and peruse his Chapbook page. "He's a good artist." She side-smiles at me. "And it's sweet that he included his dog and sister on his page."

"Lish," I say scoldingly. "This is purely a recon mission so you could see that it doesn't even matter if I contact him because he has a girlfriend."

Lish has heard not a word of what I've said besides *if I contact him.* "Ohmygod, when are you going to do it? What are you going to say? Can I be there? Or do you want to be alone?" She is wild-eyed and breathless, and it's rather terrifying.

Before she can help me pick out wedding rings, we hear footsteps approach from the hallway and Travis walks in.

I don't know if I'll ever be happy to see Lish's dopey cowboy lover.

"And that is my cue to head home," I say, as Travis kisses Lish hello like a television housewife.

"No, stay," Travis pushes, kneading Lish's shoulders adoringly.

"That's okay. I have to work early tomorrow, and you two haven't seen each other all day. I'm sure you have loads of things to catch up on." I gather myself and give a quick wave to the disgusting lovebirds before I take off.

Is that what I want? Shoulder massages and hello kisses and genial home welcoming? Maybe eventually. But I'm only eighteen. If Hendrix Cutter is indeed my MTB and we are, nauseatingly, *meant to be* together, why couldn't it wait until we both have explored what else is out there? It would give us more to talk about. He's probably exploring right now, hence the not knocking on my door.

My phone buzzes.

Hang after work tomorrow? I miss U.

I wish Luke and I had more to talk about. Or less to talk about. Or that the use of *U* didn't disturb me so. Still, I shall persevere. Because it is my choice. Even if I have to force myself to do it.

CHAPTER 30

Today was a slippery sort of day; the type when no one seems to be able to hold on to anything. Scoops plop off ice cream cones, stuffed-animal prizes gather around benches waiting for their winners to reclaim them, and not one but two separate shoes float past me in the river of the Devil's Dinghies. How those children managed to exit the ride and fully walk away is beyond me. Ace job on the parenting.

I was also feeling a bit slippery, in the trying-to-get-away-from-a-certain-person-every-chance-I-got department. I don't not like Luke. I'm just . . . confused. Was it my lack of satisfaction with the Luke situation that drove me to a Hendrix Cutter search? Or would the cosmos have forced me into an Internet search eventually whether I wanted to or not? The bad sex isn't helping. Nor are the bordering-on-clingy texts.

Take, for instance, my good-morning text from Luke (those exist now).

Can't wait to see you tonight. I need U.

There's nothing inherently disturbing about this upon first reading. But after close inspection, I can find upward of sixteen things that bother me about it. (To start, why use both *you* and *U*? Make up your mind!)

Two summers in a row, I was gushy over this guy. For two long school years I used fantasies of Luke Jacobs and the Wheel of Torture as part of my masturbatory canon.

Here we are, living the dream, as it were, and I am not enamored with any of it.

I passed him early this morning and allowed myself to be taken into his consuming hug. He smelled good. He felt pleasantly solid. Admiration remained for his structure. But that gooey, delicious, tingly feeling was missing.

I've thought about it all day, and I've come up with the following list of possibilities as to why I'm not melting in my Underoos when I'm near Luke Jacobs anymore:

1) He likes me too much. (This is the dumbest reason ever to not like a guy, but maybe a part of me thinks I'm not deserving of his love. . . . Nah. I'm deserving, I just don't know if I want it.)
2) He is different than he used to be—before he seemed all casual and laid back. Now, he's so serious with all his lovey-dovey-ness and wanting to hug and cuddle. (Have I always been this cold?)
3) That time he told Adam we had sex really pissed me off—true, but I'd be lying if I said it still bothered me.
4) He went from lukewarm to hot very quickly. Ha! *Luke*warm! See what I did there? But seriously,

ladies and germs, what changed from him wanting a casual summer fling to these boyfriend-esque texts? I know I've been considering upping the ante on *possibly* liking him *more* and for *longer*, but something isn't gelling.

5) Do we really have all that much in common? I don't know what he wants to study in college. I don't know his middle name. He doesn't seem to want to travel. The only things I can think of us sharing are our commitment to our summer jobs, a pleasure in berating Adam, and a love for my boobs, which brings us to . . .
6) Sex. This is a tricky item. As I have so eloquently shared, I do find quite a bit of enjoyment in our trysts (so fancy), up to a point. But everything else is lacking. Is it his technique? His attention to detail? My waning level of attraction? Missed communication? Or is there something even deeper than all of the above? What if it's . . .
7) Hendrix Cutter and Scarlett Dresden. Are these merely engraved onto our bodies or are they entrenched into our very beings?

I hate to believe that I do not have a choice in whom I am going to end up with. I know I'm stubborn, I am a complete and royal asshole, but I refuse to give up on the notion that our lives add up to more than a single person's Name on our chests.

My list accelerates the day, and when six o'clock comes, I round up all the slippery items that made their way up the Dinghies river: the two shoes (yet unclaimed), a sopping-wet stuffed animal that resembles a bunny but may be a bear, and a locket that was once gold, as indicated by a few remaining splotches, but ultimately revealed itself as plastic. I pass Luke on my way to the park's lost and found. He slithers his arm around my waist, and I will myself to remember how much I once wanted this. It doesn't feel terrible; it's the sensation of no sensation that is bothersome. "Want me to take your lost-and-found items up front?" I ask him.

"Thank you." He grins admiringly and then proceeds to swallow my face with a massive kiss.

8) I don't think I am down with PDAs. Particularly of the tongue variety.

After I am granted access to air again, Luke tells me, "I have to run a couple errands for my mom. Want to come with me?"

In the past, Luke would have received several gold stars for this proposal. Running errands for his mom? How sweet. Inviting me to join him? Inclusive. Asking instead of telling me? Admirable. But it's just so glaringly . . . boyfriend.

That's when it hits me. I want to be free! I don't want to be tied down. Like that balloon a mom triple-ties to the stroller until it eventually deflates and drags along the ground and disintegrates. I want to be the balloon a kid lets go of the second his mom buys it! The reason I don't like this MTB bullshit is the lack of freedom, and here I am claiming I'm going to find love other than Empty love. Love is not what I want at all! I want romance and summer flings and someone to touch my body other than me! So I say to Luke, "That's okay. Why don't you go ahead, and then meet me here for some painting?"

I want to wink at Luke, to hint that by *painting* I mean *third time's a charm*, but sadly I have never acquired the ability to wink. It's a travesty, I recognize.

"Sounds great. We've barely made a dent in the wall," he says, while I'm praying he means, "Let's get *bare* again by the wall."

I'm so glad we had this little hypothetical talk.

Luke kisses me good-bye (again!), and I'm off to grab my backpack and phone from my locker before sitting down to paint. Brian from maintenance stands above the Dinghies river like a gondolier, stick in the water. "Lots of lost items reported today," he tells me while I cross toward the grass. "Thought I should check."

"Thanks," I say.

"Someone lost a shoe!" he announces.

"Another one? They do say things come in threes," I note.

"I thought it was *bad* things come in threes," he questions.

"Yeah, but they also say third time's a charm."

"That they do," Brian concurs.

Even Brian agrees.

I paint for a good half hour then stop to snack on an apple from my bag. I check my phone and find some texts.

From Lish:

Had such a good time with you yesterday. Need to talk about something but can wait if you're out with Luke.

I text Lish back:

Here to talk if you need.

She doesn't immediately reply, so I read the next message from Uncle Jim.

Buy your plane tickets yet?

I smile giddily at the pure reality of Australia, but admittedly panic at it, too.

Lastly, a new message from Luke:

B there soon. Save a spot on the grass 4 me.

"Ignore the B and 4. Ignore the B and 4," I repeat to myself. The grass portion of the text was cute, right?

I text back Uncle Jim:

Nope. Maybe you can help me figure out how? Never actually booked a plane ticket or, you know, owned a credit card.

After I hit send, I begin a search on my phone for flights to Australia. Until I realize that, besides not having any semblance of a date chosen, I have no idea where I'd even land.

Is there an airport in Melbourne? I know there's an amusement park with a terrifying giant clown head entryway, but I don't know anything about where it is or where I'd want to live. As long as I've had the fantasy of moving to Australia, I haven't exactly done any research about actually living there. Was that because I'm lazy? Because I never truly believed the dream would be realized? Or was there a subconscious part of me that didn't want to go?

I'm jerked away from my meaningful life analysis by a bothersome sucking on my neck. I rock my head back, hard enough that I hear a crack and Luke yell, "Shit!"

Turning around, I watch Luke stumble with his hands clamped to his face.

"I'm sorry! I didn't know you were there!" I tend to him, trying to get a look at the spot where I've just head-butted him.

He moves his hands away from his nose, and nothing looks off. "It's not bleeding," I assure him. Luke holds the bridge of his nose and gingerly moves it side to side. "I think it's okay. Remind me to never get on your bad side," he chuckles. I think what a perfect segue that would be into his drippy texts, but it seems easier to pretend they never existed. Like I've been trying all summer to do with Empties. And failing.

"You've gotten a lot done," Luke says as he walks along the wall and looks at my painting.

"Yeah. It's easier to do when there are no distractions." I realize when I say this that it's a total dig, but instead of hearing a negative Luke takes it as a throwback to one of our pervier, less-clothed painting adventures. I know this because his hand is now rubbing my lower back. I glance around quickly to see if Brian's still there. He is not, and I am both grateful that he's not leering at us and bummed that he's not an excuse to stop. Maybe if we talk . . .

"Guess what?" I say excitedly, turning to face Luke without physical contact. "My uncle is going to buy my plane ticket to Australia!"

Luke looks at me with a scrunched brow. "When are you going?"

"When the summer is over, I guess. It'll be a good time to go. Our fall, their spring."

"That's really soon." His brow remains scrunchy.

"Not that soon. You'll be in school anyway. Why do you look like that?" I ask.

"Like what?" he retorts defensively.

"Like you're not happy for me."

"I'm not *not* happy for you. I'm unhappy for me." He offers this line so earnestly, I actually feel bad for the guy. His hair flops pathetically over one eye, the hazel reflecting gold and green in the setting sun, his lips tense and pouty at the same time. I don't know what to say.

So, dammit, I kiss him.

He returns the kiss, and in that kiss I feel every needy and frantic emotion he has for me. It's intoxicating and terrifying to think someone likes me this much. I attempt to match his kisses, if not with sentiment at least in enthusiasm.

I want to be able to separate my body completely: to enjoy sex with this lovely boy as merely physical pleasure, to forget for this moment that we have both uncertainty and commitments laid out ahead of us.

He grips my face passionately, his hands moving from my cheek to my chin to my shoulder. He's at my hips next, then my back. We feel so exposed, having seen Brian only an hour ago.

"Wait," I protest. "I think there are still some people on shift." Luke looks at me with heavy lids. Without speaking, he holds my hand and tugs me toward the Devil's Dinghies tunnel.

From the grass, there is a ledge leading into and through the tunnel. The ledge is only a couple of feet wide, and Luke barely fits as he sidesteps into the dark and cool tunnel. I follow him intrigued; Haunted Hollow has numerous gory legends of murder and suicide, but amid the tales of death are those of lurid trysts on every ride possible. As sinister and seedy as an old amusement park can be, there is also a sense of romance. One of the reasons I am drawn to them.

The darkness within the tunnel is not complete, due to the exit lights and the pink glow of the sky outside. I watch as Luke's lithe body carefully settles itself into a boat. He offers his hand, and I reach toward the boat with my toes until my gym shoe rests flat on the floor. Steadying myself on Luke's shoulder, I drag my other leg aboard. The ratio of Luke's body to the size of the dinghy seat is comical, and doesn't leave any room for me. Luke remedies this immediately by pulling me down to straddle him. Already I can feel how excited he is through his shorts. The position and placement hits me in a spot that gets me excited, too. I try to shut off my brain, even the part cheerleading me on. "Yay!" it chants, "This is what you want!"

I rock onto him, and we exhale together. Kissing him feels more natural now, less greedy on his part and more approving on mine. Luke lifts my shirt over my head, and I reciprocate, quickly unsnapping my bra and flinging it to land precariously on the ledge. The last thing I want is my sizable bra ending up scooped out of the Devil's Dinghies river by Brian and his handy-dandy net. In an instant Luke's mouth is on one breast, then the other. I want this portion of the show to last, but I quickly find us again transitioning to the naked part of our evening. Maybe my mom was right, and we'll never slow ourselves down enough *not* to have sex. That said, we *are* at a semistaffed amusement park, and the prospect of getting caught speeds the need along. I take a moment to stand up and drop both my shorts and underwear in one motion. Luke shucks off his shorts, then sits back down, bare ass on the small wooden bench seat. I try not to focus on the humor, kids sitting where Luke's butt has been or hearing my mom's voice in my head. *Slow down, Agatha.*

"Shit!" I say. "My backpack is out there, and so are the condoms." I can't hear you, Mom! Stop telling me what to do!

"I put one in my wallet," Luke breathes into my skin as

he peppers me with wet kisses. Deftly he continues his assault while fishing a condom out of his wallet in his scrunched-up pants. I help Luke roll it on, and soon I'm on top of him, moving carefully as to not upset the boat too much. The angle, the proximity of my breasts to his mouth, and the danger of getting caught accelerate every sensation. The boat jostles, water sloshing below us. Luke grunts, "I'm . . ." And, finally, so am I. There we are, coming together. Or at least at the same time.

Our bodies and the boat steady, and I gingerly stand up, using Luke's head for balance. Luke leans up to kiss me and continues to hold me close by my waist. Physiologically? Yowza. But emotionally? I still feel so unsatisfied.

I want to get dressed, very aware of my nakedness on a carnival ride, when Luke whispers in my ear, "I love you."

It's as though a phantasmagoric force knocks me backward, and I fall out of the boat and into the shallow ride water.

"Holy shit!" he cries. "Are you okay?" I'm grossed out that my naked vagina may currently be ingesting carny water, but at least it saved me from having to find an answer to Luke's declaration. Perhaps I can even play like I didn't hear it.

Luke effortlessly yanks me out by my armpits, the way I do to the children on my ride. Back on the ledge, I struggle to pull my clothes over my wet body. It's uncomfortable for sure, but not as uncomfortable as having to confront the inevitable fact that, even though the third time was indeed a charm, an orgasm did not change a damned thing.

I do not love Luke Jacobs.

The words *I love you* from his mouth literally propelled me away from him.

Today was indeed a slippery kind of day.

CHAPTER 31

Glazed in front of my computer, I stuff my face with gummy candies Uncle Jim ordered from Germany. You can buy the exact same items at your local Walgreens, but Uncle Jim swears they taste better direct from the source. They probably cost a shitload, too, so I hope he won't mind that I've downed an entire bag of fake raspberries and am now working my way through the peaches. There must be some weird correlation between me stressing and mutated fruit.

Lish hasn't answered any of my texts, so I try calling. No response. I hope everything's okay. What if Travis decided to leave her because he doesn't think they're as compatible as she does? Or what if she decided that she's done with this MTB bullshit and instead wants to go to Australia with me? I wish she would answer. She needs to help me figure out what to do about this Luke predicament I've gotten myself into. The scientists who said that thing about girls being more obsessed with guys after sex apparently had the conclusion backward. Having sex with Luke has turned him into an "I love you"–spurting, PDA-obsessed, gag-reflex-triggering text monster.

And he was so pretty.

I obviously have to end this. I can't hang out with him again and be seduced into becoming his girlfriend. Granted, there isn't much summer left before he goes off to college and I to Australia (I should probably get on those plane tickets). Plus, I'm about due for my period, which is a stellar excuse for just about anything where guys are concerned. It could be really awkward having to see Luke at work after breaking up–ish with him, though. As wussy as it makes me, I decide to hold off on the "breakup" until we're closer to the end of the summer. A month isn't very long. In the meantime I concoct a list of excuses for not hanging out:

1) The period excuse—the only gift my period brings.
2) My mom needs me—maybe to grocery shop. Or clean the house. Or *paint* the house.
3) Lish is having a crisis—which may or may not be true. I'm voting for not, but no one asked me.

This is not a very thorough list.

My phone cackles, and I dive for it, assuming it's a message from Lish. Alas, it's Luke.

Loved how wet you were earlier. . . .

From falling into the river, that is.

Ugh, ugh, and ugh.

My pesky chest itch flares up, and I take it as a sign to do some light stalking of Hendrix Cutter. Nothing new is up on his page. I stare at his *My Girl* picture. (Why does my stomach hurt all of a sudden? Must be all that German candy.) She looks pretty, with her annoyingly golden hair and twinkly blue eyes. It's a drawing, of course, so they're probably exaggerated. Braids. So cute. Or quirky. Or artsy. I wonder what Hendrix looks like. Is he big and brawny like Luke? Short and pudgy? Light skin? Dark skin? No skin? Does he have all his limbs?

I slide open my desk drawer and pull out a drawing pad and graphite pencil. Portraiture has never been my strongest medium, but I make an attempt at imagining Hendrix Cutter.

Instinctively I touch my hand to the letters on my chest. They're warm and bumpy, and the gesture is calming. Until I realize *the gesture is calming* and whisk my hand away. Minutes later I come up with a drawing that looks vaguely like a police sketch artist version of a man. If this man has two shadily uneven eyes and a questionably drawn nose. Damn, noses are hard.

I shut the sketchbook, and stare at my computer screen. I know I shouldn't, but I open a search engine. Why does it have to be so easy? I didn't want to want to see him, and yet I have no control anymore with which to stop myself. I type *Hendrix Cutter* into the box. My finger hovers dramatically over the return key, just like in a scene from the Lifetime MTB movie *A Name Is Forever.* That movie sucked, by the way.

I hit enter.

At the exact second my phone rings. My initial reaction

is a groan. "Luke's calling me now?" But I quickly see Lish's name on my screen.

"Hey!" I answer the Viddle with relief. "I was worried about you."

"Yeah, sorry. I was charging my phone in Travis's car, and I forgot it was in there." Lish seems calm, collected, not at all in crisis. This is good.

"So what's going on?" I press, trying my best not to look at my computer screen where a small number of links and several images appear in the results. I'm so tempted to click, to possibly see the face of my MTB, when Lish announces, "I'm pregnant, Aggy."

My mouse-clicking finger drops, as do my mouth and stomach.

I can't think of anything to say, so I sit in silence with the phone frozen in my hand.

"You there?" Lish checks. She doesn't look like she's crying.

"I'm here," I answer, even though she can plainly see me. "Holy fuck, Lish. I thought you were on the pill."

"I am. But I was stupid and only just started right before we were doing it. So I guess it didn't take. I was supposed to wait a cycle, I think. I didn't really listen at the gynecologist because I was thinking about Travis coming, and then, ha-ha, Travis came." I think Lish was implying humor, but I'm not finding any. "Get it? Came? Like with a penis. In my vagina. You love those words."

"Lish! How can you be so chill about this? You are

fucking pregnant! How did you not know how the pill works? Aren't you working for a pharmaceutical company?" I yell and leave no room for an answer. "What the fuck are you going to do?" Few things fill me with more terror than the concept of having a human growing inside me. Like a parasite in a horror movie. I'm not saying I don't want kids of my own someday, but hell to the no do I want one in there anytime soon.

"Travis and I talked—"

"What the hell does Travis have to do with this?" I'm shouting into my phone. The gummy candies are very unhappy in my tummy. "Besides putting you in this state in the first place!"

"He's the father, Aggy! Can you calm down? You're hurting my ears."

"Oh, I'm hurting your ears. What about what this baby is going to do to your vagina? That is not going to feel good."

"I'm sorry I ever brought up my vagina. Geez. Just listen, Aggy. Can you listen?"

I huff around my bedroom for a minute while Rugburn attempts to dodge me, then manage to compose myself as I collapse onto my bed. "I'm calm. Ish," I report.

"Good. Travis and I talked, and we've decided to get married." Lish sports an extra-enthusiastic plastic grin.

Is it possible to faint while lying on a bed? I look at my phone to double-check that I'm talking to Lish.

"Hello?" the person says. It's her.

"Uhh . . ." is about all I can muster, while my stomach gurgles angrily.

"Yep. We're getting married," she chuckles nervously. "And we're going to have a baby." She only sounds half as maniacal as my stomach feels. Why the fucking hell balls is she getting married?

I finally summon my voice. "You know, you don't have to get married. Or have a baby. You do have choices."

"I know. And these are my choices." She purses her lips resolutely. "I love Travis. He *is* my meant-to-be, after all."

I try to argue that point with a "Lish," but she argues right back.

"I'm sorry that you don't get it, Aggy, but I know this is right. I feel it. In my heart and my head."

"And your uterus," I add grumpily.

"Yes, Aggy, in my uterus. There's a little me and Travis in there. For some reason that doesn't disgust me. It makes me feel ridiculously, uncontrollably happy," she gushes.

"Aren't you scared?" I ask.

"Well, yeah, but isn't that part of what you're always talking about? The unknown? Just because something bigger than us brought Travis and I together doesn't mean there aren't going to be new and terrifying things. I'm beyond excited. A husband. A baby. This is going to be my life," she muses.

It is painfully difficult to be happy for Lish. I can't help but feel she's throwing what *life* she had away for some cliché prescription for love.

When I'm still mute a minute later, Lish breaks the silence. "If you don't have anything else to say, I'm going to go. We can talk after you've processed this. But don't be mad at me, okay?"

I nod at the phone, then sheepishly answer, "Okay." Lish says good-bye and hangs up.

I curl into a ball on the bed. On this occasion, Rugburn acts like a normal cat and settles in next to me. Maybe it's not these new life choices that are as bothersome to me—although fuck all, it's crazy—as the fact that if her life has an MTB, a husband, and a baby, where the hell do I fit in?

I glance at my computer screen, and it blinks to sleep. Not wanting to move, so do I.

CHAPTER 32

I oversleep by half an hour and rush to work in a dirty Haunted Hollow t-shirt and a pair of shorts that are normally reserved for around the house due to an unfortunate incident with a pair of scissors. Other girls may feel comfortable with shorts barely covering their asses, but I've always enjoyed the sensation of not having my labia touch public seating areas. The shorts will have to do because I can't find anything else without making me risk a scolding from Sam Hain. I spend the majority of the half-hour car ride digging denim out of my crotch. Chalk one up for having to stand all day.

As I walk into work, I'm painfully aware of my thighs rubbing together. How do people wear these things? I feel like I'm in my underwear. I may as well be. As if on cue, I walk past Adam sitting on a bench. I silently pray that I don't officially get my period today of all days.

"Looking good, Aggy!" he calls.

I stop and turn around. Did he just? I stride toward him, my thighs applauding me, and say, "You aren't allowed to say that anymore, remember?"

"I wasn't talking about your tits." He holds up his hands defensively, eyes definitely glued to that area.

"Then to what were you referring?" I glare.

"I was talking about your ass." He shrugs with an attempted charming smile.

Bam! As natural as a sneeze and just as lightning fast, I pop Adam in the nose with a closed fist. It hurts like fuck and makes a repulsive crunch. I'm in shock. He's in shock. Blood trickles from his nose, and I'm struck by how satisfying it all feels.

"I'm sorry," I offer, then recant. "No, I'm not. You're a sleazebag. You totally deserved that."

"You did," a voice sounds from behind me. It's Luke. "Remind me never to talk about your ass," he winks, and adds, "Which I can almost see, by the way."

I give him a perturbed look, and he says to Adam, "Let me take you to first aid. They might have to remove your hat. Can you handle it?"

I'm strangely energized for the rest of the morning. Does that make me a psychopath? Hitting Adam was sweet. Gratifying. I needed that.

Maybe I should take a boxing class.

The morning is so busy, I quickly forget about the incident until I enter the cafeteria at lunchtime. There's Adam with a cut on the top of his nose and two swollen, silvery purple eyes. I sit down next to him. We look at each other guiltily. "Sorry I looked at your ass," he offers.

"Sorry I hurt you. I'm not sorry I hit you, though. Just sorry it hurt. I guess." People nearby giggle at my semblance of an apology.

"Truce?" he asks, hand extended.

"Unless you say something again. And I'm not shaking your hand right before I eat lunch. I don't know where it's been."

"Fair enough."

Conversation disperses throughout the table, and I'm able to eat in peace for about five seconds until Luke asks, "Hang after work?" He smiles an inviting smile, and I feel for him. He has no idea I don't want to be his un-girlfriend anymore. Still, I'm not ready to speak to Lish and I would really like to work on the wall.

"I'm going to paint if you want to join me," I offer, trying not to inject even a drop of innuendo into my words or intonations.

"Cool," he nods, and I'm comfortable with his tone.

Luke and I walk back to our rides together. He reaches for my hand lackadaisically, and I hold his like a reflex. It's not a bad feeling, having my small hand intertwined with his large one, and for a second I pretend we're a blissfully happy couple. Then Luke whispers, "I've refilled my wallet," kisses me on the cheek, and walks back to the Ghoster.

He's talking about condoms.

He wants more, and I don't feel particularly right about that if I don't have strong feelings for the guy. Sure, if we were both all casual, it could be okay. But he had to send all those corny texts and then, glug, say those three little words. There is nothing casual about *I love you.*

I shudder to myself as I relieve Chaitu. He's been training on all the rides, since a lot of us may not be back next summer.

At least I don't think I will. The plan is that I'll be in Australia. Or maybe moved on to a new country, a new park by then. Gold Reef City in Johannesburg, South Africa, sounds entertaining. Who doesn't love an old-timey gold-mining experience?

I really should buy that plane ticket. What's stopping me? Is it fear of the unknown or fear that I'm fighting an impossible war of fate versus free will?

I work my stomach up into a tizzy and ask Chaitu if he can hang around while I run to the bathroom.

I hate feeling out of control. This is the antithesis of the person I want to be. Why else would I fight so hard against the Empties? Because I want autonomy in my life. And here I am, wussing out about Australia, waffling over what to do about Luke, and totally jonesing to look up more info on Hendrix Cutter.

My MTB scar itches, and I grunt, "Fuck off," at it.

I'm not in control. I'm a total mess.

I mechanically slog my way though the rest of the afternoon. At closing Luke meets me at the lockers where I'm reading a text from Lish.

Ready to talk yet? Everything's going to be okay.

I huff at my phone and throw it into my bag.

"Everything all right?" Luke asks.

"Not really." Before I have to explain myself, I ask, "You want to get something to eat?"

"Yeah. You up for Mexican?"

"If you are," I say, not to be coy but because I have no idea what I want to eat. I have no idea what I want at all anymore.

Luke doesn't make things easier at dinner. "I've been thinking about Australia," he says, and I prepare for battle. Albeit, a battle I'm not sure I even know how to fight anymore. He continues, "I think you should go." I freeze midbite on my burrito.

"Really?" I ask. "What changed your mind?"

"We're young, right? We should do all the things we want now. Things we can't do when we're older?" I'm intrigued. Luke has never sounded so analytical.

"Because I am not so sure we do have a choice," he admits.

"What do you mean?" I unravel my burrito, then attempt to reroll it, causing lettuce, beans, and cheese spill everywhere.

"Well, you know the other night?" he asks, and I raise an eyebrow in question. He leans forward in discretion. "When we fucked on the ride?"

I cover my mouth with a laugh at the bluntness of his description and instantly regret it when refried beans smear my lips. "Yeah," I say, wiping my mouth with a flimsy paper napkin. "I remember."

"I'm not sure if you heard me. God, this is weird." Luke closes his eyes and rubs his forehead. "I said I love you when we, you know, finished," he mumbles.

"Really? I'm sorry. I didn't hear." I replace the napkin in my lap, mostly just shreds of brown stains, hoping to cover the lie in my expression. I don't feel great about it, but I reconsider when Luke says,

"I hope this doesn't offend you, but I don't think I meant it."

Even though I freaked when I heard it, enough to throw me into a rusty river, it still sucks to hear my un-boyfriend say he doesn't love me.

Make up your mind, Agatha!

"Um, ouch, maybe?" I try to make light.

"Not that I don't like you a lot, and I *really* like what we did on the boats." Luke bugs his eyes to emphasize how much he liked it. I feel my cheeks warm. Will I ever regain control of this vessel?

"I've been trying really hard *not* to be obsessed with Scarlett." I wince at the reference to his MTB by only her first name. "That's why I said I love you and sent all those romantic texts."

"Oh. So that's what those were supposed to be," I realize.

"And most of my body is totally into you . . . except for this fucking Name, which won't stop itching me. I think it gets worse after we have sex, truthfully, but my brain is like,

Look Scarlett up, man. Get to know her. She's your MTB. It's driving me insane."

It pains me to admit that I'm kind of where he is. I so want to be the cool girl, grabbing life by the balls and doing what I want with whomever I want.

When I don't say anything, Luke says, "You think I'm an asshole."

"No!" I correct him. "I don't. I totally get it. I wish I didn't."

"So you've been thinking about this Hendrix guy?" he asks with a twinge of jealousy in his voice. *That* I like.

"Unfortunately," I sigh.

"Have you seen a picture of him?" he asks.

"Not yet. I've been trying my damnedest to avoid it. How about you? Have you looked up Scarlett?"

"Yeah," he says, and a warm smile grows on his face. It's not a smile he's given me before, and I know it's not meant for or about me in the least. It's both sweet and chilling at the same time.

"And?" I prod because I need to know. Not because I care what Luke thinks of his Empty; because I want to know if I'm involuntarily on the same path.

"You really want to know?" he asks.

"Sure." I shrug nonchalantly, belying the burrito churning in my gut.

"She's supercute. She's a redhead!" He's giddy as he describes her. "Freckles."

"Have you talked to her?" I question from the edge of my seat.

"No." He shakes his head. "It felt like it would be cheating on her. I mean, with you."

"Even though we aren't technically boyfriend and girlfriend."

"I know. But I also thought that once I talked to her, you and I would have to stop . . ." He trails off.

"Boning on carny rides?" I complete his sentence.

"Yeah. That."

"Probably," I agree, crossing my arms in observance of this bizarre creature who at once is "breaking up" with me because he has potentially discovered his soul mate but can't quite cut the cord because his penis would temporarily be sad. Now seems as good a time as any to give some much-needed schooling.

"So what should we do?" Luke asks seriously.

"As long as we're being honest," I say, flicking my burrito carcass with a fork. "There is something *you* should know. About the sexy times." Luke looks on intently because, of course, this part is important. "This will be helpful for your darling Scarlett, too. When a girl is obviously enjoying herself in the sexington department, don't stop to get a condom and then automatically switch to the intercourse segment of the show. It's pretty much a guarantee that *you're* going to come no matter what. A lot of girls, me included, can't easily have orgasms during sex. Always ask if she's ready, so she's not left hanging. Or at least until you figure out what works."

"I left you hanging?" He's mortified. And definitely oblivious.

"Dangling like a participle."

"I don't even know what that means, but, man, I feel like a dickstone. I thought you were into it."

"I was. Just not as much as you were. It takes me a lot longer for a buildup to turn into a gusher. That sounded weird."

"I'm feeling you. Although not enough, apparently. I guess I didn't realize you needed more time." He futzes with his napkin.

"Yeah. Sometimes, when I'm by myself, I make up entire sagas with the Tenth Doctor just to get to that point."

"When you're by yourself?" Luke asks naively and far too intrigued.

"You really do have a lot to learn before you turn into Scarlett Dresden's knight in shining armor."

"Are you going to teach all of this to Hendrix Cutter?" He waggles his eyebrows suggestively.

This discussion has gone off the rails. Sex with Hendrix Cutter? I am not equipped to consider such a scenario at this juncture. "If you ever want to have sex with me again, we should probably stop talking about our Empties," I suggest.

"So do you want to keep doing it?" The obvious answer is no, but the defiant little shit in me who likes to do things to spite the universe can't get the word out.

"Why don't we go paint, and see how it goes?" I answer and stand up to use the bathroom.

I gently lay toilet paper on the seat in the festively decorated bathroom. It is there I discover that, for better or worse, I actually do have my period. In these damn tiny shorts, too. I fold up some toilet paper and place it into my undies as a makeshift pad. After I wipe and flush, I check the bathroom for a tampon machine. A handwritten sign reading OUT OF ORDER is taped to the gray box on the wall.

Back at the table, I inform Luke, "I'm going to have to take a rain check on tonight."

"You okay?" he asks.

"Full disclosure: I got my period," I inform him.

He mulls this information over and announces, "I don't mind if you don't."

I'm impressed at this fact, but there is nothing sexy to me during this time of the month unless it involves me and two men named Ben and Jerry.

"I'm not really feelin' it," I say.

"Then I guess it's just me and my hand tonight," Luke declares, pulling back from the table and standing up. I side-eye him. "What? I thought we were talking about self-pleasuring now."

"I do see a little why you get along so well with Adam," I note.

"My true colors are coming out. You scared?"

"More like relieved," I admit. "I better get home before I bleed all over my hot pants."

"Maybe we should tone down the honest talk a wee bit."

"Probably," I concur.

My shorts make it home unscathed, and once I'm changed and padded I know what I should do.

I text Lish.

Can you talk now?

CHAPTER 33

Talking to a pregnant Lish feels like talking to a Lish who has been abducted by aliens, probed, and returned to tell the tale; it's still the same person, essentially, but there's stuff going on inside her that I am not nor will I ever be privy to. Even Travis has a one-up on me on this front; there are literally pieces of him growing inside her.

How does anyone let themselves get pregnant when it sounds this sci-fi?

I am still completely freaked out, repulsed, and maybe even a modicum of jealous. Not of being pregnant, obviously, but of this solidified "future" that Lish has carved out so quickly for herself with Travis. That has never been my goal, to settle down straight out of high school, but it sure looks convenient when I watch it from my jumbled vantage point.

Lish already knows who she will (theoretically) love for the rest of her life. He feels the same way about her. They're ready to put a ring on this piece, and her body is ready to have babies. Now all they have to do is live their lives. So easy!

And boring.

And predictable.

And vanilla, but not like that good kind of vanilla ice cream that surprises you because it has so much flavor. More like vanilla soft-serve sugar-free frozen yogurt.

I want my life to be mint chocolate chip. And Moose Tracks. And birthday-cake ice cream. All piled high onto a chocolate-dipped waffle cone and covered in rainbow sprinkles. Where my Ben and Jerry at?

Before I call Lish, I jot down some points of what I want to say, so I don't go off on a tangent-slash-diatribe.

- Hey, Lish, still pregnant?
- Is the baby kicking yet?
- Is it a boy or a girl?
- If it's a girl, consider naming it after me.
- If it's a boy, you can still name him after me. How about Angus? No, I didn't say Anus.
- When are you getting married?
- Will I be your maid of honor?
- If so, please choose a bridesmaid dress that allows for a sturdy bra.
- Where will you live?
- Will you still go to college?
- How will you survive?
- You're going to be homeless with a new baby!

I stop writing. This list is not going well. My goal was to be interested and supportive, but I think this is more irrational and apocalyptic. I decide to fake it till I make it and call her via Viddle.

"Hi, Aggy," Lish sounds warm as she answers, a close-up view of her face filling her phone screen. I envision the rest of her reclining against Travis, rubbing her gigantic belly. I realize this is crazy because she is all of one-month pregnant, but this is pretty much the first pregnancy I will ever live through and it's semitraumatic for but-a-wee eighteen-year-old like me.

"Hi, Lish" I pronounce robotically. A stellar start.

"How are you?" she asks.

"Good," I offer. "And you?"

"I'm okay," she answers. Shit. Is this where I'm supposed to begin the questioning? The concern? The prenatal vitamins talk? Lish, ever the grown-up, helps move the awkwardness off to the side. "I threw up four times today."

"Yuck. Because of the . . ." I tilt my phone toward the general vicinity of my stomach.

"Yeah. It's morning sickness, which is a bullshit name since it's been an all-day puke-a-thon."

"Maybe you have the stomach flu?" I suggest, and a morsel of my stupid brain hopes that this is all just a big misunderstanding and she is not, indeed, pregnant.

"I don't think so. After I puke, I want to eat a lot. Microwave hot dogs are the end. Weirdly, eating makes my stomach feel better. I'm going to gain seven hundred pounds before the baby is born."

Well, there it is. My body chills, as though a spirit passes through me.

I have so many questions. A lot of them start with *Why???*, but I know that's too accusatory. I try the *How*s, which have more of an interested connotation.

"How are you going to manage school and a baby?" I ask.

Lish looks down guiltily. "Travis and I decided I'm going to move to Louisville, so he can still go to school and we can be near his family. We're going to live with his parents, actually." She looks at the camera with a teeth-gritting smile.

The worst part of Viddles is that Lish can see my face.

After I scoop my dropped chin off the floor, I attempt to gather my thoughts enough so I don't go off the rails. It's impossible, though, so I do the only thing I can think of. "My mom's calling me. Can I call you back?"

Her expression, and the fact that she's been my best friend for more than a decade, lets me know that she's not buying my bullshit. That doesn't stop me from hanging up.

God, my stomach hurts. Why would anyone voluntarily put a baby in there if it makes you throw up all the time?

I'm close to throwing up myself as I walk into the upstairs hallway and yank down on the string to open the attic stairway.

"Uncle Jim?" I call. "Can I talk to you?"

"Sure," he yells back. "Come on up."

I rarely make the sojourn to my uncle's office. He's

always busy, and I hate to interrupt if Savannah Merlot is in process. Plus, the retractable stairs are precarious and petrifying. I don't know how he carries hot beverages up and down.

His office is simply decorated with a lot of furniture that looks like it's from Ikea but is most likely from a high-end Scandinavian furniture store. Savannah Merlot likes a splurge. Two complementary-patterned cushy chairs surround a stereo, and the whole room is lit by day from a skylight. There are also numerous lamps for when the skylight isn't bright enough or when Uncle Jim is having an all-night writing session to meet a deadline. If he didn't work up here, I would love to make it my bedroom. Not that I'll be here much longer.

"You want to order your plane ticket?" Uncle Jim practically scares me back down the rickety steps the second I make it up.

"No. I mean, not now. That's not why I'm visiting."

He shrugs, looking disappointed, then sits in one of the fluffy chairs. Jazzy music emanates from the stereo, probably to set the mood for a kinky boudoir scene. It is truly a testament to what a good author my uncle Jim is that this man in a Mr. Bubble t-shirt and sweatpants can become a glamorous, crime-fighting vixen.

"I have something to tell you," I start.

"Oh, fuck, you're pregnant, aren't you? I should have given you the sex talk instead of just letting you read my books. What a shitty uncle . . ."

I interrupt with a laugh. "No, I'm not pregnant. I use condoms."

"Thank god." He puts his hand to his chest.

"But Lish is," I add.

He looks dumfounded. "Little Lish? She was always such a good girl."

"What are you saying about me?" I ask defensively.

"I'm not saying anything. Lish just has that air of innocence surrounding her that you never had."

"I guess." I try not to be offended.

"Anyway, so she's pregnant. Who's the father?" Uncle Jim asks.

"Travis," I say with an eye roll. "Her Empty."

"You're still calling them that, huh?"

"Yeah. I learned that from you, you know."

"Oh, you did?" He sounds disappointed. "I'm teaching you all kinds of bad stuff, aren't I?"

"What's so bad about calling them Empties?"

"Because maybe there's more to it than we want to believe. What if it's real? What if instead of Empty, they're meant-to-be and they make our lives full?"

"Oh God, you didn't," I accuse.

"Didn't what?" Uncle Jim asks.

"Find your Empty. You're going to move out with her, aren't you? Leave my mom alone?"

"It's not like that, Agatha. I'm not moving out. But a man can't live off fan mail and writing oral sex scenes alone, now can he?"

"So have you talked?"

"A little," he demurs.

"Who is she? Where is she? Does Mom know?" I ask.

"Mom does know. And she is okay with it. We're taking it very slowly anyway."

"But how can I go to Australia if you're leaving Mom, too?" I hadn't realized that part of why I was comfortable going so far away was that my mom had a partner in Uncle Jim. Now what if I'm gone, he's gone, and her MTB is dead?

"Your mom is an adult. Hell, she's never home. Did you know she went out for coffee with that fish counter guy?"

"What?" I'm both excited and disgusted at the thought of my mom on a date.

"Your mom is a trooper. She is resilient and brave and stubborn as hell. Where do you think you got it?" he asks.

I fill with pride at the notion that I could be like my mom, who, completely without me noticing, has built a pretty cool life without my father or her MTB.

"Don't you feel kind of like a traitor, finding your MTB?" I ask.

"Aggy, dear, it's not the MTB that I'm so against, and I don't think that's what you're opposed to, either. It's all about choice. If I choose to find this person, and if I like them, aren't I still making a choice? And if you don't want to find yours, that's your choice to make. And if Lish wants to throw her life away by having a baby at eighteen and settling down with a cowboy, who are we to judge?"

I snicker at his snark.

"My brain wants so badly not to end up with my MTB, just to prove the system wrong," I sigh.

"But it's not a system, is it? We don't know what it is. The Name that's on your body is yours alone, Agatha. And your name is out there on his body. Doesn't that excite you in the least?"

My chest itches. My heart hurts. My stomach jumps.

No matter how much I wish he didn't, Hendrix Cutter turns my body electric.

CHAPTER 34

A week passes, and so much and so little happen. In Lish's life, a baby is growing, a wedding is being planned, a move is being scheduled. In my life I go to work, come home, and play video games. Luke and I, as friends, paint the wall. We're getting closer to finishing. Only a few more detailed devils, and the wall will be back to its satanic majesty. While we paint, I pontificate about the future of the wall.

"You realize our work will be here even when we've long moved on," I say. "It's crazy to think we might not be back next summer."

"You'll probably be painting murals in Australia. Kangaroos and koalas and boomerangs." I laugh. "And I'll be . . . I don't know." He puffs out some pensive air. "I did something last night," he tells me very guiltily.

"What?" I demand, concerned by his tone.

"I contacted Scarlett." He looks at me from his place at the wall, where he adds flames to a faded fire. The setting sun brings out the green in his eyes.

"Oh," is all I can muster.

"Are you mad?" he asks.

"I don't think so," I admit. "I feel like I could be, but, first off, we're not really un-dating anymore. We haven't kissed in, what, more than a week? And it's been really nice not having the added pressure of the sex and relationship stuff."

"Totally," he agrees enthusiastically.

"Of course part of me wants to be eternally desired. I mean, who doesn't want to feel wanted?" I ask.

"Right. And in a way, I wouldn't mind if you were a little jealous because that would mean you still had feelings for me, and that's cool, too."

"We're total assholes," I say.

"But honest assholes," Luke adds.

"So what was she like?" I ask, turning back to the wall to paint. I figure if my face belies my feelings, it won't be a problem if he can't see it.

"She seems pretty cool. Smart. Funny. Ambitious. She's really into the circus arts."

"What does that mean?" I ask, hoping the bite in my voice didn't register.

"It's kind of performance gymnastics. She hangs from scarves. Like Cirque du Soleil. I guess she's really flexible."

"I guess she's really flexible," I mimic under my breath. Oops. I guess I'm more jealous than I thought.

Luke must notice because he approaches me. "Do you want me to stop talking about her?"

"No, no." I wave the thought away. "It's fine. It's cool. Go on," I say completely unconvincingly.

"This is going to sound really stupid, but after talking with her, I don't even feel like having sex with you anymore."

"What?" I'm dumbfounded at the ridiculous statement.

"That didn't come out the way I meant it to. I guess what I mean is that I still really like you, and think you're adorable-slash-hot, but my body isn't reacting to those thoughts anymore. Does that make sense?"

It's like the same aliens who abducted Lish have now taken over Luke, and he's spouting gibberish just so he doesn't have to touch me anymore.

"I get it." I look at anything but Luke. "You're not into me anymore. You've moved on. It's cool. We already agreed to be friends, so no big."

"Aggy." Luke gently takes my chin so that I'll look at him. "I want you to understand. Even though we're here, and the sun is setting, and there are a whole lot of empty boats just waiting for us to get buck naked, I don't want to. Something happened when Scarlett and I spoke. It sounds so crazy, but it's true!"

"It's the whole 'it's not you, it's me' thing," I clarify.

"But, like, for real. Not an excuse. Not a line. For real."

I look at Luke quizzically, then dive in for a kiss. It's a short one, no tongue, and Luke barely has time to reciprocate before I pull away. "Anything?" I ask. He looks pitifully at me. I grab his hand and place it on my shirt-clad breast. "How about now?"

"I still like the way it feels, for sure, but I don't want to do anything with it."

"So it would be pathetically desperate of me to strip right now?" I check.

"If that's what you want to do, go for it. But I'm not going to act on it. I hope that doesn't offend you. Like I said, it's not you." I try not to slump and to accept what Luke says. It's what I wanted, I guess.

The conversation dies, and we clean up the paintbrushes. At our cars, Luke warmly, and completely without sexual connotation, hugs me good night. I receive it stiffly.

I drive home baffled. Did Luke choose to stop feeling a certain way about me? Is he so smitten with Scarlett that he doesn't have eyes (or lips or hands) for anyone else? Or is there some freaky chemical reaction that happens when MTBs meet? Maybe it's different for everyone. Maybe Luke is an extreme case.

Maybe the only way I'll ever know the answers is if I talk to Hendrix Cutter.

I'm home, the glow of my computer screen illuminating my dark bedroom. My uncle is asleep; my mom left a note on the kitchen table alerting me that she is out—not on a date, she stressed—with the seafood guy. I am essentially alone. Just me and the entire rest of the world that is available at the click of a button.

If I want to, I can do more than lightly cyberstalk

Hendrix Cutter. I can send him a message. I can find his home address. Hell, I can order a drone right now to bring him a cookie bouquet.

I'm antsy. I need to reach out to someone, to know that I'm not the only person left over the age of eighteen who doesn't know what she wants. Sure, there are obvious others, the zealots who tattoo over their Names, the ones who stay with their current partners, but I don't fit into that. Maybe Sahana hasn't succumbed to her Empty. Her parents had an arranged marriage; they could want the same thing for her. Or she could want the same thing for herself. We all still have a choice, don't we?

I text Sahana to see if she's home. The minute it takes for her to reply is too much time, and my eyes burn from staring at my screen's background pic, a childhood photo of me and Lish with balloons stretching out our Phineas and Ferb t-shirts like enormous breasts. The irony. When Sahana finally gets back to me, she writes:

At my aunt's. Can text under the table if you need.

Me: *Quick question: thoughts on MTBs?*

Sahana: *Hardly a quick question. My mom gave me choices: College plus no dating or find my MTB and we'll talk.*

Me: *Are those good choices?*

Sahana: *I hate making decisions, so I appreciate concrete options.*

Me: *This is love we're talking about, not groceries.*

Sahana: *Love can grow where we want it to. My parents showed me that.*

Me: *So where do you want it to grow?*

Sahana: *Not at a local college for damn sure. I'm going to Brown. As for the love part...*

Me: *Keep me in suspense, why don't you.*

Sahana: *I've been chatting with my MTB all summer. He's adorable AND Indian, so win-win.*

Me: *Why didn't you tell me?! Congrats!*

Sahana: *You've been going off on "Empties" diatribes for years. Why would I put myself through that?*

Me: *Fair enough.*

Sahana: *What's your plan?*

Me: *1) Australia*

2) Fuck if I know

Sahana: *Sounds like a perfect plan for you. Gotta go. My mom is giving me the stink eye.*

Me: *Ciao*

I really am the only one I know.

But wait . . . Hendrix Cutter is still out there *not* talking to *me*. Therefore, I am officially not alone in my crusade against . . . what is my crusade against at this point? It's not against love. I don't even know if it's against choosing your MTB over actual, falling-in-love love. What once felt like a crusade really just feels like me marching in protest in front of a Dunkin' Donuts when they run out of Munchkins. Nobody else gives a damn and, really, if I'm that unhappy I should either go to the other Dunkin' Donuts three blocks away or buy a full-size donut and be done with it.

Why do we never have donuts in the house?

At least Hendrix Cutter has a girlfriend. He has love. He has commitment. He has . . . MY NAME FLARING FORTH FROM HIS CHEST.

I can't take it anymore. Whether I'm compelled to do so out of resignation or a cosmic ray of bullying, I log on to Chapbook. I haven't visited since the night Lish told me she was pregnant. Immediately after talking with her, I shut it down. I didn't want to see the Hendrix Cutter search; something about Lish's news felt like a bad omen when looking at a picture of one's meant-to-be.

Three messages await me. The first, from Lish, was written soon after she broke the pregnancy story, wondering when I would talk to her. The second was from Adam, the week I punched him, offering me a dozen virtual roses as an apology. The third was sent yesterday from Pippa Cutter.

The instant I read the last name, my heart threatens to extract itself through my mouth.

Pippa Cutter is Hendrix Cutter's sister.

I can barely swallow as I open the message.

Dear Agatha,

My name is Pippa Cutter, and I'm fifteen years old. This is probably totally wrong of me, but I had to write to you to let you know that my brother is your MTB. You probably already know that, seeing as his Name is also on your chest. Unless it's not, and you are one of the few unmatched people. Also, I am assuming you are my brother's MTB and not the four other Agatha Abramses I found who are all over sixty. Do you live anywhere near Brunswick East? It's a suburb of Melbourne, in case you live in a different state.

I'm babbling. I don't even know what I want to tell you except that my brother is a great guy who is dating a total dag and is super stubborn about meeting you. He keeps going on and on about free will and choice, and I think he's a dick for it. You look really cute in the pictures I found of you online. (Yes, I am stalking you, but not in a creepster way. I merely want you to find my brother so the two of you fall in love and then I get a really cool sister-in-law. Is that too much to ask?)

Please don't hate me for being nosy, and I know this is none of my business. The thought of finding true love is just about the most romantic thing I can think of, and since I have to wait three years, I'm going to force my brother to find it if it kills me.

Also, please don't kill me.

Signed,
Your hopeful future sister-in-law,
Pippa
PS Do you like dogs?

Clearly this family is horrible and evil and WHY IS SHE SO CUTE?! I can't even. There is far too much info to be gleaned from this e-mail that I spend the next two hours scrutinizing:

1) Hendrix Cutter has a loving sister. A sister who loves her older brother means her older brother is probably not a dickwad.
2) She is sweet in her own right, so probably good parenting.
3) Hendrix Cutter still has a girlfriend. But she sucks. According to Pippa anyway.
4) They live in a suburb of Melbourne. If that means what I think it does, there is a realistic chance that my mind will explode and I won't have to worry about Hendrix Cutter or MTBs ever again.

Does Hendrix Cutter live in Australia?

I text Lish, forgetting for a moment that not only is she practically married but also with child, and pretend that we are as we once were: plain-old best friends.

Me: *Help! Hendrix Cutter's sister messaged me. Need analysis pronto!*

In a second, Lish texts back: *TELL ME ALL*

Me: *Sending message over Chap.*

I cut and paste the message from Pippa into a letter

for Lish. Instantly a bubble from Lish pops up on my Chapbook.

Give me 5 minutes.

I use the five minutes to go to the bathroom, twice, and drink approximately a gallon of water. Then I go to the bathroom again.

When I return to my computer, Lish has sent me a highlighted and annotated version of Pippa's letter. Sections of it stand out in blue-colored blocks with handwritten notes like, "Conscientious!" "Complimentary!" "Polite!" "Honest!" Lish especially enjoyed the signature of "hopeful future sister-in-law," as evidenced by the halo of red hearts.

As I read her comments, my Viddle rings. The second I answer, Lish's too-close-to-camera face looms. "Find him!" she commands.

"And hello to you," I try to make light.

"You have to find him, Aggy. He's perfect for you!" She draws out the word *perfect* like she's Catwoman.

"How do you know he's perfect for me?" I want to be defensive, but my cheeks are fighting to smile. Why do I feel so giddy?

"Because he is stubborn just like you and claims he doesn't believe in MTBs, just like you, but you are crumbling and so will he!" Lish clasps her hands maniacally.

"You are crackers, and I am not crumbling. I didn't send the message. He didn't send it. His sister did. That would be like you sending Hendrix Cutter a message."

And before I finish saying that, I'm kicking myself.

"Thank you for your permission! Good night!"

Lish is gone. Off the phone, and off her rocker.

She's kidding, right? She's off-balance from her pregnancy hormones. She won't actually do it when she knows I don't want her to. But if I truly don't want her to, why do I feel so stupidly excited?

CHAPTER 35

My face is bugging the hell out of me. I want this dopey smile to go away. I have no reason and no right to be happy about essentially nothing, and yet here I am making my breakfast like I'm Snow Fucking White or Sleeping Dipshit Beauty or whichever obsolete Disney princess surrounds herself with joyous animals. I swear Rugburn is dancing.

I pop a slice of rye bread into the toaster to a beat that plays in my head, and I rap on the counter with the butter knife. Hell, I blow bubbles in my orange juice glass with a straw. A straw? At breakfast? Have I lost my mind?

No news yet from Lish. Will there be news? Was she just screwing with me? I care way too much.

Uncle Jim walks into the kitchen and eyes me suspiciously. "Do you have a boy in your bedroom? Is that what I just saw zipping through our backyard?"

"If you saw a boy in our backyard, I'm thinking you should up the prescription on your contacts. It was probably the Schusters' cat. He has thumbs, you know."

My lips pucker in a whistle, then somehow I manage to stop myself. I am not a whistler. Nor am I someone who wakes up bright and cheery. And I certainly am not, nor have I ever been, a person who gets all giddy because she may soon be in contact with her MTB. Her EMPTY.

"Well, since you're in such a good mood, and really, I don't need to know, I have something I want to tell you," Uncle Jim says mysteriously.

My toast pops enthusiastically, and I catch it. At least I would if my toast flew out of the toaster instead of lethargically peeping a mere two inches above the slot. I pinch the tip of my toast with disregard for the fact that my bread has turned into "toast" through the process of being heated. The toast is so toasty that, as I had earlier desired, it is now flying through the air. The slice lands on the floor with a crumbly thunk.

"Sit down, Aggy. You're wound up today, aren't you?" Uncle Jim eyes me as he helps me pick up the toast and put it on a plate.

"Thanks." I laugh. "I don't know what my deal is." I bounce in my seat. This is getting very annoying.

Uncle Jim sits across from me, without breakfast or coffee, and looks at me intently. "I have some really big news, which may be hard for me to get out, so please don't interrupt. And, for god's sake, sit still."

"Yes, sir," I respond mockingly at his attempt at authority.

"Agatha, this is serious."

"Sorry. I'm listening. Even if I can't stop moving, I promise you I'm listening." I wiggle my butt in my chair.

"Okay. Away we go. . . ." Uncle Jim takes a few deep

breaths and closes his eyes to center himself. "So, I am going to meet my MTB next week. In Houston, of all places." Uncle Jim smiles to himself at the thought of Houston. I don't know if it's the specific city or that he will have to leave the house to get there.

"She must be pretty special to get you all the way to Texas," I interject.

"That's the piece I want to talk to you about. Not Texas, exactly—"

I can't resist interrupting with, "I hear they have excellent toast in Texas." I'm chuckling to myself with pride at the corny joke, when Uncle Jim explodes.

"I'm gay, Agatha!" He covers his mouth with his hands the second he emits those words, as though he can't believe he let them escape.

It takes me all of two seconds to process, before I shout, "Why the hell didn't I figure that out? And why the fuck didn't you ever tell me?" I feel angry at Uncle Jim for hiding this fact from me, hiding it from the world by holing up in our attic for the last five years. But mostly I'm angry at him for holding it in so long. What a complicated burden to live with every day, seeing himself in the mirror with a man's Name splayed across his chest, and not wanting to admit to it. "I'm not mad at you," I add hastily to clarify. "I'm mad *for* you."

"I get that you deal with a lot of your issues through anger, Agatha, but that's not how I work. You have to imagine what it was like for me when the Naming happened, and there was Michael Delacorte on my chest. God, I haven't said his name to anyone but your mom." I think Uncle Jim is blushing, but it's hard to tell under his stubble. "I've never been what you'd call a dater. I mean, I had one 'girlfriend,'" Uncle Jim air-quotes, "in high school, but that was all hand-holding and group dates. In college, I studied. Really, I thought I was asexual."

"But you must have known you were leaning toward guys. Didn't you want to test it out?" asks the teenage horndog.

"No, Agatha, I'm an introvert and an agoraphobe on top of it. Not to mention I've never been a hugely sexual person, even when I allowed myself to think about men. To admit that I was gay would mean adding a whole lot of other complications to my life. I preferred to deal with it by locking myself in your house and writing smutty fiction for people in need. It was a hell of a lot easier than touching real humans."

I mull this over for several minutes. Uncle Jim gives me space and makes his coffee. When his mug is poured he sits back down.

"What changed your mind?" I finally manage to ask.

"You." Uncle Jim smiles at me.

"Me?" I sit back in surprise. "What did I do?"

"You lived your life honestly, Agatha, and passionately, which could not have been more opposite to how I've been living mine. Talking to your mom about Australia, that was very brave. Dating outside of your MTB, that was, too. I admire you. And now your mom has started dating."

"Allegedly," I add.

"Get a grip, kid. They've already schtooped."

"No! TMI! TMI!" I cover my ears.

"Anyway, your mom is moving on, and she doesn't need her spinster brother getting in the way. Plus, Michael sought me out, and it felt so good to be wooed like that. We get along famously, so we're going to see how that works in person."

"I am very happy for you. Really." I check the clock and realize I'm late for work. "I have to go to work. We can talk more later." Uncle Jim squeezes me into an endearing hug, and my heart fills with joy at how open and relaxed he seems. "One more question: Would you still think all those good things about me if I ended up meeting my MTB?"

Uncle Jim blinks with blissful bewilderment. "My dear, like your mother, what I want for you is happiness. Go after it, wherever it may be found. Don't wait until it comes to you." He laughs and rolls his eyes up to the ceiling. "Or you could be sitting in an attic imagining love instead of living with it."

And that is why Uncle Jim writes the books.

CHAPTER 36

Uncle Jim's news has me driving well over the speed limit to work. I'm barely able to focus on the road, let alone how fast I should be going on it. It's amazing how his life has completely changed just because of the Naming. First, he was a guy, albeit an in-the-closet guy, but still living his life. Then the Naming happens, my dad moves out, and Jim moves in and never leaves. And here he is: gay and possibly in love. I wonder what this all means for Savannah Merlot.

More important, what does this mean for me? Still no word from Lish. At a stoplight, I text:

What did you do?

The light turns green, and I drop the phone onto my seat. I never thought I'd say this to myself, but there are too many choices. It would be one thing if falling in love was the way it used to be thousands of years ago: Someone hits you over the head with a club. *Bam!* You're in love. Then you have babies and live to the ripe old age of twenty-two. Phones and computers have added infinite ways to find people, also adding infinite choices. Then *whammo!* The Naming goes down, and things are supposed to be easier: Look, now you don't have to choose! Your perfect mate has been selected for you by . . . whom exactly? That's the shiftiest part, the piece that throws me more than choosing someone: How do any of us know the Name on our chest is the real deal? What if it wasn't the science of pheromones or the divine intervention of God helping us find a mate? What if Satan is playing a joke on the human race, yucking it up in hell when everyone's love lives go to shit and the divorce and murder rates skyrocket? What if his goal was to turn the next generation, the kids who result from Empty love matches, completely against the idea of love so that reproduction ends altogether and the human race dies out?

What if Hendrix Cutter is super ugly?

God, I'm an asshole.

I arrive at work, head swimming with Uncle Jim's news and the cacophony in my brain. Reluctantly I relinquish my phone to my locker. Nothing a repetitive day at Haunted Hollow can't fix.

My desire for normalcy is blown out of the electric blue river when I pass Luke at the Ghoster.

"Aggy!" he calls out to me, and I meet him at the ride. Luke clutches me in his arms and spins me around. "I have the best news! I'm going to visit Scarlett next week!" He doesn't wait for my reaction. "Sam Hain said he'd give me the week off. Anything for love, he said. Can you believe it? I knew he was a softy."

I'm glad Luke isn't giving me room to speak because I have little to say. I knew turning eighteen would change things, but I had no idea how much.

"Aren't you going to say something?" Luke looks down at me with an expression reserved for Great Dane puppies.

"That's . . ." I search for the appropriate word. "Awesome," I announce. I don't think that was the word I was looking for, but it came first alphabetically.

Luke hugs me again obliviously. "Park's open. I'll tell you all the details at lunch!"

I toddle off to the Dinghies, questioning how I went so quickly from sexified un-girlfriend to his girl/friend.

Again, I have to wonder: A chemical reaction, or is Luke just a really intense boyfriend kind of guy? Uncle Jim seemed to turn pretty quickly from hermit to husband. Lish is on her way to domesticity and mommyhood (I gag a little every time I think about that tiny Travis inside her). It's as though Choice has become a myth or legend, a concept so imaginary and fantastical I'll be locked away if I continue to pledge my allegiance to it.

If my morning hadn't been so busy with a steady stream of children boarding the Devil's Dinghies, I might have stolen a trip to my locker for a check of my phone. Lunch can't come fast enough, and by the time my break arrives and Keely moseys to my booth I'm bolting full-speed to the staff room. I zip past Adam, my breasts bobbling in every direction, and I dare him with a sneering glance to look at them. Unable to avert his gaze, he simply turns around and I win.

I rip my locker open and fish out my phone. There's a text from Lish; an annoyingly minimalist line reads:

I did something. . . .

Why is she so infuriating? Does she think she's funny? This is only my life we're talking about here.

Or not.

Why am I getting so worked up?

I attempt to fool myself into calm. What's the big deal if Lish messaged Hendrix Cutter? I don't care. Who is this guy anyway except some Australian dude whose name is surreptitiously written upon my physical being?

When I say it that way it sounds so important.

I type to Lish:

I have a short break. What did you do? Did you send him a message? What did you say? Did he write you back?

I hit send, and wait for a reply. When she doesn't respond instantly I type:

I'm waiting.

When she still doesn't respond in a timely enough fashion, I grab my lunch and stomp outside to a bench, phone gripped tightly in my fist. I make it through half a PB and J plus four Doritos before she decides to stop torturing her best friend.

I wrote him. I have not heard back. Found a pic. Want me to send?

This text is too much for me, and I simultaneously knock over my can of Grape Crush and spill my remaining Doritos. Both are instantly swarmed by a colony of bees.

I switch benches and type frantically:

a) What did you say to him?

b) I don't know, do I want you to send it?

My knee bounces frantically as I watch the bees pollinate my chemically flavored corn chips. Is this why they're going extinct? Because of my careless Dorito-dropping?

My phone cackles, and I can't unlock the screen fast enough to read it.

a) A LOT.

b) Hell to the yes.

Carolyn, my supervisor and anti-MTB-er extraordinaire, passes my frazzled form on the bench. The tattoo she chose to cover her MTB is blantantly on display, jeering at me while I writhe in confusion. Or maybe she just says hi.

With only two minutes left in my meager lunch "hour," I don't have time to read Lish's message *and* look at a picture of Hendrix Cutter. I weigh my two options: Either I can see the words my best friend wrote to a dude whose name is currently on my body, or I can see the dude whose name is currently on my body. Let's not forget that Lish could have said or told him anything, and I should probably be rolling on the ground among the bees in mortified agony at the embarrassment she's caused me.

Break is over. I have to return my phone to my locker and get back to work. Hastily I type:

Send the pic!

Not even a millisecond after the text goes out, I receive a chimed reply.

I knew you'd say that. Here you go!

And here he is.

Hendrix Cutter.

At least, I hope it's Hendrix Cutter and not some other guy Lish found in a botched web search. Or potentially another guy named Hendrix Cutter.

But I really do hope this is him.

He has short brown textured hair that looks effortless but like he probably fixes it every day. His left ear peaks into a point, although not enough to be elfish. His eyes are dark, but they look more green than brown or black when I zoom in. His nose, a tad crooked, I'd like to imagine from a bout he had over a Vegemite sandwich as a child, is peppered with freckles. Not entirely perfect, but not snaggly, teeth peek out from his full lips in the picture's smile.

You know that part in *How the Grinch Stole Christmas!* when the Whos are singing, and the Grinch's heart grows three sizes bigger? That's not how I feel. It's more like my heart, so engorged with the possibility of love, is pressing out of my rib cage and reaching out to touch the picture. Or better yet, the Name on my chest.

Even if Lish didn't seek this picture out, I instantly know I would recognize him anywhere as Hendrix Cutter.

And this scares the shit out of me.

CHAPTER 37

After seeing—and experiencing—Hendrix Cutter for the first time, I'm happy to sequester my phone to my locker for the rest of the day. In fact, I'm so freaked out by my reaction that instead of taking my phone out of my locker after work, I stay late to paint without revisiting my locker at all. I buy a burger and fries from Concessions before the park closes and pop a squat at the Devil's Dinghies wall. The transformation is rather wondrous, if I do say so myself. The colors are much brighter, and the lines are cleaner, which makes the wall visible from farther away in the park than it used to be. Maybe that's why my guest numbers seem to be up. I'm busy admiring my handiwork, thus am startled when a gravelly voice says, "Nice job. Looks real good." It's Brian from maintenance, wielding his trusty pole for lost-item fishing.

"Thanks," I reply. "I think so, too." We look to the wall as if it might give us something else to talk about. It does not. Brian begins shuffling away, when I say, "Brian, do you mind if I ask you something?"

"You already did," he yuks. One of *those.*

"How about another question, then?"

"Did that, too." Lord.

I ignore the witty banter and inquire, "Do you know your MTB?"

Brian's expression rarely fluctuates from unenthused, but he looks like he just saw the ghost of the guy allegedly killed on my ride.

"Sorry. Too personal?" I backtrack.

"Yup." A major wordsmith, this one.

I watch Brian drag the net through the fake river, and I can't help myself. "You don't have to tell me specifics, but did you have anything happen to your body when you found her? Or him? I don't judge."

Brian slowly sloshes the net back and forth at nothing in particular. I can tell he's thinking by the movement of deep lines on his forehead.

"Hey, you two." Sam Hain approaches the grassy area where Brian and I stand. When Sam begins talking to me, I see the worry relax on Brian's face. He slinks away from us and into the tunnel like Gollum. Maybe he'll find his precious.

"Not much of a talker, that one." Sam nods in Brian's direction.

"I think I might have offended him." The corner of my mouth tugs town in embarrassment.

"I don't know if Brian gets offended. He is a private man, though. What did you say?"

I move closer to Sam Hain, but not too close. His short stature and muscular build remind me of a sumo wrestler but with clothing; a waft of incense drifts from his hair. At least, I think that's what the smell is: something sweet and smoky. Perhaps it's barbecue sauce aftershave.

"I asked him a question about his MTB," I whisper.

Sam Hain lets out a raucous laugh, a sound I would never guess could come out of this man. He rests his hands on his stomach, as I imagine Santa does. When he finally manages to settle himself, he confides, "Brian doesn't talk about his MTB. He lives with his mom, who needs lots of assistance, and he hasn't had a girlfriend since he started here in 1993. I suspect it's a lot of pressure for a guy like that, going through life a little lonely but okay with things, the ladies of the Internet keeping you company, and then you find out there's a girl somewhere who you're supposed to be with? What does a guy like Brian do with something like that?"

"My uncle ignored his MTB for six years. Then it turned out he's gay." I shrugged.

"The Naming really fucked us all up, didn't it? I feel bad for you kids, never getting a chance to sow your wild oats like we did." Sam winks at me in commiseration.

"It does complicate things," I concur.

"You and Luke seemed to do all right for yourselves." Sam Hain winks at me again.

Oh God. Does he know we had sex on one of his rides? Is this the part where he fires me?

"I always liked when my kids found summer love here at Haunted Hollow." Sam looks off into the distance dreamily. "I though the Naming would end that for sure, and then Brian finds a condom wrapper in the river here at the

Dinghies." Is there a way to stop one's face from turning as red as a cherry snow cone? "Warms my heart," Sam muses. "Anyway, what did you want to ask Brian? Maybe I can answer for him."

My voice has mortifyingly receded into the far reaches of my throat, and I have to clear it several times before I'm able to eke out, "I was wondering if he—*you*—had a physical reaction to your MTB before you met them. Or after. Or at all. I want to know if what's going on with me and my friends is normal."

"None of this is normal, darling. You got a world of people trying to find and figure out love and then—*wham!*" Sam smacks his hands together zealously, and I jump. "All of a sudden a Name is going to make life simple? Fuck that," he scoffs.

"Aren't you with your MTB?" I ask.

He resigns, "That I am. But I didn't go willingly. I fought it tooth and nail. Sleeping around with whomever I could. Avoiding my computer, my phone. Spending all hours at work."

"So what happened?"

"I couldn't shake this nagging sensation. In my brain, in my chest, in my . . ." He blinks his eyes downward, and I feel the blush creep back into my cheeks. Sam Hain's crotch is one area I try not to think about. "I finally thought, to hell with it. She's another woman out there, why not at least try her out? I found her easily through an app, chatted her up, and that was it. We've been together ever since. Fuck all if I ever thought I'd end up with a lawyer," he chuckles. "I hate to admit it, but whoever had their hand in these MTBs might have got something right."

"Who do you think did it?" I ask, enthralled by this man who I revere and slightly fear.

"Balls if I know. God? The devil himself?" Sam points at the images on the wall. "A mad scientist trying to rule the world? Does it matter? It happened, and we all gotta deal with it. Poor Brian's probably losing his hair because of it." We both look off into the tunnel, as though we can see the receding top of Brian's lonely head. "What's your plan?" Sam asks me.

"I guess I'm moving to Australia." I shrug.

"You guess? That's a plan? What's in Australia?"

"Luna Park. Thought I could teach them a thing or two about scary rides." Sam puffs at the flattery. "And aside from a kick-ass amusement park? It turns out my MTB just happens to live there. Unbeknownst to me until after I chose to make the move."

"Ain't that a kick in the balls?" Sam asks, and I have no idea to what he's referring specifically. "You're still going, right?"

Hesitantly I answer, "Yeah. I think so."

"You think so? That doesn't sound like you, Agatha. You know why I hired you?" I shake my head no. "You came in here all tiny but held yourself so confidently. You told me some story about Halloween being your favorite holiday and how you wanted it to last all year. And since it couldn't, working at Haunted Hollow would at least give you the chance to relive it all summer. Then you told me a story about a disturbing book you liked to read as a kid about amusement parks where people died."

"*Abandoned Amusement Parks*," I interject. "People didn't die at all of them. Some were just haunted."

"See! That's it right there! Even if you were going to freak out a potential boss, you didn't care. You really knew what you wanted, and I admired that."

I'm taken aback that Sam Hain, after the hundreds of kids he's interviewed, remembers mine from three years ago. "Why don't you know for sure if you want to travel halfway around the world?"

"I want to go because I choose to. Not because of this bullshit Name on my chest."

"They always say listen to your heart. What is your heart telling you to do, Agatha?"

"It's telling me that I have no choice," I say, frustrated. "Even if I want to be with whomever I want. Even if I tried to like someone else. Even if I had sex with someone on the Devil's Dinghies, say, I still would rather be with my stupid MTB!" I'm exasperated.

"That was you?" Sam slaps his knee hysterically. "You are part of Haunted Hollow lore, my friend."

"You didn't know it was me?" I ask, horrified.

"It's all good. Your secret is safe with me." He zips his

lip with an imaginary key. "I can't say I'm not a little bit of a proud papa." Sam beams, and I kick my shoe in the grass awkwardly.

"Look, whether your body is telling you to do it on rides or go find this lucky fella whose name is on your chest, it's still your body guiding you. Take it where it feels good. Does thinking about your MTB make you feel good?" Sam pats his hand on my shoulder in a fatherly way, if my father were covered in tattoos and could bench press seven thousand pounds.

"Annoyingly so."

Another jarring clap. "Well, there you go! Fly to Australia! Box some kangaroos, and go find your MTB. If it stops feeling good, you can always choose to do something else. You've got chutzpah, kid."

Who is this man? "I suppose," I concede.

Sam Hain slaps me on the back encouragingly. I fall forward several feet. "That's my girl! Now about this wall . . ."

Sam is so pleased with my work, he offers me an extra $666 for my summer pay. I tell him Luke helped, and he says he'll give him a little something, too. "I know it was all you, though, kid. Consider . . . ," he pontificates, "if you ever make your way back to this neck of the woods, you've always got a job waiting. Hell, maybe I'll give you this place when I die."

"Uh . . . uh . . . ," I stutter.

"Just kidding!" Another backslap. "But think about it," he mutters and walks off.

When I get home, my mom is at the kitchen table paying bills. I inform her of my bonus.

"That's awesome, Aggy! Money like that can help pay for books," Mom starts about college but catches herself. "Or kangaroo burgers. I hope you won't actually eat kangaroos."

My mom and I talk for a long time about my summer, Luke, Sam Hain and his advice, Uncle Jim and his revelation, my mom and her seafood guy. His MTB died, too, albeit after he met her. Car accident. It must be confusing for both of them, losing their supposed meant-to-bes so soon. Kind of magical they found each other. Definitely not fate. I refuse to cave. My mom seems content, excited about school and work, and there's a rosy incandescence in her cheeks that hasn't been there in forever. It's comforting and encouraging, and I know my mom will be okay when my uncle Jim leaves.

When *I* leave.

I will myself to listen and chat as long as I can, knowing that Lish's message to Hendrix Cutter awaits me on my computer. When my mom says she has homework, I feign disappointment at the end of our conversation. She hugs me and kisses my forehead. "I'm so proud of you, Agatha."

I bound up the stairs, wishing my legs were long enough to take them two at a time. Rugburn is balled up on my bed, and acknowledges me with a logy head lift. "No. Don't get up," I drawl.

My computer takes forever to wake from its slumber, and

I bounce my foot, crossed over my knee, impatiently. Finally, the screen is aglow, and I click to open Chapbook. There, I have five messages waiting. Displayed in a list, I can see the names of the senders and the first few words of each message.

The first is from Luke. It begins with, "I can't wait to meet . . ."

That message can *certainly* wait. The next three are from Lish. The first begins, "Dear Hendrix Cutter," and I laugh at the use of his complete name. The next two, also from Lish, begin with, "Aggy," followed by numerous exclamation points. One would think I'd open her letter to Hendrix Cutter immediately, dying to know what my best friend wrote to my potential MTB. And I am. But the name on the fifth message causes my hand to shake over my computer. I check to be certain I'm not reading it incorrectly. Maybe it's the first line of another e-mail from Lish. Or I'm blurring the name of his sister to read something else.

When I steady myself, I read the name aloud carefully. The fifth message is from Hendrix Cutter.

CHAPTER 38

This goes against protocol! Hendrix isn't supposed to write me a letter! It should have gone: a letter from his sister, a letter from Lish, and then there would be comical back-and-forths, and one day, when I am ready, *I* would contact him. I am not ready!

I don't know what to read first. Do I dive right into Hendrix's e-mail? Do I read them in order, so I'll know what Lish said and to, naturally, build suspense?

"Rugburn!" I shout, and the cat bolts upright. "What do I do? Tell me!" I scream. He shoots out of my bedroom. "Not helpful!" I yell after him.

My stomach churns. It's rotating at a rapid pace, and I question whether I'll have a chance to read a single e-mail before I must rush to my trusty toilet. I could always bring the laptop with.

No! I shall persevere. Too terrified to read actual words from actual Hendrix Cutter (holyshitholyshitholyshit), I open the initial message from Lish.

Dear Hendrix Cutter,

My name is Lish Heins, and I am the best friend of your MTB, Agatha Abrams. I'm hoping this is the correct Hendrix Cutter, but you look to be the right age and, frankly, I couldn't find anyone else with that name. Can't wait to learn about its origin. You can tell the story at your wedding! I'm probably getting ahead of myself. Forgive me if I'm all over the place. I'm pregnant. Don't let that give you the wrong idea about Aggy (that's what most people call her, but maybe you'll have an adorable pet name for her like Aggles or Agalong. Or not). It's not like the two of us are out there sleeping around with everyone. I was sleeping with my MTB and—oops!—now I'm having his baby. You and Aggy will be smarter about the birth control. I know she is big on carrying condoms.

Am I telling you too much for an intro e-mail? I just feel like you guys are meant to be and all, so is anything off limits? (I know Aggy's answer, and she will probably kill me when she sees what I wrote to you. Not really kill me. She's not violent. Except for that time she punched a guy in the nose. He totally deserved it for talking about her boobs. She has great boobs, so get ready.)

I feel like I'm blabbering. The whole reason for

writing you is that I love Aggy and would do anything for her, and since she is still hesitant about this whole MTB thing I wanted to help move things along for her. What are best friends for, if not for writing mortifying e-mails to potential husbands, am I right?

I was going to keep my big mouth shut, but I learned something about you, Hendrix Cutter: You live in Australia. And guess where Aggy plans on going after the summer (our summer, your winter): That's right—Russia! Just kidding. Australia. But not because of you. She has wanted to live in Australia for years and years and had no idea you even lived there until your sister wrote Aggy an e-mail (she's adorable, btw). That's got to mean something, don't you think?

Actually, I have no idea what you think since you have made zero effort to get in touch with Aggy (what's up with that? Are you some kind of a dick? Beware the wrath of a pregnant best friend). Even you, Hendrix Cutter, must admit that's weird. So, I am putting the ball in your court. If you are the guy my amazing best friend deserves, you will get in touch with her. I'm not saying you have to fall in love and get married and have babies so my kid has a friend, but that would be nice.

She's on Chapbook under Agatha Abrams.

Sincerely,

Lish

(maid of honor at your future hypothetical wedding)

PS Dump your girlfriend.

PPS Don't tell Aggy I mentioned her boobs.

You know when you first get your period, and your dad doesn't know what to do when he finds out so all he manages to say is, "Congratulations?" I feel seven hundred thousand times more mortified right now. Let us recap all the humiliating details I learned about myself in Lish's message:

1) I am getting married.
2) I am constantly prepared to have sex, with my arsenal of condoms.
3) I only punched one guy, so that's okay.
4) MY BOOBS.
5) My best friend basically called Hendrix Cutter a dick.
6) I am supposed to have babies with him.

All of this, and he wrote me back. What if his e-mail is him telling me never to contact him? What if Hendrix Cutter puts a restraining order on Lish? On me?

I open the next message from Lish with a modicum of terror.

Aggy!!

Hendrix Cutter wrote me back!
See below:

Hi Lish,

Funny you should write. I've been thinking about MTBs a lot lately. My girlfriend, ex-girlfriend, has galloped off into the sunset with hers. Truthfully, it made me want to find mine even less. But your message intrigued me (and not just the breast part). I think a lot about fate and choice and destiny and free will. I don't know what I've concluded, but the fact that Agatha (I like her full name, if that's okay) is coming to Australia—learning that has me all mixed up. What are the odds? Or is it more than odds at work? This new life we have drives me batshit. It was a lot simpler when we could sneak off with someone after homeroom, right?

I have to figure out what to say to Agatha. I don't know if I'm quite as open as you. I'm guessing most people aren't. ☺

Thanks again for writing,

Hendrix

PS Don't tell Agatha, but I have a massive . . . big toe.

Aggy! He's perfect for you! I love him!!! Manners and depth, and he's funny! His girlfriend is out of the picture! I can't stop using exclamation points! Get home from work, so you can fall in love already!

I am completely, utterly, blissed out to the max. The ridiculous attention from Lish that I've missed so deeply combined with the fact that Hendrix Cutter seems the complete opposite of a dick makes my head spin. It's too good, and I'm not ready to read the message from him. Impeccably timed, Uncle Jim knocks on my door frame.

"Aggy, I have something for you," he sing-songs while holding up a folded piece of paper. He smacks the document into my hand, and I peel open the flaps. It's an airline itinerary, my full name listed for a flight from Chicago to Sydney, stopping in Los Angeles, on September 7.

"I knew you weren't at one hundred percent certainty, so I took the liberty of getting you there. You'll be done with work by then, right? After Labor Day." I nod, dumbstruck. "And it's a Tuesday. I always liked Tuesdays. Plus, seven's a lucky number, or so they say."

"I . . . I," I stutter. "I don't know what to say."

"Thank you is always appropriate."

"Yes, thank you, of course, but . . . Uncle Jim. This is so confusing." Uncle Jim sits on my bed and puts on his listening face. "Hendrix Cutter sent me a message."

"That's great, Agatha!" Uncle Jim jumps up and leans over my shoulder to look at my computer screen. "What did he say?" His enthusiasm is slightly grating.

"I haven't read it yet," I admit.

"What?!?" This newly liberated version of Uncle Jim is too animated for my currently fragile state.

"Uncle Jim! I need you to calm down or leave. It's too much," I say.

He puts up his hands in surrender. "Sorry. It's exciting is all." He sits down again. "Why aren't you feeling the excitement?"

"I am, but it's also hella terrifying. I've been anti-Empty for years. I wanted to live my life the way I choose and not have it dictated to me by love, right? And then Hendrix Cutter somehow becomes all I can think about, and it turns out he lives in Australia. And when I'm about to read a real honest-to-fuck message from this guy whose Name magically is on my body, you walk in with a ticket to Australia. It's unsettling. How is this actual life? Meant-to-bes can't be real, and yet all of this"—I gesture hysterically to the computer, the plane ticket—"what if I never had a choice all along? What if every moment of my life is carefully crafted by some god or demon or maniac scientist? What's the point of living it?" I hate myself for crying, but like everything in my life these days, I have zero control over it.

I wipe my nose with the heel of my palm.

"That's gross, Agatha."

"I'll do it if I wanna!" I blubber like a child. Except that I'm not a child. If I were a child, I'd have my whole life ahead of me. But I'm eighteen, and everything has been decided for me.

"I guess I have to go to Australia," I mumble.

"Oh, God, Aggy, poor you! Snap out of it! You are going on a trip to an amazing country, and you are going to meet a boy there! Maybe you'll fall in love, and maybe you won't."

"But I don't have a choice. It's all over," I weep.

Uncle Jim heaves an overzealous sigh, "Agatha Bea Abrams. Stop being such a whiny assbutt." I sit up straight. "You will still have a billion choices to make. What cell phone company to use. What deodorant scent to buy. What you want to eat for every fucking meal for the rest of your goddamn life! Stop acting like you're chained to a wall. You have a wide-open life ahead of you, MTB or no. Let me tell you one of my favorite quotes. I heard it on an HBO program years ago called *Mondo Beyondo*, hosted by one of my people's icons, Bette Midler. I'm allowed to say that now. Like when you see another Jew and you can refer to each other as MOTs."

"What's an MOT?" I ask, wiping the drying tears from my cheeks.

"Member of the Tribe. Don't kids know anything these days? Anyhow, there was a short film about a man on an airplane telling his story of flying to America for the first time. He spoke in an odd British accent, I think it was, and he had a very clipped, enunciated way of speaking. The stewardess also played by him because it was a one-man show, gave the man this bit of advice: 'Build yourself a life, and live with it.' I've kept that line in my pocket for more than twenty years."

"Your sweatpants pocket?" I ask.

"My figurative pocket, Agatha. Are you even listening?" I nod, and he continues. "Build yourself a life, and live with it. Make choices for yourself, but accept that things are happening and go with them. It is, and will always be, your life."

"So what you're saying is, just because some creepy shit is going down and it is all too coincidental, I should go with it because I'm still, technically, making a choice whether to go with it or not."

Uncle Jim looks at me resignedly. "Something like that," he acknowledges.

"Then, if you wouldn't mind leaving, I kind of want to be alone with my message."

"Say no more. But I get a report at some point, right?"

"You got it, dude."

"You really should stop watching *Full House* reruns."

"I know. They're terrifying. Now leave, please."

Uncle Jim walks out, and Rugburn strolls back into my room.

"Glad you're here. I could use the moral support." Rugburn shrugs indifferently and begins licking his butthole. "You're the best, Rugburn. Never change."

I inhale through my nose, exhale through my mouth like we learned in the yoga unit in gym class. Then I click open the message from Hendrix Cutter.

CHAPTER 39

Hi Agatha,

I'm guessing you know who I am, from the name on my message. It's crazy to think that my name is printed on your body. I hope it's legible. My mom's always getting on me about my handwriting. Because that matters, apparently. I like the way the As in your name look like stars. Even though I've barely said anything, I already feel like this is too personal. Is it supposed to feel natural? Should we subconsciously know things about each other? All I know about you is what your friend Lish told me. She seems nice. Very enthusiastic. My best friend's name is Patrick. We met in primary school.

Truly I don't know where to begin. I feel pressure to tell you everything all in one go, but that's not how it usually works. In my vast dating experience (cough cough), you meet a girl, you like her, you go out, she cooks for you (kidding). I don't know. Even though you and I have this connection, I will admit

I'm skeptical. It seems impossible that a phenomenon like this could help people find partners. (So you know, I deleted about fifteen different words there and wound up with partner. It felt the least traumatic.)

I'm curious about your thoughts on the matter. I'm quite curious about a lot of things about you, actually.

Do we write? Chat? You're coming here, aren't you? Do we wait until you get to the airport, then have a brilliantly awkward first hug? Perhaps we can have a TV crew document it for added discomfort.

I feel compelled to write more, everything really, but my band has a show tonight and I have to go. I play drums. Do you play any instruments?

I need to stop writing. Stop writing, Hendrix. Send the message, Hendrix. Stop talking to yourself, Hendrix.

Hendrix

PS If you ever doubted what my first name was, please see the last paragraph.

I wish this were a real letter. A letter on notebook paper, written in smudgy pen, so I could hug it to my chest and read it and reread it and smell the pages for remnants of Hendrix's scent. I want to see the way he writes all his letters, not just the ones in his name.

I scurry to my uncle's room and rap on the door. "Uncle Jim, can I use your printer?" He helps me print a copy of the e-mail, as long as I also print one for him to read. I tell him I will, on the condition that he won't speak to me about it until I am completely ready.

Back on my bed, Rugburn at my side (more like on top of my head), I read every sentence fifty times. One hundred times. I am enamored with this message. Every word makes my breath hitch and my skin tingle and my stomach butterflies do their happy dance. I refuse to believe this is love. It's a single message. There is no possible way I am in love with this guy.

I realize something, and I jolt upright in panic. Rugburn flies off the bed and darts out of the room.

I have to write Hendrix Cutter back.

CHAPTER 40

"You're overthinking it," Lish tells me over Viddle. "He's going to like you instantly, so you don't have to be all flowery with your words. I certainly wasn't."

"Yeah, and you used the word *boobs* three times."

"Sorry about that. Pregnancy brain," she sings.

"That's already getting old, Lish."

"Prepare thyself for eight more months of it."

"Did you notice how he called them *breasts* in the e-mail he wrote you? Serious bonus points," I note.

"Quit stalling, and write your lover a letter," Lish commands.

"My lover?"

"Agatha! Do it!" Lish hangs up on me.

I would like to say that I went with my gut and wrote exactly what I felt, but in truth it took me two hours to write four measly paragraphs.

Hi Hendrix,

I'm glad you wrote. I've been pretty stubborn about the whole thing, to be honest. It's still hard for me to believe in MTBs even though there you are, hovering over my breast (that didn't come out quite as I meant it to). I am going to admit flat-out that I'm nervous, and I don't always present my best self in messages. There are so many words to choose from, and I fear that I'm always picking the wrong ones.

This is all to say: Yes, I'm coming to Australia in September. No, I don't want our first meeting to be an awkward airport hug, although I have always wanted someone to hold up a sign with my name on it at an airport. Doing anything September 7? You don't even have to hold up a sign. You can just stand there with a flower in your lapel. Or not. Can we plan a time to Viddle before then? I have to look up the time difference. I'm in US Central time. I work most days (I'm a carny! That is, I run a ride at a children's amusement park called Haunted Hollow), so evening (my time) is best. Unless that doesn't work for you. Maybe you're out every night with your band. What's your band called? What kind of music do you play? It feels like I could write a message with two thousand questions. Maybe we should send each other multiple-choice quizzes to break the ice. Or those notes we used to send as little kids.

Do you like me? Check the box:

- ☐ *Yes*
- ☐ *No*
- ☐ *You smell*

Did you do that in Australia, too? That sounded ignorant. Like, oh, do you have paper and pens in Australia, too?

I'm going to stop typing before it makes you not want to write me back.

Good night (here at least. So, maybe good morning?).

Agatha

There seems very little chance that I'll sleep tonight. I do a search to figure out the time difference between Chicago and Melbourne. Seventeen hours. What an awkward number. At least it's a prime. Because that makes all the difference. And now I'm starting to have that wacky late-night brain that thinks about prime numbers even though I've never given two shits about prime numbers in my entire life, even when my math teacher, Mr. Stubbs, gave us that prime-number assignment where we had to come up with prime numbers in our daily lives. I wish I could call him up right now and tell him, "Hey! Mr. Stubbs! I have the perfect prime number for you. It's the time difference between Chicago and Melbourne, Australia. That means that since it's two a.m. here in Chicago it's seven p.m. in Melbourne. Bye, Mr. Stubbs! Take care of that gout!"

I try sleeping, but every time I'm about to fall asleep I feel the urge to check my computer to see if Hendrix wrote back. At three a.m. I convince myself to only check for messages on the hour. I even manage to fall asleep for a solid twenty-three minutes before my biological clock (is that what keeps waking me up?) alerts me that it is 4:02, and I am well past my four o'clock message-checking time.

I blink at the screen, my sleep-deprived eyes blurring at the overly bright pixels.

And there it is. Written at 8:57 p.m. Hendrix time (3:57 a.m. my time).

Agatha,

Chatting sounds good. We should wear something identifiable, so we know it's us. I'll have a white carnation on my lapel.

(I hope you know I'm kidding. You were kidding, right? Part of the problem with messages, I guess.)

Does tomorrow night at 8:00 your time (1:00—next day—my time) work for you? Actually, I guess it would be later today for you. Sixteen hours from now. I'm writing this at 9:00 p.m. my time, so 4:00 a.m. your time. Holy fuck this is confusing.

Let me know. Do I call you? You call me? Chapbook chat okay?

Have a good day at work, carny.

Hendrix

I want to message him back immediately. I want to chat with him immediately. I want to sit on his lap and kiss his neck and contemplate prime numbers with him this very instant.

Instead, I attempt to sleep the paltry three hours I have left before I must get up for work. Two hours is the best I can do.

In the shower I shave my legs and armpits, as though Hendrix Cutter and I will not be sharing a video call but will actually be meeting face-to-face and there is a possibility he will want to touch my silky-smooth legs and armpits.

I dash off a quick message to Hendrix before I leave.

Eight my time, one yours—the next day!—sounds great. Call me? See you later!

I spend my drive berating myself for how casual my message sounded, then regret how uncool it was. Damn me and my exclamation points! No turning back now.

Daydreams about our impending conversation fill my workday. What if we don't hit it off? What if he's not as cute as he is in his picture? What if he doesn't think I'm attractive? What if we have nothing to talk about?

At lunch, conversation turns into a debate on what I should wear.

"As little as possible, obviously," Adam advises. I glare at him. "What? You're trying to hook the guy, right? You got the perfect ammo right there." Adam points his fork in the most predictable direction.

"May I remind you that I already punched you once this summer, and I will not hesitate to do it again."

"Why not show a little cleavage?" Jerry B. agrees. "Boys are stupid and easy."

"I don't want *my* boy to be stupid and easy. I want him to be interesting and funny and able to look me in the eyes when we're talking."

"So wear a muumuu." Adam sounds annoyed.

"Can I borrow something from your mom?" I crack.

The longest afternoon in history passes second by second, as children enter and exit the Devil's Dinghies in slow motion. I'm ready to power out of the park at six p.m. on the nose, but the guests are particularly poky today. I nearly screamed at that dad who brought his daughter to the Dinghies at 5:58 and said, as though I have nothing else to do with my time, "One more ride won't hurt, right?" It will after I beat your face, mister!

Finally, at 6:42 p.m. I am in my car and on the road. Two road-blocking accidents later (assholes! Your shitty driving is getting in the way of my destiny!), I walk in the door of my house at 7:37. That is not enough time to take a shower and blow-dry my hair. I don't want to look like a wet dog on my first interaction with Hendrix Cutter. I opt for washing my face, brushing out my hair so it rests semi-gloriously on my shoulders, and changing into my mom's old Monkees tee. It seems fitting the shirt I wore the first day I read Hendrix Cutter's name will be the first shirt he sees me in. I examine myself in the mirror and try to determine if the thin fabric is too sheer for a first meeting. I decide it's okay, particularly because the light in a VidChat isn't going to capture everything perfectly anyway, and also because fact: I have large breasts. He's heard about them already anyway. If he is my MTB, he will be happy I have them. Not in a slithery, Adam-ogling way, but in an appreciative way that one's *partner* (hee hee) has for their *partner's* body parts.

I settle in front of my laptop. 7:57. I think about the days leading up to this moment. The years. Before the Naming, when our dolls married each other for no reason other than whose hair matched best. After the Naming, when there was so much speculation about the what and the how and the why. I turned eighteen, and Hendrix Cutter's name was there, on my chest, over my heart. I wanted none of this, yet here I am bursting with anticipation. It could all be for nothing, merely a short romance or a friendship that fizzles when one loses interest. Or it could be everything: love, family, future, life.

I am choosing to do this. I am building my life, and I will live with it.

The Chapbook VidChat rings, and my heart leaps, then

pounds rapidly underneath his name. I take my yoga breath, and click to answer.

A boy with short brown hair and dark green eyes, freckles, and an off-center nose looks at me on my screen. Whoever he sees looking back at him makes him smile, then laugh, with what appears to be both happiness and nerves.

"Hi . . ." is all I manage to get out.

"Hi," he replies, and there's his beautiful Australian accent.

"I'm Agatha Abrams," I introduce myself because it seems like the right, if absurd, thing to do.

"Hi, Agatha Abrams. It's a pleasure to meet you." He pauses and looks down to fumble with something. I study every movement, as if they will tell me what I want to know about this fabled creature. He directs his eyes back at the camera, blinks twice, and pronounces, "I'm Hendrix Cutter."

Acknowledgments

(True) Love and appreciation go out to the following:

Becky/Rebecca for introducing me to fan fiction,
Brian and John for their amusement park expertise and countless entertaining meals,
Caroline for the amazing outline of all things Six Flags,
Mike for the brilliant idea of six years and lots of analysis,
Jim for the friendship, support, and French fries,
Lish for being such a great writer, reader, and friend,
Allyx for the discussion of sexy names,
My very first beta readers: Kara and Liz,
My SPNFamily: Kris, Katie, and Mishka,
Jean, Liz, Anna, Rich, and all of my Feiwel and Friends family,
My wonderful agent, Rosemary,
Mom, always, and
Matt, Romy, and Dean, who are so special they get their names at the beginning and end of my book.

Thank you for reading this Feiwel and Friends book.

The Friends who made

Meant to Be

possible are:

Jean Feiwel PUBLISHER

Liz Szabla ASSOCIATE PUBLISHER

Rich Deas SENIOR CREATIVE DIRECTOR

Holly West EDITOR

Anna Roberto EDITOR

Christine Barcellona EDITOR

Kat Brzozowski EDITOR

Alexei Esikoff SENIOR MANAGING EDITOR

Kim Waymer SENIOR PRODUCTION MANAGER

Anna Poon ASSISTANT EDITOR

Emily Settle ADMINISTRATIVE ASSISTANT

Carol Ly DESIGNER

Ilana Worrell PRODUCTION EDITOR